In *Songs for a Sunday*, Heath[barcode]
nates how familial bonds are
sonal regrets, and life-changing choices are exposed and dealt with.
Perfectly capturing the unique yet challenging relationship between
sisters, Smith takes us on a journey that may seem familiar. Not
because we've read similar books but because we've lived it within
the pages of our own life story. Readers will remember this poignant
tale of faith and family long after they've turned the last page.

—**Michelle Shocklee**, award-winning author of *Under the
Tulip Tree* and *Count the Nights by Stars*

Songs for a Sunday is a lyrical exploration of two women who've sacrificed much for the sake of others, a God who can heal any wound,
and the unbreakable bonds of family. Intriguing characters, powerful
scenes that speak to the soul of a musician, inspiring spiritual arcs,
and authentic historical details make this a story that will stick with
me for a long time. Fans of Amanda Cox's family-centered Southern
split time will find much to love about *Songs for a Sunday*.

—**Amanda Wen**, award-winning author of *Roots of Wood
and Stone* and *The Songs That Could Have Been*

Heather Norman Smith has already proved her adept ability to perfectly convey the culture and faith of rural North Carolina in her pre-
vious novels. Now, in *Songs for a Sunday*, she's once again brought to
life—through her trademark laugh-out-loud on one page and reach-
for-a-tissue on the next storytelling genius—a Southern family and
community with profound depth and gracious style. You will walk
away from *Songs for a Sunday* with a melody in your heart and a mini
revival in your soul.

—**Amy Grochowski**, award-winning author of The Amish
of Prince Edward Island series

Songs for a Sunday is the sweetly poignant tale of two women separated by generations but bound by love. With heartfelt honesty,
Heather Norman Smith has created characters that are as real as
the people gathered around our dinner tables. This story is a candid

journey through the trials and heartaches of the choices they've made, but it ultimately points to the truth that when we give up the things we want, God gives us exactly what we need. With grace and mercy, she reminds us of the joy to be found in our acts of sacrificial love. This is a book for every woman who has ever wondered if it was worth it.

—**Lori Altebaumer**, award-winning author of the Turn-around in Texas series

Songs *for a* Sunday

HEATHER NORMAN SMITH

IRON
STREAM
FICTION

Birmingham, Alabama

Songs for a Sunday

Iron Stream Fiction
An imprint of Iron Stream Media
100 Missionary Ridge
Birmingham, AL 35242
IronStreamMedia.com

This is a work of fiction. Names, characters, and incidents are all products of the author's imagination or are used for fictional purposes. Any mentioned brand names, places, and trademarks remain the property of their respective owners, bear no association with the author or the publisher, and are used for fictional purposes only.

Iron Stream Media serves its authors as they express their views, which may not express the views of the publisher.

Library of Congress Control Number: 2022912423

All Scripture taken from the New King James Version®. Copyright © 1982 by Thomas Nelson. Used by permission. All rights reserved.

Cover design by For the Muse Designs

ISBN: 978-1-56309-613-6 paperback
ISBN: 978-1-56309-614-3 eBook

1 2 3 4 5—27 26 25 24 23

To my sisters—who, no matter how alike or how different we may be, are an extension of me. By the bonds of blood and of shared experience, and much more laughter than tears, you are part of my heart forever.

Your eyes saw my substance, being yet unformed. And in Your book they all were written, The days fashioned for me, When as yet there were none of them.

Psalm 139:16

And above all things have fervent love for one another, for "love will cover a multitude of sins."

1 Peter 4:8

Prologue

May 2002

A BLOOMING DOGWOOD IN THE BACKYARD made an excellent subject. Equipped with a fresh set of watercolors—a gift for her ninth birthday—Melissa brought the painting to life with each deliberate, delicate brush stroke. Brown, green, and a muted red in place of pink; her best work yet, for sure. Robins cheered her on with their song as she leaned in close to the canvas, taking in the cottony smell of it. With one eye almost closed and the tip of her tongue clamped between her front teeth, she formed the final flower just right. For the signature, she used orange, placing it above the grass line on the right side. *MH.* Melissa rocked forward on the toes of her tennis shoes and back down again. Perfect.

She dropped the brush into the plastic tray that hung from the wooden easel then turned and ran across the yard. Her feet pounded the deck steps as she ran to get her father.

"Daddy, come see."

Dad's eyes smiled from just above his newspaper. "Okay, Picasso. I'll be there in a minute."

She found her mother wiping the bathroom sink. The mirror in front of her sparkled with a fresh Saturday shine.

"Mama. Come outside. I want to show you something."

Without a word, Mama dropped the rag, turned on the faucet and washed her hands.

Melissa ran back outside, but as soon as her feet reached the grass, she froze. "Erica! What are you doing? You've ruined it."

In Melissa's short absence, her six-year-old sister had added a fat, smiling sun in the corner and a blob that *might* have been a dog at the base of Melissa's beautiful tree.

"I'm sorry, sissy. I wanted to paint, too." Erica stuck out her bottom lip.

"Well, you should have asked." Missy stomped. "I'm telling Daddy. He told you this morning to stay out of my things, right after you cut Barbie's hair without asking."

"Missy, please don't tell. He said if I got into any more trouble this week, he'd take a switch to my legs."

"Oh, c'mon, Erica. He never actually whips you and you know it."

Tears formed in Erica's eyes, tears that threatened to spill down her cheeks. "He will this time. I know he will. Please don't tell on me. I don't wanna get a whippin'."

The girls turned at the sound of their parents' voices. They'd stopped on the back porch to inspect a small tear in the window screen.

"Please, Missy. Please." Erica's eyes pleaded as she whispered.

Missy looked at the painting—her beautiful dogwood tree. That dumb dog and stupid sunshine.

"What did you have to show us?"

Missy turned at the sound of her father's voice. Her parents stepped nearer to her and Erica. "Got some new artwork?" Mama came close to examine the painting.

"Yeah, I—I thought you'd like to see that we painted one together," Melissa said.

Erica mouthed a silent thank-you.

"Now, that's my girls." Mama ran her fingers through Erica's long ponytail.

"It's very pretty," Daddy said. "I especially like this little brown dog. Look how cute he is. And what is this? Is that a rosebush?"

Missy barely heard them. She'd already headed back inside.

Chapter One

S OMETHING STICKY.
Missy Robbins' bare feet met with the unattended residue of sugary liquid on linoleum. The subtle sucking sound it made as skin separated from floor was all too familiar.

Little Bit's juice spill.

Missy sighed. She'd dried it right away but had neglected to mop it for *what,* three days now? If it were warmer outside, the ants would have already found it. But they were all underground, hiding away and resting. On hiatus. No such vacation for mamas whose babies needed to be fed and bathed and bandaged no matter the season.

Missy retrieved a discount brand diet cola from the fridge. Not her favorite, but they had been on sale, and the caffeine content mattered most anyway. Standing at the kitchen island, she took a slug and set the can down. The aluminum sides popped inward under the pressure of her thumb and forefinger. The feeling was back. An uneasiness. The tiniest measure of anxiety bubbled under the surface of every action and thought, just enough to keep her distracted. The last time she'd felt this way, a car had fallen off the hydraulic lift only seconds after Ray crawled out from under it.

Then again, past-due library books made her anxious, so the range of possibilities was wide.

She pressed a hand hard into one side of her face and drew a deep breath that could push her voice into the next room. "Turn that television down. It's too loud." The brashness of her own voice brought her shoulders up near her ears and made her nose wrinkle.

The usual volley of *you do it* and *no, you do it* came from the bookend babies—her thirteen-year-old daughter and four-year-old son—until Missy finally went to the family room to *do it* herself.

"Where's the remote?" She stood over them, each sprawled on the couch at opposite ends. "Did you lose it again?"

"Little Bit lost it."

The boy sat up and pointed a finger as he pushed blond bangs from his eyes. "*Nuh-uh*. Emma lost it."

Missy huffed then walked to the set and mashed the black down-arrow button until relief came to her overwhelmed ears. She should shut the television off and send them outside to play. That would be the best thing. It was too cold for ants—unusually so for a North Carolina October—but not too cold for jacketed children. One more show and she'd insist they get outside.

Around the corner, she peeked in on the two middle children playing in the dining-room-turned-chaos. Seated across from one another, they rolled out playdough on the third of the table that wasn't occupied. A half-put-together puzzle map of the United States, whose condition hadn't changed in the last month, occupied most of the space, along with stacks of random things too important to throw away just yet—bills, kid drawings, graded spelling tests, coupons. She tiptoed backward from the doorway, leaving them to their peaceful play.

Just as Missy returned to the kitchen, hoisted herself onto the stool at the island, and took out her phone, a mischievous guffaw from the boy rang out from the dining room followed by a loud and drawn-out *ugh* from his sister.

"You're a disgrace to the family, Joshua," Piper said.

Piper's inner drama queen came up with the absolute funniest lines, especially for a ten-year-old. Never a dull moment with that one. "Piper Grace, what's he doing in there?"

"He took off his shirt and covered his nipples in Play-Doh."

Disgrace indeed. But it might make for a hilarious Instagram post. If only Missy felt like getting up to snap the picture.

"Joshua, don't cover your nipples in Play-Doh." Missy didn't look away from the phone. The monotone admonition was only necessary to prevent the diatribe about fairness that she knew Piper was getting ready to unload. If *she* couldn't take off her shirt and apply fake molding clay underwear, *he* shouldn't be able to either.

All four kids had gone crazy on the same day. But of course, it had to be at staggered intervals, assuring that any hope of finding a semblance of peace was snatched away the moment Missy felt it. And she couldn't sneak to the garage for a cigarette. The kids were getting older and could figure things out. No. Saturdays and Sundays were off limits for her two-a-day habit. On weekdays, right after the three oldest left for school and again right before they got home, she'd leave Little Bit with her smartphone and escape for three minutes. Inhale, exhale, and step back from the cloud, retreating into the garage with each puff until it was done. Then she'd dispose of the evidence in the old Folgers can she hid in the corner and rush back to make sure Little Bit hadn't climbed into the pantry to help himself to the cookies.

Again.

Once, she had forgotten to change clothes and brush her teeth before the kids got home. They'd almost caught her, but she told a fib about burning popcorn in the microwave and they bought it.

Missy again shook off the uneasy feeling that had plagued her since she first opened her eyes that morning, and she blocked out the sound of bickering siblings as she opened the email app on her phone. Finally, the message she'd been expecting, all the way from Nashville. Her thumb and pointer finger moved in opposite directions on the glass, and the image on the screen became bigger. Bright blue words on a black-and-white pinstriped background read: *Help us celebrate Thomas T. Hall's 60th birthday. Saturday, November 7. Twin City Moravian Church. 2:00 pm – 4:00 pm.*

Perfect in every way. Wording. Font choice. Design. She expected nothing less from her baby sister.

At least the invitations were taken care of—literally the least Erica could do. Everything else would be up to Missy. She'd reserved the church fellowship hall, ordered the cake, clipped coupons for mixed nuts, and taken all four kids to the party store to buy decorations, where the middle two had spent the entire time begging for every cheap, plastic, made-in-China trinket that caught their eyes, while the oldest, who couldn't be corrected without either snapping back or bursting into tears, kept her face buried in her phone's screen and nearly ran into three separate displays. Then, as Missy put her card back in her wallet at the cash register, John Thomas let out a groan from the front of the buggy and the two packs of peanut butter crackers he'd scarfed for afternoon snack came back up in a massive mess all over the floor. Missy's normal inclination to apologize profusely and offer to help clean it up was quelled by the growing intensity of a headache just above both temples. She'd wiped his mouth with the bottom of his shirt and pushed the buggy out the door without a word as the other three followed behind.

Yeah, taking care of invitations was the least Erica could do.

She slipped off the stool and tip-toed to the living room to check on the kids again. A show had ended, and another started. Piper and Joshua had apparently tired of Play-Doh and had joined Emma and John Thomas in front of the set. Brightly colored characters with giant eyes and angular features jumped and danced on the screen. The kids' anime phase had already lasted longer than the classic cartoon phase from a couple months back and didn't seem to be going away any time soon.

The phone in Missy's hand rang, giving away her position, and she froze. Four heads turned and eight round eyes looked up at her. All at once, children spoke.

"Mama, can I have a drink?" Piper batted her eyelashes.

John Thomas pouted. "Can you get my blanket?"

"I want another sandwich." Joshua rubbed his tummy and grinned.

"Kids, cool it. I have to answer this. It's Aunt Erica." Missy's tone dipped and rose like a bow across a fiddle string. Her normally subtle accent was replaced by the voice of Minnie Pearl whenever she was agitated. It was a Pavlovian response—though she was helplessly aware—that frustration added extra syllables to her words.

She tapped the answer button on the screen. "Hey, sis. I just got the invitation. It looks great." Her speech had regained its normal timbre.

"Hey, I'm glad you like it."

Loud music came through the phone along with Erica's voice. Missy raised her volume.

"I think we sent them just in time. Only two weeks away. When are you flying in?"

Missy's question was met with a long silence, save for the blaring of polka music. No . . . mariachi. The vihuela stood out. Erica's taste in music had become somewhat eclectic since college.

"Um . . . yeah, that's what I'm calling about. Something's come up. Um, I'm not actually going to make it to Dad's party."

A rock-like knot formed in Missy's throat. Was this why she'd felt so anxious? Her mouth gaped for a moment, and she stared at the kitchen wall without blinking. Then she closed her eyes and drew a loud, deep breath through her nose. Her jaw clenched and her back stiffened.

"Erica, what on earth do you mean, you can't make it?"

"Oh, great. Here we go with the accent. Look, some things have just come up. I can't help it."

"You can't do this to him. You *cain't*."

The background music quieted.

"The truth is, I thought that since the tour was over, I'd have time off until after the holidays. But Justin's agent booked some charity shows, and the first one is that weekend. In Des Moines."

"Don't you think Daddy is more important, Erica? I mean, Justin Trent can do charity shows without one back-up singer." Missy walked across the kitchen and pulled a chair away from the table with a screech, then sank into the seat, letting her free hand slap the tabletop as she sat.

"I caught that tone. You don't have to say *back-up singer* like it's a bad word."

Missy picked at a tiny tear in the lime-green vinyl tablecloth. Erica was right. An apology was on the tip of her tongue when John Thomas barreled into the kitchen. He sped by, arms outstretched. Their Labrador retriever ran ahead of him, and John Thomas's stubby fingers wiggled inches from the tip of the dog's tail.

Missy held the phone away from her mouth.

"Little Bit, don't chase Mr. Peanut. And you better not pull his tail. He's liable to bite you."

She came back to her sister on a different train of thought.

"Well, how am I supposed to greet guests, cut the cake, serve punch, take pictures, and clean up afterwards, *by myself?* I really want this to be special for Daddy."

"Mom will be there to help. And Gran——."

"Don't even bring our sweet grandma into this. She's not as able-bodied as she was the last time you were home, Erica. And while you're trotting around the country doing concerts, who do you think helps Daddy and Mama look after her? And who helps look after Daddy and Mama, too?"

"Sheesh, Missy. Daddy and Mama are still young. They're in their prime." Erica let out an exasperated puff. "And come off your pity party. It's not like you're George Bailey stuck tending the Building and Loan while Harry goes off to college."

Completely out of touch. She has no idea what it's like for me. Missy's top teeth pressed into her bottom lip. "But I have things I need to do, too, you know. And goodness knows I don't get much help from Ray."

"Like what, sis? What do you have on your calendar that is so important?"

Of all the . . .

"If you must know, I have the Southern Kitchen conference in January."

"You mean you're actually going to the national conference this year?"

"Well . . . January is just the regional conference." Why had she gone down this path?

"Like, for the Southeast?"

Of course, she would ask. "A little bit smaller region."

"North Carolina?"

Missy hesitated. "No, but it's for the entire Piedmont Triad, and there'll be at least a hundred other consultants there." She gritted her teeth, pinched her eyes closed, and held her breath through a long silence.

"Hey," Erica said. Her voice was gentle. "That sounds great, sis. I'm—I'm proud of you."

Missy relaxed, and her bottled-up breath came out harder than she meant it to.

"Thanks." After a long pause, she spoke again. "He was really looking forward to having you sing at his party, you know."

"I know . . ."

"You'll call soon to tell him, won't you?"

"Of course."

"And what about Thanksgiving?"

"Not looking good, sis. I'm sorry. Hey, let me say hello to the munchkins."

Missy perched her forehead on her fingertips, her elbow on the table. "Okay, one sec." She sighed as she raised her head, then held the phone away from her mouth again and yelled. "Hey, kids. Aunt Erica wants to talk to you."

The brood came running—all barefoot, like Missy—entering the kitchen in order from oldest to youngest.

Missy couldn't help but laugh. "Why can't y'all move like that when I need help with the groceries?" She lay the phone on the table and hit the speaker button. "Okay, sis. They can hear you."

Before Erica could speak, the children yelled their hellos, all at the same time.

"Hey, Aunt Erica."

"I miss you."

"I love you."

"When are you coming back to visit?"

Erica's bubbly laugh echoed through the kitchen, and the sound painted a picture in Missy's mind. Erica's eyes glimmered whenever she laughed.

"Hey, guys," she said. "I love and miss you all, too. I hope to see you at Christmas, though."

"But that's so long," Emma whined. The other children sounded off in agreement.

"It'll be here before you know it. And I'll be sure to bring awesome presents. Hey, I gotta run, but we'll video chat in a couple of days. Okay?"

Emma, Piper, Joshua, and John Thomas cheered, sending both of Missy's forearms to cover her ears. She ducked and yelled goodbye over the din, but Erica had already hung up.

"Okay, y'all," Missy said. Before she could say another word, the kids scattered like cockroaches. "Hey, get back here. I'm not giving out chores." They slowly reassembled. "Go get shoes and coats on and get outside to play. You need some fresh air. Oh, and Little Bit needs pants, too. Emma, help him."

The command was met with whines and groans, though Joshua cheered. But Missy insisted. Maybe with the kids outside, she could think about how she was going to throw Dad's party without Erica's help. She swallowed hard. The truth was, their mother *would* do much of the work. The guilt trip she'd given Erica wasn't completely fair. But she deserved it anyway for letting Dad down. Maybe one day Erica would understand the importance of family.

Missy milled about the kitchen as the kids scavenged for clothing. Once they were all at least three-fourths ready for the outdoors—some with shoes or coats that belonged to someone else—she shooed them through the sliding glass door that led to the patio and fenced backyard. She zipped up the youngest's jacket and pulled on his hood, then she swatted his backside as he ran to join the others.

Missy's focus zoomed in from the kids running around the backyard to the vague reflection of her face in the glass, just inches from her nose. Her wild, dark curls—the trait she'd passed on to her firstborn, though Emma's were slightly tamer—were past due for a trim. Missy had chopped her long locks after baby number three and liked to keep it just past chin length. It was always air-dried. In sixty seconds or less, she could brush it and pull it back from her face with a hairband or put a bobby pin on one side.

Large brown eyes stared back at her from the glass—the trait she'd passed on to John Thomas. Time would tell if he'd inherited her poor eyesight as well. Missy's eyes had been behind corrective lenses since she was ten.

She stepped back and studied her outline in the glass, turning to one side and then the other. She sighed, the kind of long breathy utterance only made when she was alone and didn't have to explain to anyone. The extra pounds of pregnancy weight hadn't gone away postpartum and had only accumulated with each baby. When it came to heredity and size, her third-born, Joshua, had won the prize there. But Ray always said he didn't mind her figure, that she looked fine. Maybe he'd even said she looked great. But saying it and showing it . . . .

Missy's focus went back to the children. Her youngest daughter threw a tennis ball, and the dog ran the length of the yard after it. Did Piper Grace have any of her features? It

seemed she was one hundred percent her daddy's girl, in attitude *and* appearance. Quick-witted and short-tempered, Piper
loved being the center of attention.

Missy's phone rang again, a happy melody of guitar strums,
and her father's picture appeared on the screen—the one
she had taken last Christmas of him opening the leaf blower
she and Erica had bought. Well, Missy had picked it out and
ordered it, but Erica paid for half, a week into the new year.

"Honey, I'm sorry to ask," Dad said when she answered,
"but I need your help."

Missy's stomach tensed. Her anxiety hadn't left after Erica's call.

"What is it, Daddy?"

"I know you have your hands full, but Mama has taken a
nasty spill down the front steps."

"Is she okay?" Missy pictured the brick steps and concrete walkway in front of her parent's rancher. She'd tumbled
off those steps before herself, years earlier. How she'd let her
younger sister convince her to try skipping rope down them
she'd never understand.

"I don't think she broke anything, but we're at the hospital
getting her checked out."

"Wait. You said *Mama*. Are you talking about *my* mama or
your mama? Who fell?"

"It was *your* mama. My wife, your mama."

"That's what I thought." Imagining her mother on the
ground, hurt, brought tears to Missy's eyes in an instant.
"Which hospital?"

"Forsyth. Waiting in emergency now."

"Is she in pain?"

"A little. Mostly her shoulder."

"Is she bleeding?"

"No. Just a few scrapes. But she landed on the shoulder pretty hard."

Missy paced around the island. "How did it happen? What do you need?"

"We were getting ready to move your grandma's stuff inside the house . . . *my* mama, not your mama." Dad's attempt at humor fell flat as Missy was reminded of what they'd all deemed "Moving Day." *That's* why she'd been so anxious. It had to be. Like a first-rate heel, she'd forgotten to offer to help, and now Mama was hurt.

"We had just gotten all her things off the back of your cousin Jeff's truck and into the yard when he got called into work and had to leave. Your mama carried something inside and was coming back out to help me move a dresser when, somehow, she just missed the step. All the years we've lived there, you're the only person who ever fell off them until now."

"What on earth were y'all doing moving furniture that heavy?"

"Melissa, stay calm. It isn't like she got hurt moving furniture. There wasn't even anything in her hands when she fell. And like I said, there's not that much to move. The two of us could have handled it, but now it's all out in the yard and it looks like rain."

"Oh, that's not good."

"Mama's furniture will be ruined if someone doesn't bring it in soon. Can you call Ray? If not, it's okay. I'll call your uncle. Or someone from church."

She looked at the clock. Ray wouldn't be done at work for at least another hour, and she knew he was short-handed at the shop. Uncle Tim lived twenty-five minutes away. And Missy didn't care to ever ask anyone from her parent's church for help, no matter how much they needed it.

"Don't worry about it, Daddy. I can take care of it. Call me as soon as you can to let me know how Mama is."

"I will, honey. But she'll be fine."

Missy offered to fix supper for them when they got home, and she said goodbye with an *I love you* as always, then she returned the phone to her jeans pocket as she peeked out at the kids. They were all on the swing set now, seemingly unaware of the dark clouds forming over their heads. The boys chased one another up and down the slide and the girls were side-by-side on the swings, their legs pumping back and forth at the same time, hair windswept from their sweet faces. At least the four of them were already wearing shoes. One less battle to fight.

She looked up at the sky again and hurried outside to gather her brood. Playtime interrupted. Life interrupted.

And no way to sneak that cigarette.

Chapter Two

April 1963

$\mathcal{A}$NNIE BREATHED deeply, taking in the earthy smells of the forest around her as the wind hit her face with welcomed freshness. She smiled at her reflection in the convertible's side mirror. Her caramel-colored hair was pulled to the side in a tight braid, but little wisps danced free in the breeze and tickled her nose. The large, round lenses of her glasses shielded her eyes from the flashing of sunlight between trees as Julian drove, but they also concealed the joy that she knew shined there. Never could she have imagined a better day.

The car took the curves like a fish in water, and her body swayed gently with each turn, a romantic dance with the mountain road. The curves to the right were her favorite—they brought her that much closer to the handsome man in the driver's seat. Only a few more minutes of driving into the next county and they'd be at their destination.

"I haven't been to Hanging Rock since I was a little girl," Annie said. Her voice floated, tiny amid the roar of the engine and the wind. "I absolutely love it up here."

R.C. spoke up from the back seat, her voice monotone. "You came when you were thirteen. A teenager. Not a little girl. It was May 1, 1956. A Sunday. I was nine."

Annie turned around and gave her sister a smile. Her special gifts never ceased to amaze. Did Ruth Claire even comprehend how unique she was? How awesome she was? If she did, she never showed it. Her strawberry blond curls blew wild and loose in the wind, and she looked into the fast-moving forest through squinted eyes. Expressionless. As if everyone could pull seven-year-old memories out of their heads with such details.

As Annie turned back, the expression on Julian's face made her stomach muscles tighten.

"Um . . . she's just really good with dates," Annie said. "It's her thing." That was all. What else could she say? Julian would just have to be around R.C. more to understand, or at least come close to understanding. The things that made Ruth Claire different were hard to put into words. Annie wasn't sure there were even words for it. But if she had her way, Julian *would* be around them both more. *Much* more. Hopefully forever. And as the days and weeks of their courtship passed, she grew more confident that he felt the same way. Only a few weeks ago, he'd used the word *love* for the first time. They'd taken an evening stroll at Salem Lake, and he had busted out with it as if he would have exploded to wait a second longer. She'd been shocked to tears, so much so that it took her a moment to be able to say it back.

"We're here." Nervous excitement coursed through Annie's body. She was at one of her favorite places with two of her favorite people.

Julian turned the car into the parking lot nearest the main trailheads. He had suggested Hidden Falls and she had agreed. It wasn't the most magnificent of the waterfalls in the park but, from what she could remember, was pretty nonetheless, and most likely wouldn't be as crowded. The hike would be nothing short of perfect, as long as the terrain wasn't too rough. She'd put on saddle shoes with her pink pedal pushers, not tennis shoes or hiking boots, and Ruth Claire wore the same, though with a knee-length twill skirt. R.C. despised the way trousers rubbed against her legs.

"So, are you going to tell us what's in the picnic basket, Julian Lane?" Annie said with a lilt in her voice. "It's too late for lunch and too early for dinner."

"Not until we get to the falls," he said as he opened her door.

He gave her a wink that made her breath hitch, and from that spot where she imagined her soul must live—above the belly button and toward the back—warm electricity radiated out to the rest of her body.

Julian was always planning little surprises. He left notes in her dance bag, and last week he'd shown up at the studio to give her a single flower. He said it was so beautiful that it reminded him of her, and he had to bring it. All the little girls in her class had squealed with delight, and they all made kissing noises when he gave her a peck on the cheek to say goodbye.

Following the sign for Hidden Falls, Annie and Julian started out on the wide, easy trail hand-in-hand, fingers locked. Ruth Claire followed behind, and as they hiked, Annie turned every few yards to check on her. Sixteen-year-old R.C. studied her surroundings as if there'd be a test at the end of the outing. She stopped to examine the rhododendrons in bloom and the blue-tailed lizard racing along a dead tree. She studied the bright green ferns and ran her hand along patches of spongy moss. R.C. seemed to see things in a way no one else could. Like she wasn't even seeing, but instead using some extra sense that couldn't be explained to the likes of ordinary people.

"Thank you for letting R.C. come with us, Julian," Annie whispered. "She's been so out of sorts since she broke up with her boyfriend. And she won't talk to me about it, which is strange. I want to help her, but I don't know what's going on."

"Hey, no problem. Poor girl." His tongue clicked behind closed teeth. "Maybe some sunshine will help cheer her up. And I bet what's in the basket won't hurt, either." He nodded toward the brown woven basket in his hand and gave her another wink and a half smile.

Dark blond hair, blue eyes, tanned skin, and muscles. Oh, those muscles. Julian Lane was the cat's meow. The moment she'd first laid eyes on him six months ago, when he picked up his little sister from dance, she cursed the distance between them. Then a few weeks later, he approached her on an otherwise ordinary Tuesday afternoon and asked her to the drive-in. Mama wasn't too keen on the idea—even though Annie was twenty years old—until she heard his last name. Lane was right up there with Reynolds, Hanes, and Gray in Winston-Salem. It also didn't hurt that he'd be graduating from Wake Forest with a business degree and aspired to run for office one day. But Annie would have fallen just as hard if he'd been an exterminator or a car salesman, and from a poor family like hers.

"Daddy helped build this trail," Ruth Claire called out loudly from behind them.

"You're right, R.C.," Annie said, without turning around.

Julian looked at Annie, an eyebrow raised.

"Our daddy was in the CCC before he met Mama," Annie said. "Camp 3422. He never talked about the war. Not once that I remember. But he talked about the Civilian Conservation Corps all the time. He brought us here a lot when we were little. Never tried to hide how proud he was of this place."

She surveyed the forest on either side of the once-familiar trail. Nostalgia washed over her, and she could hear her father talking about blasting quartzite and assembling walls along the trails out of the native stone. *We couldn't improve on God's creation,* he used to say. *We just made it easier to enjoy.*

Her father's efforts made Annie proud, too. His spirit lived on there in the Sauratown Mountains. The "mountains away from the mountains" they were called, being so far removed from the Blue Ridge to the west. The small chain jutted up sharply from the earth, where no other mountains stood, declaring itself a unique monument to be respected.

Annie stopped in the middle of the trail while her brain caught up with her. "I can't believe it's been so long since we were here," she said. "The last time we were here was . . . it was the last time Daddy brought us before he died. That's one reason R.C. remembered." She closed her eyes and laid her fingers across the bridge of her nose for a moment before checking on R.C. again. She was about ten yards behind, looking upward as she took half steps.

Annie looked back to Julian standing next to her. He offered a sympathetic smile and put his arm around her shoulders. His arm was a strong shield and a soft blanket all in one, just like Daddy's had been. Under the comfort of it, she began walking again.

After a few hundred more feet of trail, they came to a series of rock ledges that resembled stairs going down.

"R.C., stay close behind us," Annie said. "It's a little steep getting to the base of the falls."

The trio navigated single file with Julian in the lead. Annie bit her lip in concentration, careful to land her slick soles clear of the edge of each step.

"Go slow," Annie called over her shoulder.

Ruth Claire was quiet.

"The next one's tricky." Annie reached for Julian's offered hand, though it wasn't strictly needed, and she hung on to it as they continued their descent.

Annie tossed another encouragement over her shoulder. "Almost there. Doing good."

Julian let out a staccato chuckle as he put his foot down on level ground. "Annie, she's sixteen. She's not a baby."

Annie jerked her hand away as she stepped down beside him. "I know she's not a baby. But she's *my* baby sister. It's my job to look out for her." She tamped down indignation like a stray ember and made her voice calm, turning to watch R.C. join them at the bottom.

"Look!" Ruth Claire pointed toward the cascading water with her mouth open. Her eyes, so wide and blue, just like Daddy's, were filled with a wonder not often seen, as if the three of them were standing on the edge of Niagara or Kilimanjaro, or at least as if it were her first time seeing Hidden Falls. Her voice and figure were that of a woman, but her excitement gave her away as a child.

Annie's heart swelled at her sister's joy. It didn't matter that Julian and R.C. didn't understand her maternal feelings.

The narrow waterfall was as pretty as Annie remembered, and the gentle percussion of water over rocks took her back to childhood, when she could stand on the banks and skip rocks across the creek for hours.

"Hey, why don't we try over there?" Julian led them to a rock wide enough for the three of them to share. The girls sat first and crossed their ankles. Then Julian sat down between them and raised the hinged lid on the basket.

"*Ta da.* Stopped and picked these up on the way to your house." He waved one hand in a circle, palm-up, over the treasure.

Annie and Ruth Claire reached into the basket at the same time, but it was Annie who brought out the white box with the familiar Dewey's Bakery logo. Her favorite dessert peeked through the cellophane window.

"Thanks, Julian," Ruth Claire said as Annie opened the box and handed her a cupcake. She consumed a third of the cake in the first bite, and the smile on her face as she chewed held no hint of heartbreak. It was just the joyful expression of a child whose sweet tooth had been satisfied.

Desserts of any kind had become a luxury at home. After twenty-five years at the mill, arthritis had set in, and now it was impossible for Mama to work the loom. An old woman at forty-five. Annie had picked up extra hours from Miss Melinda at the dance studio, but things were still tight. Any more hours and her studies would suffer. She had to keep her classes a priority.

When Daddy was alive, he'd scraped and saved to afford dance lessons for his girls, until Annie became so good, she started teaching classes in her early teens. She lived it, breathed it. Dreamed about it most nights. As soon as Annie's business certificate was completed, Miss Melinda would put her in charge of the studio. That's what Annie wanted more than anything else in the world, other than Julian Lane. Then she'd be able to help Mama even more with the bills.

Dancing had never been Ruth Claire's thing. She preferred to sit in the corner and read Tolkien. Like him, she'd created entire worlds in her head, populated by different creatures with unique abilities and languages. She shared them only with Annie.

"Ruth Claire, don't make yourself sick," Annie said. She handed her sister a napkin from the basket.

"But they're so good." R.C. licked the white icing off her lips. She peeled the cupcake liner back further. An already empty one lay in her lap.

"I shouldn't eat these, you know." Annie made her eyes smile at Julian. "If I keep letting you spoil me with treats, it's all gonna go straight to my hips."

"Nah. Not the way you dance. You must burn four thousand calories a day just dancing." He looked her up and down.

"At least half that many." Annie fluttered her eyelashes.

"Hey, speaking of dancing . . . guess what? My father and I were talking about the new conservatory this morning, and about Governor Sanford's planning committee for it." He gave a wide grin.

"Oh, do you really think it will happen? A school just for the arts here in North Carolina?"

"Most definitely. A high school and a college, with departments of drama, dance, and music. And later, visual arts, too. Dad says the plan is set to go before the General Assembly soon."

It sounded magnificent. Like a dream come true for anyone lucky enough to attend.

"And where will it be?"

"They don't know for sure, but Father thinks it will be in Winston-Salem. We were the first place in the country to have a city arts council, so it makes sense. And I know of several local donors with big pocketbooks."

"How wonderful. Maybe some of my girls will go there."

"Or maybe you will. You never know. Or maybe you'll teach dance there."

Annie wrinkled her nose. "I'll be much too old for school by the time it's done, I'm sure. And I'd need more formal training before I could teach at that level. I'm not even sure what kind of training I'd have to get."

"Don't sell yourself short, Annie. You're amazing. You can do anything you set your mind to."

Her cheeks went warm. He took her chin gently in his hands and turned her head toward him.

"And don't forget, my family knows people. If you wanted to teach at the new arts school, I'm sure I could help make it happen for my future wife."

He leaned in and she closed her eyes as their lips met. Her mind raced, the word *wife* having ignited every synapse in her brain, until she was intoxicated into mindlessness from the passion of his kiss.

"Girlie, don't mess with that," a loud, deep, drawly voice called out. Annie pulled away from Julian's face and turned toward the voice. It belonged to a man who stood on the other side of the creek, and he and his female companion shared the same look of shock and fear. Annie followed the path of their gaze to where R.C. sat, on a boulder about twenty yards away. Her face was leaned close to the rock, and her eyes were fixed in study. A foot from her nose was a coiled-up snake with its head raised and snout pointed at R.C.

The last bite of Annie's cupcake fell to the ground as she jumped up and bolted to R.C.'s side. Her sister let out a half-grunt, half-scream as Annie grabbed her by the shoulders and pulled her backward. The snake lunged forward with its mouth open wide and landed in the spot where R.C. had been sitting, then it slithered off into the forest.

Annie helped R.C. up from the ground and pulled her several steps, walking backward to make sure they were clear of the creature. With trembling hands, she spun her sister around by the shoulders to face her.

"*Ruth Claire.* What were you thinking getting that close to a snake?" Annie screamed. "What's wrong with you?"

R.C.'s eyes clouded with confusion, and her half-open mouth contorted in a misshapen O.

"Y-you . . . you don't do that," Ruth Claire stuttered.

Annie put her hand over her racing heart and pressed into it as she tried to steady her breathing. "Do what?"

R.C. looked away to answer. "Talk to me like other people do."

The painful truth pinched at the corners of Annie's heart. "Oh, R.C., come here." She pulled her close and rested her chin on top of her head. She held her tight, wishing she could take back her words. "I didn't mean to say it like that. You just scared me. That's all. There's nothing wrong with you, R.C. Not a thing in the world. You hear me? Nothing. You just gotta be more careful." She stroked her baby sister's hair, just like she had done since R.C. first had hair.

Julian, who'd been lingering at a distance, came to Annie's side. "Y'all okay?"

"We're fine," Annie said. "Just a little too fascinated with snakes, apparently." She breathed out hard, finally able to process the situation with a clear head. "What kind was that anyway, R.C.?"

"A timber rattler. You can tell by its pattern. There aren't too many up here. I'd never seen one in real life."

"A timber rattler? Aren't those poisonous?"

"Venomous," R.C. said.

Annie rolled her eyes and pressed her lips together. It was better to leave well enough alone with R.C. She was calm in the most stressful of situations—until she wasn't—and the last thing Annie wanted was for Julian to see a meltdown.

Julian gave R.C. a gentle pat on the back and suggested they pack up then go for a short hike before heading home. Another thing for Annie to love about him—he was great in tense situations.

On the first step of the ascent from the falls, R.C. said, "You know, I knew what I was doing, Annie. They don't strike unless you scare them."

"I'm sure you're right," Annie said.

"*You* scared it, Annie."

"I'm sorry, R.C. I was worried about you. You're my baby sister, and I don't like seeing venomous snakes so close to your head. Okay? Seems like I'm always pulling you out of some kind of jam." She tousled her hair playfully. "But don't you worry. I'll always be here to rescue you. You can count on it." She passed her on the trail to try to catch up with Julian.

"I'm glad I didn't get bit."

"Me too."

"Hey, Annie?"

Annie turned to see R.C. place a cupped palm over her midsection.

"Do you think it would have hurt the baby?"

Chapter Three

October, Present Day

MISSY KEPT a heavy foot on the gas pedal and scanned every side road for patrol cars. The last thing she needed was a speeding ticket.

For the fifth-largest city in the state, Winston-Salem had plenty of roads that could have inspired the lyrics of a country song. Communities untouched by urban expansion dotted the perimeter of the city, a glimpse into the past of the original twin cities founded so long ago by Moravians. In these places, the city limit signs had only to do with zip codes and tax districts. There was no city here. The winding roads, void of stop lights, hid the story of the skyscrapers that stood a few miles away—a couple of them over four hundred feet tall. The roads that took Missy from her house to her parents' led past cow pastures, barns, and mom-and-pop gas stations on their third generation of ownership. Missy loved it here. Not as exciting as Nashville, probably, but this was home.

The sky taunted her as she drove. A gray cloud rolled in front of them, foreboding, then the sun peeked out, offering hope and spotlighting the deep reds, oranges, and yellows of the leaves, only to soon be chased away by another, even darker cloud.

"The Wheels on the Bus" rang out from the van's speakers. When it got to the part where the mamas on the bus say *shh, shh, shh,* John Thomas's childish giggle rang out. "It sounds like you, Mama."

Emma sat in the front seat, playing a game on her phone. The two boys occupied the middle row of the van, the youngest in a booster seat. Piper sat in the far back, since she'd promised to let Joshua sit there on the way home.

Less than ten minutes after they'd left her house, Missy's green, nine-year-old Kia pulled into the paved driveway of her childhood home. Almost a record.

The brick rancher sat half a football field-length back from the road. As she approached the house, there was her grandma, sitting in a glossy oak rocking chair in the grass, just off the walkway. Around the chair, a headboard, footboard, and bed-rails were scattered in the grass. A matching nightstand and chest of drawers were positioned on the sidewalk behind her. It looked as if the older woman had taken up residence in the front yard, her long legs stretched out into the grass and her knees bending slightly with each back and forth of the rocker. Her arms were crossed in front of her, buried in the folds of her oversized lavender sweater. The top of one beige knee-high stocking had rolled down to sit below her ankle, leaving a small strip of leg below her slacks exposed to the chill.

Missy parked the van. "Kids, you stay here for a minute."

Emma looked up from the phone. "Is Gigi alright?"

"I'm not sure, honey. Just make sure your brothers and sister stay put until I say. Okay?"

Emma nodded.

The rain came the moment Missy opened the van door, but only a sprinkle.

"What are you doing out here?" she called, keeping her tone upbeat.

"Hey, there, baby. Just waiting on the rain, I guess. Worrying about your mama mostly." Her tone was much lighter than her expression conveyed, with a sort of resignation about her current state. Missy could only imagine what she felt, having moved out of her home, now sitting with all her things outside about to be ruined, and with a daughter-in-law at the hospital.

"I know. I'm worried, too. But we have to take care of your stuff now. Gotta get this pretty furniture inside before it gets all messed up."

Missy bent down to hug her grandma. The woman's long, slender arms wrapped around Missy's neck, and she gently pulled Missy's face close to her own. Then she kissed her cheek tenderly, silently saying *thank you* and *I love you* at the same time.

"I'm afraid I can't be much help with the way my back's been lately. That's the whole reason I'm moving in here, after all—these doggone back problems. Can't hardly get up and down by myself without causing a scene."

Missy straightened and scanned the yard again, her hand poised on her hip in a fist. "I'm sure you can help. You'll supervise."

The ornate, real-wood furniture in the yard was nothing like the pressed particle board stuff at Missy's house. There was less of it than she'd feared, but the sky turned a darker shade of gray each minute. Grandma Annie looked up, then back at Missy with silent concern, just as the rain picked up and cold drops began bouncing off their skin and soaking into their clothes.

"I know," Missy said. "We need to hurry." She smiled. "Good thing I brought my own moving crew." Missy waved the kids out of the car and started giving instructions.

"Emma, you're going to have to help me with the big stuff. Piper Grace, you hold the door open for us, and boys,"—she snapped her fingers at the boys who were traipsing through the shrubs— "you'll bring in these bed rails when we're finished with the other stuff." Joshua stood at attention and gave his mother a soldier's salute in response. "Good man." She smiled and winked at him.

The older woman's eyes twinkled. "I'll go get a towel to dry off the furniture when we get it in." It took effort to push herself up, using the chair's arms for leverage, and she made it no more than a couple inches above the seat before she plopped down again with a huff.

"Here." Missy helped her to her feet, then started to work.

The first thing to go inside was the rocker, which Missy carried easily by herself. As she held it by the arms and hoisted it up the front steps, her mind went back to story time at her grandmother's house, when Missy had sat in Grandma's lap, listening as she read Little Golden Books, one after another, until Missy fell asleep. When Erica came along, Missy had been demoted from the chair and had to sit at their grandma's feet instead.

The heavy lifting began as the rain stopped, teasing them before it started up again a moment later. Emma was strong for thirteen, and the headboard and footboard were brought inside without incident. Piper seemed to relish her role as doorwoman, even directing them to watch their step. The boys ran around the front yard in the rain while they waited their turn to be movers.

Missy went back for the nightstand. Wet leaves clung to the bottom as she lifted it. Burdened with the square piece of furniture, she fought off shivers as a burst of cold wind blew against her bare arms, and she bit back an ugly word—as Mama called them—when she scraped her knuckles on the door frame.

Exactly the kind of thing Erica's missing out on in Nashville.

There in the modest living room, surrounded by furniture and the mattresses that had been brought in before Missy's mother fell, Grandma Annie was busy drying every drop of rain from the bedroom suite. After she set the nightstand down on the hardwood floor, Missy stood upright, then tugged her shirt down and the waist of her blue jeans higher. She looked out into the yard.

"We'll never be able to move the chest all together. I'll start bringing in a drawer at a time."

"I'm sorry about this," Grandma Annie said. "I really hate that you and the kids had to rush over here to help me." Of course she felt that way. She was the one who had taken care of everybody else for so long.

"Don't worry about it, Grandma. That's what family is for."

Missy took one big deep breath. *Now for the hard part.*

The chest of drawers was even more challenging than she expected. It didn't make sense that her parents hadn't packed Grandma's things in boxes. Instead, all five drawers were filled to the brim—some with clothes and accessories, others with what appeared to be a random collection of items from an old woman's life story, reduced to the space of a few cubic feet.

Missy had just removed the bottom drawer when John Thomas let out a cry of pain from somewhere behind her. She turned to see him lying on the driveway, and she quickly put the heavy drawer down on the sidewalk. *Oh, we can't have two family members in the ER on the same day.* Nausea overtook her as she approached and saw blood running from his mouth. *Please don't be his teeth. Please don't be his teeth.*

"I didn't push him," Joshua said. "I promise. He tripped."

Missy ignored her oldest son, who was backed against the van. She could sort out the cause of the fall later.

A quick inspection revealed just a busted lip. If it had been teeth, she would have had to call Ray at the shop and ask him to come home right away, short-handed or not. The only things she couldn't deal with as a mother were wiggly or broken teeth.

Grandma Annie called out from behind her. "Is he okay? My *things.*"

Missy turned to see her grandma standing on the front stoop, pointing to the drawer on the ground. The sprinkle from the sky had become a downpour.

Piper, still at her post, pushed the dark, wet bangs off her forehead and looked at Gigi. Her face read of sympathy. The week before, her favorite teddy bear, aptly named Snowflake, wound up in the washer with a brand-new dark red blanket. She'd cried for hours, and Missy still felt terrible.

"It'll be okay, Gigi," Piper said. "Mama, hurry. The drawer."

Missy yelled for Emma to come attend to her brother then ran for the drawer. The rain dribbled down her glasses, and she wiped at the lenses with her fingertips. Fueled by a sense of urgency and a desire to be finished, she rushed to bring all five drawers into the house, one by one, growing more exhausted with each trip.

All the children except the doorwoman had gathered in the living room. Emma held a paper towel to John Thomas's lip. Joshua used the drawers as hurdles until Grandma Annie told him to stop.

"Okay, Emma," Missy said. "We're going to have to get the chest in, and it won't be easy."

"Be careful," Grandma Annie said. "I don't want you to hurt yourself."

"Hey, Mom," Piper called from the small porch. "Couldn't I slide this little metal piece on the arm thingy to hold the door open?"

In all the excitement, Missy hadn't even thought of it.

"Yes, baby. Do that and go on inside and dry off," she said. "Good job."

Piper smiled wide and gave a dramatic nod of satisfaction, then made an even more dramatic pivot to turn and march into the house. Emma rolled her eyes and huffed.

The chest stood taller than Emma, and the hardest part was easing it down for them to get a hold. Both grunted as they maneuvered up the two front steps. Emma's face was scrunched up and turning red, but she didn't say a word. Just before the door, Missy's cell phone rang in her pocket. Probably news about Mama. That, or Ray had gotten home and was wondering where everybody was. The call would have to wait. There was no way to answer it now. If the caller were Ray, he'd figure it out, and if it was about her mother . . . No. She had to be all right. Her heart raced as she allowed herself to think about it. Once upon a time, she might have said a prayer for her mother, but it seemed like a waste of time now.

A few more grunts and a couple stumbles later, all the wood furniture was finally safe inside the house. Missy dropped onto the sofa. The bed rails could wait until her father got home. Besides, she heard thunder in the distance, and the last thing the boys needed to do was hold big pieces of metal outside in a storm.

After Grandma Annie got all the furniture dry and Missy had a moment to rest—and to check the missed call, which turned out to be a telemarketer—they got the children settled at the kitchen table, each with a cup of hot cocoa in their hands and each with a bath towel wrapped around their shoulders. Then Grandma Annie shuffled back to the living room, and Missy followed.

"Missy, can you lift that drawer to the couch?" she said. "I can't bend down there to it."

With the drawer placed on the brown microfiber, Grandma Annie sat beside it and started examining the contents that had been exposed to the rain. She patted items on top with a towel, then dug around and patted at the bottom of the drawer. "Oh, thank the Lord," she said. "It doesn't look too bad."

Missy knew her grandma well enough to know that her thanks to God wasn't idle talk.

"What is all this stuff?"

"Just the things that mean the most to me. The things I couldn't bear to put in storage. See here?" She held up a small black book with a tattered cover. "This was my granddaddy's Bible. Got his handwritten notes all in it." She shook her head. "Priceless. And here's the only picture I have of my father in his Army uniform."

Finding out what precious treasures could have been damaged made Missy grateful that she'd hurried, despite the fact that her face still stung, and her legs were like gelatin.

Missy peered into the drawer for other treasures. There were framed pictures of her Daddy when he was young, including one black-and-white photo of him as a baby, being held by her great-aunt, R.C. "These would be great to set out at Daddy's party. I especially love that one with your sister. Can we use them?"

"Yes, of course." Grandma Annie picked up the nearest frame and ran her fingers atop the glass with a faraway look in her eyes. She handed it to Missy.

"Oh, it looks like this folder got pretty wet," Missy said. She reached into the drawer and pulled out a plain beige folder with papers peeking from the edges. "I'll go spread the papers out to dry."

Grandma Annie stood with a quickness Missy hadn't seen in years. Like a miracle had happened and the osteoarthritis and two slipped discs were just a memory. Her hunched frame became rigid.

"No. Let me have that. Give me those now." She grabbed the folder then whisked it behind her back. A secret flashed in her grandmother's eyes. Behind all the tired and worry, it jumped out for only a second, just long enough for Missy to see it. Grandma Annie's panic was palpable, even more intense than Missy's when the kids had almost caught her smoking.

"Grandma?" The coldness from the outdoors left Missy's face and was replaced by the kind of heat that always accompanied the twisting sensation in the pit of her stomach. Her grandmother was never brash, never rude. Even when Missy had misbehaved as a child, her grandma never scolded severely. Missy didn't recognize *this* grandma.

"I'm sorry, honey. It's just—I—I have personal things in here. You understand." Grandma Annie's shoulders slumped as she sighed. She eased herself back onto the couch.

"Of course, I understand. And I wouldn't read them. I just wanted to help dry them for you."

"I *don't* want anyone else to touch them."

"Sure. I'm sorry."

Missy searched her grandmother's amber eyes, while an awkward silence passed. Her panic regressed behind the irises, like a coin sinking to the bottom of a deep fountain.

Turning back to the drawer, Missy tried again, asking permission with her slow movements. She needed something to help change the subject, diffuse the tension that had never before existed between them. Her lower eyelids filled with water, like the rain gutter on the roof. Any more tears and they'd all spill over.

There in the drawer, peeking from beneath a small blanket, was a pair of silky pink ballet slippers. The soles were dark and worn thin.

"What about these?" Missy held up the shoes. "Who do these belong to? I know they're not Daddy's." She faked a giggle.

Grandma Annie's scowl melted into a remorseful expression—furrowed brow, quivering mouth, and kind eyes which she then closed as she drew in a long breath. She opened her eyes again as she breathed out. With a wrinkled hand, she laid the folder behind her on the couch, then reached for the shoes in slow motion. She took them from Missy and brought them to her chest, cradling them like a newborn baby. Her eyes closed once more, for a moment, and a wistful smile spread across her face.

"These were mine, dear one," she said. "These *are* mine. The last of probably a dozen or so pairs I owned when I was young." She looked at Missy and smiled before returning her gaze to the shoes. "They wear out quickly when you dance as much as I did back then."

Missy could hardly believe it. In all her thirty years, Grandma Annie had never spoken of being a dancer. She couldn't even imagine it. All the late-night talks and browsing through old photo albums, all the family stories around the dinner table, it never came up. Daddy never talked about it either. Surely, he knew.

"I didn't know you used to be a ballet dancer. I bet you were good."

"Yes. I was."

With those three words, Missy's curiosity multiplied. Grandma Annie was a modest person. Never boastful. Her answer said there was a story to be told, and so did the look on her face as she clung to the shoes.

Missy looked from Grandma Annie's face to the shoes in her arms, then to the folder lying on the couch and repeated the scan twice more as her head swirled and her insides trembled. What more could there be to know about this woman whom she thought she already knew so well?

Chapter Four

April 1963

"**D**o you think she's going to be mad?" R.C. said.

Annie held her sister's hands as they sat on the bed they shared. Ruth Claire didn't show emotion like most people. She didn't seem scared about being pregnant, and she hadn't cried. She'd kept an even tone the whole time she spilled the story of her and Tommy Jacobs in the hayloft of his grandfather's barn two months ago, with details Annie didn't need to know. But those details were just facts to R.C. She told it like reading a story from a newspaper, including how Tommy had completely stopped talking to her after she told him she'd missed her cycle and that she might have a baby growing inside her. For all her lack of emotion relaying the story, a tiny bit of fear showed when she mentioned telling Mama.

"It will be okay, R.C.," Annie said. "She's going to be upset, but it will be okay. I'll be right there with you. Mama loves you. It will be hard for her to accept, but she'll forgive you. Just like Jesus forgives you. You made a mistake, and now we have to accept what comes with it." She nodded once. "The good and the bad."

We. Ruth Claire was the one who was pregnant, but no doubt, it affected all three of them. Annie tried not to think about the consequences. It would do no good to worry.

"But do we have to do it tonight?" R.C. said. "We could just wait a few weeks, couldn't we?"

Annie studied the innocence on her sister's face. The orange freckles across her nose and beneath her eyes were so evenly distributed and so perfectly symmetrical; she resembled a china doll with painted-on features. Her eyes were a stunning transparent blue with hints of gray. No wonder the boys couldn't stay away.

Annie had objected to Ruth Claire's dating, but Mama had allowed it. She said it would be good for R.C. to do some of the same things other girls her age did. After all, she *was* sixteen. But R.C. wasn't like other girls.

Annie had tried to warn her of certain things, and R.C. had learned the basics from health textbooks, but the complicated emotions of being a teenage girl couldn't be taught. Annie should have tried harder.

"You need to tell her right away, R.C. The sooner, the better. And you should probably see a doctor. I mean, just to make sure, anyway. Mama will want to take you to Dr. Steelman soon."

R.C. picked up her worn-out stuffed rabbit from the pillow and rubbed her thumb down the length of its ear in a steady motion, over and over, as she stared at nothing. She was quiet for a long time then drew a deep breath.

"Will they give me a shot?" R.C. finally said. "I don't like shots."

"I don't think so, baby girl." Annie drew her sister close. She rested her head on top of R.C.'s. "I don't think so."

*   *   *

Annie sat hunched around a four-top kitchen table alongside R.C. and Mama. The light from the simple fixture above glared off the varnished wood of one long-vacant chair.

"You've hardly touched your cornbread and milk, Ruth Claire," Mama said. At least four nights out of seven they had pinto beans, corn bread, and milk. Sometimes without the beans. That's the way it had been even when Daddy was alive.

"She's probably still full. We had cupcakes this afternoon," Annie said. "Julian brought them for us when we went up to the mountain."

"That's nice, dear, but your sister can speak for herself. Can't you, Ruth Claire?" She reached to pat R.C.'s hand.

"Yeah, Annie. I can speak for myself." R.C. shot a defiant look toward her big sister, then her volume dropped. "But what Annie said, Mama. Too many cupcakes."

"Mr. Lane is full of surprises now, isn't he? You're a lucky girl, Annie. But then again, he's pretty lucky, too."

Annie wanted to talk about Julian now, gush about his good looks and how happy he made her. She wanted to tell Mama that he'd hinted at marriage today. Why, by this time next year she could be Mrs. Julian Lane. But the heaviness of R.C.'s news trumped her joy for the moment.

"Mama." Annie squared her shoulders and pressed her palms against her legs. "R.C. and I need to talk to you about something important."

Mama's eyes lit up. No doubt she anticipated something good, until she looked at both girls. Annie fixed her face in a serious pose, and R.C., across the table, looked down.

"R.C.," Annie said. "You said you could speak for yourself. Do you want to?"

The young girl looked up just long enough to shake her head.

"What's going on, girls?" Mama said. "You're making me nervous." She massaged at the crooked fingers of her right hand with the equally crooked fingers of the left.

"Mama, I don't want you to get too upset, but . . . there's no other way to tell you. R.C. thinks she might be pregnant."

Over the last hour, Annie had played out the moment in her mind several times. She imagined the shock, the sadness, the anger. She planned on comforting her mother until acceptance came. Maybe for an hour or two. Then they'd eventually celebrate the new life together when the dust settled. But none of Annie's daydreams had prepared her.

Mama stood from the table slowly and carried her bowl and cup to the sink in stone-cold silence. When she turned around, her face was expressionless, save for a hopelessly desperate look in her eyes.

R.C. rocked back and forth in her chair, gripping the seat. Annie's stomach muscles tensed, and her limbs went icy. After Mama sat again at the table, R.C. jumped up and ran to her room. Neither of them called after her.

Mama's forearms pressed into the table; her eyes fixed straight ahead. Annie waited in silence. Finally, her mother spoke. "There's an herb," she said, barely above a whisper.

"*What?*"

"An herb. Something that grows in the mountains. My granny talked about it. I think it's easy enough to come by."

"Mama, what are you talking about?"

Her mother broke her gaze at nothing to see Annie. "It might be able to solve this. But if that doesn't work . . . I know this girl from the mill. When she found herself in a bad way, she went to see a man. A retired doctor. I'm not exactly sure what was done, but he was able—"

"Mama, stop. Stop talking like this. Please." Fear washed over Annie. This wasn't the woman who had raised her. She sat at the table with someone completely different.

"She can't take care of a baby." Mama pressed at her temples with the heels of her hands. "*We* can't take care of a baby. Don't you see, Annie? It would be better off not to be born." The eerie calm of her voice broke over into sobbing. This once-strong woman, who'd withstood the pains of birth, death, and poverty, fell onto the table in a heap of fearful sorrow.

"Mama, now listen to me." For the first time Annie could remember, her own mother needed a scolding, and backward as it was, Annie was the only one there to do it. With her jaw clenched and a fire in her belly, she stood and pulled Mama by the arms into an upright position. "That's your own flesh and blood you're talking about. A living soul. And if you believe the Bible like you say you do, then you know that tiny person already looks like God somehow. It says so. You know it's true. Made in His image."

She held Mama there, squeezing just below the short sleeves of her white and green-checked house dress, and leaned close to her face, searching Mama's eyes for any sign of sense or reason. Leeta Swaim had been a God-fearing woman all her life, had taught Annie and R.C. the ways of right and wrong. But she'd let the devil slip in and whisper in her ear.

"She's just a baby herself," Mama said. The words came out staccato between gasps for air. "She just can't have a baby. She can't." She shook her head. "The shame of it. The shame of it is too much."

"Shame?" Annie released her grasp and stood up straight. "Shame is nothing, Mama. We all have shame. Think of what it would do to Ruth Claire to make her carry that kind of pain around the rest of her life, knowing she's responsible for making and killing the same life." Annie cupped a hand over her mouth, then dropped it. "Whose shame are you worried about, anyway? Hers or yours?"

Annie walked to the sink and looked out the window at the small patch of backyard blanketed in darkness. The reflection in the windowpane was her mother's twin—amber eyes and light brown hair with just a hint of wave—only not so tired and used up. How long before that would change?

After a long time of silence, Mama spoke.

"Was it Tommy?" She'd regained enough sense to keep her voice down.

Annie looked over her shoulder and nodded.

"Did he take advantage?"

Annie sighed as she walked back toward the table. There was no black-and-white. No way to measure how much Tommy might have persuaded, or how much either of them understood about their choices. He was a kid himself. She sat with her mother, whose face had been rearranged back to solemn and wiped dry. "I've talked to her, Mama. I think she knew what she was doing, mostly. But it's hard to understand exactly what R.C. knows or feels about a lot of things."

Mama looked away, and Annie read her face like Morse code. If her mother hadn't accepted R.C.'s differences before, now wasn't the time to help her see them.

"But there's no blame to place here," Annie said. "What's done is done. She's doing okay, and she's going to be okay. That doesn't make Tommy any less of a horse's rear-end, though." When Mama looked at her for further information, Annie continued. "He won't talk to her anymore." Annie's jaw tightened and she whipped her head to the side. "I know he's probably scared, but to make her go through this alone . . ."

"I guess we should . . . I guess *I* should talk to his parents," Mama said. "Make sure they know." Mama's eyes begged Annie for confirmation.

"I think that's the right thing."

Annie placed her hand over her mother's, then Mama let out another loud groan. It was different than before, more pain-filled than desperate.

"Annie, forgive me. May God forgive me. *God forgive me.*" The reality of what she'd suggested sent Mama into another crying spell, and Annie breathed a silent sigh of relief that repentance had caught up to her sooner than later. "I just don't know how I can keep you girls in school and take care of a little one again. Not to mention keeping the four of us fed."

"You don't have to figure it out alone, Mama. I'm here. And the Lord is, too. Didn't He see you through while Daddy was in Europe? And when you lost your job? And when Daddy died?"

"And countless times before those things." Mama placed a gnarled hand on Annie's cheek.

"Just pray then, Mama. He'll show us what to do."

*   *   *

Annie stepped out of the car in front of Farmer's Dairy Bar on Stratford Road. Her jaw was clenched, and her insides shook, but she managed to turn and smile at the young woman in the driver seat. "Thanks again for the ride, Mrs. Johnson." The lady smiled, and Annie waved as a little girl in the back seat, wearing a pink tutu, called out, "'Bye, Miss Annie. See you next week." Her students' parents were so kind to help with transportation after work on those days when Mama had the car.

She turned back to face the building and the unpleasant task at hand. After the doctor had confirmed R.C.'s pregnancy the day before, Annie decided to confront Tommy Jacobs. Someone needed to educate him about a man's responsibility. For certain, R.C. was better off without him, but Annie's niece or nephew deserved to have a father.

Annie peeked through the window of the restaurant as she silently rehearsed her plea. Tommy was there as she expected, working the after-school shift. She watched as he put the finishing touches on a banana split and handed it across the counter to a customer, then she turned and pressed her back against the warm brick of the building as she drew a deep, steadying breath. She thought of how rude Tommy's parents had been when Mama called, and it made her blood boil. "How do we know y'all aren't making this up, to try to get money out of us?" his mother had dared to say. Then she'd informed Mama that even if R.C. was pregnant with Tommy's baby, they wouldn't have anything to do with the child. Before hanging up, she told Mama not to call again. Annie's stomach churned at the memory of Mama's tear-stained face as she told her about the call. Mama'd started having chest pains within an hour later, and when they didn't let up for a day, Annie insisted she make an appointment to see the doctor.

And that's where Mama was now, with the car.

Annie needed to refocus. She walked around the side of the building to the adjoining A&P Grocery, where she pretended to peruse the hanging baskets near the entrance. As mad as she was at Tommy and his parents, she had to approach him in love. She had to put herself in his shoes for a moment. He was probably just scared. Maybe she could reason with him not to shut R.C. out completely, for the sake of their child.

A favorite verse escaped her lips in a whisper. "And above all things have fervent charity among yourselves: for charity shall cover the multitude of sins."

Seconds later, she found herself standing inside the brightly lit dairy bar, searching again for Tommy. It wasn't the time or place to have a long conversation, but if she could convince him to meet her after work to talk, that would be success. The kitchen door swung open, and curly-haired Tommy and a cute blonde came out, each carrying a tub of ice cream. Tommy set his tub inside the freezer as Annie walked up to the counter like any other patron. He hadn't spotted her yet, but Annie watched him give his coworker a pinch on the behind as she leaned into the freezer. The girl turned to him, feigning disapproval, and Tommy winked at her. The girl winked, too, and gave him a sly smile. In that moment, every thought Annie had about reasoning with Tommy vanished. She cleared her throat.

Wide-eyed, Tommy faced Annie and greeted her with a jittery and barely audible, "Oh, hiya, Annie." Then he seemed to take a deep breath and hold it while shifting from one foot to the other. His childish fidgeting almost made her feel sorry for him, but then she thought of her sister. Leaning with one hand on the counter, Annie reached across with the other closed in a fist, and with as much force as she could summon, socked Tommy squarely on the nose. He immediately covered his face with his hands and stumbled backward. The blonde let out an excited yelp, and customers seated near Annie gasped, but nobody said a word as the toes of her saddle oxfords spun around on the terrazzo tile and she walked out the door with her head held high. No doubt she'd regret it later, but for now, Annie didn't even look back.

Chapter Five

"**Y**OUR MOTHER needs surgery." Daddy kept an even tone as he delivered the news.

A gentleman to Missy's left in the Emergency Department waiting room sneezed in her direction, and she flinched in spite of herself.

"I thought it wasn't that bad." She tried to keep her voice low. There were plenty of people there with their own problems, without having to hear about her family's.

"It's *not* that bad, honey. Just something that needs attention. A torn rotator cuff." Daddy's voice reassured her. "Sometimes it heals on its own, with time. But the doc said he's pretty sure they'll need to go in and repair it."

Missy sunk back in her chair, against the same multi-colored fabric of all the other thirty-some chairs in the space. She'd rushed to the hospital after getting Grandma Annie settled and after Ray finally got home to watch the kids, only to find out there wasn't any reason to rush. She couldn't see her mother until another doctor finished examining her anyway. And they'd be sending her home soon, to wait until surgery day.

"They gave her medicine," Dad said. "At least she's not in pain."

Missy checked the time on her phone. Almost seven. She wondered if Ray had bothered to warm up the frozen pizzas or if he was waiting to see if she'd be home in time to feed the kids before bedtime.

Daddy seemed to read her mind. "Go on home to your babies. We'll be fine. You can see Mama tomorrow."

"No, Daddy. I'll stay here with you for a while. I want to wait to see her. Did they say how long it will take to get better after surgery?"

"She'll have to keep her arm in a sling for about six weeks. Full recovery in six months."

Not too bad, considering what could have happened.

They settled in—Dad with phone in hand, head down and pointer finger hovered over the screen, and Missy browsing the newest Southern Kitchen catalog. She only needed one big sale to land her in the Bronze Division. Then her name would be on that big screen during the level-up presentation at the regional conference.

"What did Erica say when you told her about Mama?" Missy asked without looking away from her catalog.

"Oh, I haven't called her yet. No need to worry her. There's nothing she can do out there, anyhow."

Of course not. Why should Erica be bothered? The woman who gave birth to them was only lying in a hospital bed in need of surgery. Missy could do the worrying for the both of them.

Her father looked up from his word game and turned toward Missy. "You know, sweetie, I realized earlier that . . . well it might be a good idea to cancel my birthday party, or . . . I don't know, maybe at least postpone it. Don't you think so?"

A team of EMS wheeling someone in on a gurney distracted her, talking over each other with a kind of urgency that meant bad things. It was a jumble of sound, but each seemed to under-stand what the others were saying.

She came back to herself as the double doors of the wait-ing room swung closed, forming a barrier that separated one kind of chaos from another. "What do you mean by cancel?" She shoved the catalog back into her bag and sat up straight. "You really think we should cancel the party?"

"Well, since your mom won't be able to help you, and since Erica can't be there now."

"Wait—I thought you hadn't talked to her today."

"She left me a voicemail a little while ago."

An ugly word formed in Missy's mind but didn't escape her lips.

"You mean make all the work that I've already done count for nothing, just because Erica is too busy to celebrate your birthday?"

"Well, it's mostly because of your mom. I just thought . . ." His words trailed away.

Missy huffed. All she could think about was the look on the party-store clerk's face when Little Bit upchucked in front of the register. All for some tissue paper balls and streamers that might not be used.

"Don't be upset, honey. It was just an idea. We can see what your mother thinks."

The look on his face and the way he shrank back into his chair told her she'd been too harsh, and a wave of Southern good-girl guilt made her stomach hurt.

"Daddy," Missy said softly, "I'm sorry. I just think it would be a shame not to celebrate your birthday like we had planned. I really want to make it nice for you. You're *worth* celebrating. I mean, you haven't had a big party since you were a kid, right?"

The normal twinkle returned to Dad's eyes. "Well, I was a young adult, I suppose. Your grandma always made my birthday special. Every year. But every *fifth* year"—he turned to her and gestured with both hands as a wide smile peeked from beneath his graying mustache—"she threw the biggest party you've ever seen. Went all out. Maybe not by today's standards, but it was a big deal to us." He combed his fingers through the top of his thinning salt-and-pepper hair. "She said that it made the celebrations more memorable to go that long in between, 'stead of having a big party every birthday. And I think she was right. Five, ten, fifteen, and twenty. Four giant parties, and I remember each of them like they all happened yesterday."

If only I could parent that way. Planning four parties every year was exhausting, but what else could she do? They'd come to expect it. Her kids weren't spoiled rotten, but the fruit flies were sure starting to hover—a natural effect of new toys at every drive-thru window and not even having to sit through commercials like she used to do.

"It really is a shame Erica can't make it, though," Dad said. "I guess that's what I get for having a daughter on the rise to country-music fame."

"She's been singing back-up for five years, Daddy. I don't think I'd call that fame."

Dad slowly put his phone in his shirt pocket, gripped the arm rests, and turned toward her again. His tired eyes narrowed. "Why do you talk about your sister like that?" His voice held curious concern.

"Well, it's true. People get all worked up over Erica being this successful singer, and I just don't see it. I mean, don't get me wrong, I'm proud of her. I think it's great. But, well, it's— it's just not all *that* impressive."

"Where did this bitterness come from, Melissa?" The curious tone was gone. Stern and deliberate, his voice made her sit up straighter, and hearing her given name brought back the guilt, though it was strangely comforting. Fathers didn't chastise children they didn't care about. She'd heard that somewhere, a long time ago.

"What do you mean, Daddy?" As if feigning ignorance had ever worked on Thomas Hall. He'd honed his lie-detecting skills during his years as a middle-school math teacher.

"You know what I mean. Every time you say her name, I hear it in your voice. You're bitter. Now, what is it between you two?"

Missy pushed the short curls from her face and swept them behind her ear. "I don't know what you're talking about. I love my sister."

"I know you love her. But you're still bitter about something. Now what is it?"

"Hall," a shrill voice called with unnecessary loudness. Missy and her father stood in unison and looked toward the reception desk. The receptionist looked at them, then to another family approaching. She pointed at the other family. Wrong Halls.

Missy and Dad took their seats again. The tense conversation interrupted, they sat in silence for at least a minute.

"I have an idea, Missy," Dad said. He turned to her again, pulling his knee into the chair and leaning on the armrest. His eyes were wide. "I want you to sing at my party."

Missy's fingers tugged through the tangle of curls that rested on the back of her neck as her emotions went from shock to dread to the familiar bitterness of which she'd been accused. She sighed. "As my sister's replacement, huh?"

"No, no. Don't think of it that way. Everyone is expecting to hear a special song, and I think you could do it."

"There's no way I could—"

"Missy, promise me you'll never tell your sister this?"

He had her attention. She nodded.

"I've always liked your voice more. It's richer. Fuller."

Missy knew the shock was written on her face. Dad really liked her singing more?

"Don't get me wrong. Erica's a wonderful singer, but your voice has a certain quality to it that . . . I don't know. It's just beautiful."

"But I don't sing anymore, Daddy." She retrieved her phone from the bag. Checking social media had become her nervous habit.

"But you could. Remember that solo in high school choir? The most angelic thing I've ever heard. Your teacher raved about it. Then you quit."

Truth was, she'd been too busy running around with Ray to take it seriously. And he wasn't into choral music. Alt-country was his thing back then. Then, right after a Dwight Yoakam concert, he'd asked her to marry him. Goodness knew, she wasn't sure what kind of music he liked now. He could have been into rap, for all she knew.

"And those Christmas programs at the church when you were little. I loved hearing you sing in church." He smiled at her. "I miss it."

"We've talked about this, Daddy."

"I know. I know. You're a grown woman. I can't make you come back to church. But you know how I feel."

The phone vibrated in her hand, and she looked down. "Ray," she said to her daddy as she swiped the phone's face. She gripped the phone tighter. A text from Ray usually meant trouble.

When are you coming home?

He didn't have to say he was in over his head, or the kids were going nuts. She already knew.

Missy locked eyes with her father.

"It's okay, honey. Go on home."

She sighed. "Okay, but call me when they let y'all out of here. And tell Mama I love her."

"I will. And Missy?"

"Uh-huh?"

"Will you think about it?"

"Okay, Daddy. I'll think about it."

"And just one more thing." He placed a gentle hand on her forearm. "Grandma is more upset than she shows about moving in with us. It's been hard on her. Maybe you can show her a little extra attention for a few days? Especially while your mama's recovering."

She considered telling Dad how Grandma had scolded her earlier. He might know something about the folder and why her grandmother had been so protective over its contents. But he had enough on his mind, and she didn't have the time, anyway.

"Sure, Dad. I'll try," Missy said.

If she could make the time, it *would* be nice to visit with Grandma Annie again soon. She'd left in such a hurry to get the kids home and then get to the hospital. Maybe their next visit would be more relaxed, and she could persuade her to tell her about the ballet shoes. Maybe even about the private papers in the bottom dresser drawer.

*　　　*　　　*

Daddy's words plagued her all the way home, even while she imagined the worst about the shape of the house with Ray there alone with four kids. Was she really so bitter toward

Erica? Quick answer: *Yes.* Erica was self-absorbed and had an over-inflated ego, pumped up in the beginning by years of "but she's the baby" logic, fed to her by everyone from their parents to the mailman.

"Remember that time she put a snake in the mailbox? Dwight just laughed and told her she was too cute to be so mean."

Great. She was talking to herself. First sign of a mental break.

But why had her growing discontentment festered from just beneath the surface to bubbling out to the point that Daddy could see it? She was mature enough to admit her jealousy, and even her resentment, but Missy refused to believe that all her attitude problems were about Erica. It wouldn't be fair. Everything had always been about Erica. Not this. It had to be something more. What was it that she wanted? What was missing?

As if someone else was in the van with her, Missy heard a small voice. Second sign of a mental break.

What do you really want, Melissa?

The voice used her real name. Was it channeling her father?

What do you really want?

She gripped the steering wheel tighter as she turned into her driveway. Every light in the house was on, illuminating the yard toys left out since late summer and the shrubs that needed trimming. She hoisted her bag onto her shoulder and moved to open the door, then froze. The voice would not be ignored.

What do you really want, Melissa?

She locked eyes with her dim reflection in the rearview mirror and fixated on the only visible portion of her tired face— from the bridge of her nose to the middle of her forehead. She drew a deep breath to force out the words. "I want to be seen."

Chapter Six

*T*HE WORLD had gone on as normal for months. The temperate spring had melted into a miserably hot summer—usually Annie's favorite season, marked by cookouts with old high school friends and trips to the pool with Ruth Claire. But there would be no swimsuits. The roundness of R.C.'s belly now threatened to give them away. Something had to be done.

For all Annie's talk of shame, she refused to let R.C. endure it—not if there was another way. There had to be a way to keep her from public ridicule and the little life inside her safe. Then there was Mama to worry about. The only thing standing between Mama and a nervous breakdown was Annie and the Good Lord. Yes, something had to be done soon. And she finally had a plan.

Between teaching classes, Annie had worked out the details in her mind as she practiced dancing, alone in the studio. Think and pirouette. Plan and plié. And pray. Always pray.

A soulful melody rang out from the record player in the corner. Annie felt the music deep inside as she swayed and dipped. It wasn't Tchaikovsky, but she could dance to Elvis Presley and "Peace in the Valley" even better than *Swan Lake*. There was something about his voice that helped her focus.

Julian was the only one who knew about the Elvis routine. "I know it might sound strange, but I feel close to God when I dance to that song," she had told him. "It helps me sort things out sometimes." And though he had smiled and had called her *honey* as he told her how nice it was, she thought she saw him roll his eyes as he turned away. Julian didn't share her faith—his one and only flaw—but she was certain he would come around one day.

Julian was privy to most of Annie's secrets and innermost thoughts. They talked on the phone until late into the night most nights, but she still hadn't divulged the circumstances that plagued her mind. She'd managed to keep the secret even from him. Only she, R.C., and Mama carried the burden of R.C.'s pregnancy since Tommy Jacobs and his parents wanted no part. But the time was coming when she'd have to tell Julian, too.

Two Annies danced in the studio there—her flesh and bones in all their sinewy strength, and her reflection floating and swaying in the mirror. She'd grown up in front of that mirror and used to it to master her form. The mirror had seen her go from pigtails and crooked teeth to a grown woman and a masterful dancer. How strange that she'd somehow grown up to be someone's aunt, too—someone who would be arriving in a few short months.

Annie had landed a perfect *grande jeté* as Elvis sang about the lion laying down with the lamb, when the studio door opened, and Miss Melinda walked in. She sported her three trademark features—a warm smile, an impossibly tall beehive hairdo, and equally disproportionate black cat's-eye glasses. Annie stopped dancing and wiped at her brow with the back of her hand as she hurried to turn off the music.

"Hey there, sweetie," Miss Melinda said. "Say, that's a song for a Sunday, ain't it? Doesn't sound much like ballet music to me." Her broad smile said she was teasing, but Annie's cheeks still went warm.

"I guess not." Annie said, smiling back. "It helps me think, though."

"Shoot. As good as you are, you could probably do ballet to 'Jailhouse Rock,' though I would never let you do it in a recital." Miss Melinda let out a chuckle followed by a staccato snort. "Hey, I brought you an updated roster. Couple newcomers to your beginner class. Cutest little twins."

"Oh, good. That class is full now."

"Well, word has gotten around. All the parents want their little girls to learn from you."

Miss Melinda handed out compliments like the perfume girl at the store gave away samples. Always encouraging. She'd been like family for years, even giving Annie and R.C. little presents each Christmas. And when Daddy died, she'd sent a giant peace lily to the funeral home to pay her respects. Annie thought of that often, for some reason. Probably because the plant was still alive at their house. Six years they'd managed to keep it from withering away.

Miss Melinda took a rag from her pants pocket and began to wipe down the barre that ran the length of the mirrored wall. She'd once confided in Annie how much she hated that mirror. "Such a rude a reminder that getting old stole my ballerina figure," she had said. And despite a colorful disposition, she always wore black from head to toe, because, she said, it was slimming. But Annie thought she was beautiful. Classy and kind. Much older, but more filled with life than Mama.

The clock on the wall read ten 'til three. Enough time to say what needed to be said. Elvis had soothed Annie's nerves and Jesus had reassured her heart. All would be well. She only had to ask.

"Miss Melinda, I need to talk to you about something before my students get here, if you have time."

"Sure, punkin. What is it?"

The lack of chairs in the room made it awkward. Her toes fidgeted in her pointe shoes as she stood face-to-face with her mentor.

"This will probably come as a surprise. And I hate having to ask. But . . ."

Miss Melinda drew still, her face pensive. "What is it, child? You're making me nervous."

Annie bit at her bottom lip. "Well . . . I'm hoping I can take a little time off."

"Is that all? *Puh.* I don't know why your face went white to ask me that. You know I can give you a few days off if you need it, sweetpea. You hardly ever take any time."

Annie brought the clipboard to her chest, the one with the class list that Miss Melinda had given her.

"Actually, it . . . it would be more than a few days. I need to take about four months. Maybe five. I'm going away for a while."

Miss Melinda's mouth went into a small *o*. The eyes behind the cat's-eye glasses begged to know why, though she didn't speak.

"I'm sorry I can't tell you why. Personal reasons. You've been so good to me and my family, and I hate to do this to you. If there was any other way, well, I wouldn't dream of leaving, but . . . I just need some time. And I'll need an extra semester to finish my business program. Then I can take over management of the studio like we've talked about. If you can just give me a few extra months."

Miss Melinda stepped toward Annie and took her shaking hands in both her own. "Whatever it is, I'm sure it's a good reason. And I hope you'll come to me if there's anything I can do for you." She took a breath before adding, "Annie, if you're in some kind of trouble, I'm here to help."

Relief washed over Annie and chased away nausea. She considered telling her the truth about R.C. She owed it to her, really. But she and Mama had decided that no one would know about the baby. Not even Miss Melinda.

"I'll be okay. But thank you," Annie said.

"When do you plan to leave?"

"In about two weeks, I think."

Miss Melinda let go of Annie's hands and turned, looking up at the clock on the wall. "You're timing is actually good, Annie. And I've been meaning to talk to you, anyway. I had planned to take you to lunch to talk about it, but . . . do you remember my niece, Alexandra?"

"Of course. She's a couple years older than me. I remember when she used to visit you in the summers. From New Hampshire, right?"

"That's right. My poor sister went and married a Yankee. But he's a good one." She gave Annie a wink, then let out a chittery laugh that went on longer than it should have. "Well, Alexandra has decided to move to North Carolina. Here to Winston-Salem, actually."

With her only son buried in the sands of Normandy and her husband ten years gone from a massive coronary, Melinda Bennett had no ties by blood or marriage within a hundred miles. "Oh, Miss Melinda. How nice it will be for you to have family here."

"Yes, dear, I am excited. She's quite an accomplished dancer herself, you know."

"I know. Maybe she can teach some classes for us." Annie's mind raced. Another teacher would be great for business. She had plans to take Melinda's School of Dance to a new level.

"Yes, I'd thought of that." Miss Melinda looked at the clock again. "Actually, she's taken some business classes, too. At a university."

"That's great. And what does she plan to do here in Winston-Salem?"

Miss Melinda took Annie's hands again.

"Annie, you know I think the world of you. And I really had no idea things would turn out this way. But family is family." She pressed her lips into a straight line and looked away. "I'm going to let Alexandra manage the studio when I retire. She's coming in a couple of weeks, and I was hoping you would mentor her until she learns the way of things 'round here. But it's okay. I can teach her."

Every muscle in Annie's body became a coiled spring under an industrial press. She searched Miss Melinda's eyes. There had to be a punchline coming, but Miss Melinda wasn't prone to joking around.

Suddenly hot and clammy on the outside, Annie had the sensation that her stomach had turned itself inside out, like the lining of a purse being pulled to shake out old crumbs. The reality threatened to set in, as Annie's vision went blurry on the sides, then it made good on the threat. Her life plan wasn't being put on hold by R.C.'s pregnancy; it was being destroyed in an instant by a mix of familial obligation and an out-of-town niece. But wasn't *she* like family? Eleven years of dancing there and two years of teaching, studying business to take over managing the studio, countless hours by Miss Melinda's side—and now for what? This couldn't be happening. Julian had suggested she get a contract, but she'd foolishly thought there was no need.

"I'm sure Alexandra would do a great job, Miss Melinda, but this is all I've ever—"

Miss Melinda placed her finger in front of her lips, shushing Annie as the studio door opened and little girls with innocent, smiling faces began filing in, all wearing light-pink leotards and tights. Miss Melinda gave one last sympathetic nod then turned to go. It was time for class, and dancing must come before anything else.

On her way out the door, Miss Melinda greeted the parents in the lobby with a loud and chipper, "Good afternoon. So nice to see you today."

The room spun. Annie's breaths came faster and faster. She was shocked into focus by two little arms that grabbed around her waist in a surprise hug. She patted the girl's head.

"Thank you, Jacqueline. I've missed you, too." The blond-haired little girl smiled up at her, then ran off to join her friend who had just arrived.

"Okay, girls," Annie said, willing her voice steady, "go ahead and start your stretches."

If not for her love of the students, she would walk out before the class started and not look back. But that wouldn't be right.

Her hands trembled as she flipped through the record box, searching for the right music for the day's lesson. The tightening in her chest made her mind flash to one summer day when she was eight. She'd been visiting her uncle's farm in Iredell County and hadn't paid attention to the warnings about the animals. She had been trying to braid a horse's tail when she ended up with a hoof to the chest that knocked the wind out of her so hard, she was unable to even cry. That's what Miss Melinda's news had done. Annie wanted to cry but could barely breathe. She had taken a swift kick to the chest from a dark-haired mare—one that she'd trusted.

Chapter Seven

October, Present Day

Missy stood with her arm raised and pressed into the stove's vent hood. Her forehead rested on her arm as she stared into the milky depths of a bubbling pot of potato soup—her mother's favorite. She thought of how Mama wouldn't be able to raise her arm like that for weeks, not even to put on a shirt, and brought it back down to her side. It had been four days since the fall, and Missy had spent much of the time cooking. Lasagna, chicken casserole, potato casserole, squash casserole, name-a-casserole, soups, and stews galore—the art of which had escaped many in her generation. But Grandma Annie and Mama had taught her well. Her parents' freezer would be stocked until Mama was able to cook for herself and Daddy and Grandma Annie again.

The bubbles popped on the surface of the soup in a musical rhythm. Steam rose toward Missy's face, fogging her glasses and bathing her tired eyes. With John Thomas napping and the big kids at school, she was alone with just the soup and her thoughts. But in moments like this—the rare quiet and calm—her peace was short-lived, broken by an invading memory from Saturday, of the scolding she'd received from Grandma Annie, and, in particular, the look in her beloved grandmother's eyes as she snatched the folder out of Missy's hand.

What could possibly be in those papers to make Grandma so upset? What would make her so protective?

She set the long-handled spoon on the rest and popped a couple of chalky, fruit-flavored antacids from the cabinet beside the stove. *What if she's in some kind of trouble?* Were there debts Missy didn't know about? A new thought hit as she choked down the medicine. On an episode of that cold-case mystery show, they'd had a story about a woman who'd spent years living a double life as both a housewife and a hit-man. Missy could see the side-by-side photos on the screen. On the left, the woman wore a shoulder-padded dress with a frilly collar and a string of pearls, her smiling face posed in a slight tilt. One hand rested on the other. In the grainy image on the right, the woman sported black from head to toe and had a rifle slung over her back. It sent a cold chill down Missy's arms, but Grandma could never have a secret that bad. *Surely not.*

The phone rang from Missy's pocket, and she fumbled to answer and put the lid on the soup pot at the same time. "Hello?"

"Hey. Sorry it took me a while to call you back, sis, but you wouldn't believe how busy we've been. Extra rehearsals, a publicity shoot, wardrobe fitting. You just *would not* believe it." Erica's voice was an octave too high. "And you're never gonna guess why."

I left a voicemail three days ago saying I needed to talk, but sure, let's make this about you.

"Justin's agent got him booked on *Good Morning, USA,* and he wants to use the full band."

Missy sat at the kitchen table, leaned the chair back on two legs—something she fussed at Joshua for all the time—and brought it down again. "Hey, you've been wanting to get on a show like that for a while." The news brought a tiny smile. "That's wonderful. I bet Katy and Tamara are beside themselves."

Erica talked about her other "sisters" often—the two women who crooned with her, behind and slightly to the left of Justin Trent, at every show.

"Oh, they are. We've all been downright giddy. And you know how those morning shows are, Missy. If ratings are good on one, the others will want him, too. He could be booked clear up to the new year."

"That's awesome."

Such a strange bag of emotions Missy carried. Her jealousy had never precluded her from being happy for her sister. Even proud; she'd always been proud. But she choked on celebration.

"So, anyway, you called me. What was it you needed? Is everything all right? I talked to Mama and Daddy last night. She's not enjoying wearing that sling, is she? Poor thing. She went on and on about not being able to do her hair."

At least Erica had made time to call their parents.

"She's managing okay. I just wish the surgery would be scheduled soon, so she can start getting better. And she is upset about the hair."

Both sisters giggled. It was no secret how meticulous Mama could be over her hairdo.

"But everything else is okay?" Erica said.

"Yeah. We're fine." Missy thought to tell her about the folder, share how hurt she'd been when Grandma Annie snatched it from her. But she tucked those words away. "I'm going to get Grandma tomorrow afternoon so she can spend some time at our house. I think she gets bored there, just her and Mama during the day, and Mama not being able to take her out. And I get the feeling Mama could use the alone time." She took a deep breath. "Hey, the reason I called is . . . I wanted to ask you about the party. Your song."

"Missy, I really wish I could. I feel so bad about it, but I just—"

"No, it's okay. Daddy knows you have more important things to do." She hadn't meant to say it like that. Nothing to do now but press on, and the words came out fast. "I just wanted to know what you had planned to sing. Daddy asked me to do it now, since you're not coming, and . . . I told him I'd think about it."

The line went quiet for a second.

"Oh . . . okay. That's . . . that's nice. Yeah, that'll be great."

Missy's nose wrinkled. Wait a minute. Did Erica sound jealous . . . of her? Or was she surprised that Daddy would ask Missy to sing in her place? Maybe she didn't think Missy was good enough to sing in her place. And maybe she should do it, just to prove to Erica that she could. She'd show everyone. She might not be as pretty, or as smart, or as popular as the famed Erica Hall, but she *could* sing as well as her. According to their father, even better.

"I was planning to sing 'Amazing Grace,'" Erica said. The regret was audible.

Missy stood up fast from the kitchen table, and the chair screeched across the linoleum. "That's not a party song. That's a church song." Her heart began to pound.

A memory from forever ago rose within her. Sandwiched between two old ladies in long dresses, standing in the soprano row, feeling the hot collective breath of the altos on the back of her neck, a much-younger Missy opened her mouth in preparation for the first word of the next verse as the rest of the choir hushed. Her first solo. She could still see Daddy's smiling face in the front pew, though in her mind, he looked the same as he did today, not the Daddy of almost twenty years ago.

"Well, the party *is* at a church, Missy, and it's his favorite song." Erica's voice brought her back to the present. "What did you wanna sing? 'Tequila Sunrise'?"

"Well, I don't know." Missy paced. "I guess I was thinking 'Wind Beneath My Wings' or something like that. Maybe 'Bridge Over Troubled Water'."

"Daddy hates sappy stuff like that. What's wrong with 'Amazing Grace' anyway? Everybody loves it. I mean, have you ever known anyone in the history of hymndom that didn't like 'Amazing Grace'? C'mon."

Missy strained her brain in search, as if it were actually possible or mattered to think of someone who, in the history of hymndom, didn't like "Amazing Grace." She gave up. "I guess you're right." She looked at the clock. The school bus would be there soon. "I gotta go, sis. Thanks for calling me back."

"So, are you gonna do it? You're gonna sing at the party? I'd hate to miss hearing you."

Missy walked to the china hutch and picked up a framed family picture. They had tried to match by wearing black, but the background was dark, making them look like floating heads. Erica's pretty face with the bright eyes and perfect complexion, topped with gorgeous, flowing hair, floated near Missy's round and unassuming image. "I don't know. I still have to think about it. But thanks again and let me know when you're going to be on television. I'm happy for you, sis." She hung up before Erica could say goodbye.

Missy pressed a balled fist into her forehead as she slid the cell phone into her back pocket with the other hand. "Amazing Grace." Now she was doubly sure this was a bad idea. Not only had she not performed in front of anyone since high school, now she had to consider taking a sacred anthem of the church and reducing it to an act. But it would make Daddy happy, and that was most important. And it would give her the chance to prove that Erica wasn't the only talented daughter. But how could she possibly sing about a saving grace she didn't believe in anymore?

John Thomas walked into the kitchen, yawning and rubbing his eyes, wearing only a pair of pajama shorts he'd had on all day. Missy sat down at the kitchen table and opened her arms wide to him. He climbed into her lap and she rubbed his back. One of her favorite parts of the day. He was so calm and cuddly right after a nap. Within five minutes, though, he'd be bouncing off the walls again. John Thomas only had two speeds.

She rocked him and tried to forget her frustrations. As she swayed, she hummed a quiet melody in his ear.

John Thomas raised his head and looked at her.

"What's that song, Mama? Sing it to me. I love it when you sing."

She smiled at his sweetness. Her children had been her only audience for so long.

"Let's see. What was I humming? I wasn't even thinking about a song."

She picked up where she'd left off and realized that the very hymn which she'd balked at the idea of singing had slipped into her subconscious. "How about 'Twinkle, Twinkle' instead?"

John Thomas shook his head, then jumped down and ran to the toy box in the hallway. Missy took the phone out of her pocket again to check the time. She'd missed her afternoon cigarette.

*   *   *

"I think you should do it," Ray said. "You've got a great voice, and none of us get to hear you sing enough. It would be fun."

He rifled through the fridge with grease-stained hands, then brought out the bologna and set in on the counter next to the loaf of bread.

"I don't know . . ."

"I remember back in high school, that solo you did for all-county ensemble. It brought the house down." He assembled the sandwich right on the counter, not bothering with a plate, or even a paper towel.

"I think you're remembering Erica's performance, Ray."

"What?" He shot her a puzzled look as he slapped on the top piece of bread. "No, I'm talking about *you*. Three or four years before Erica did all-county. You were great, honey. I remember it like it was yesterday. The only sophomore to get a lead part. Remember?" Ray bit into the sandwich, sending a glop of mustard onto his shirt.

How funny he would remember that detail.

Of course, she remembered the concert, and every detail leading up to it. How shocked she'd been when the director picked her, out of all the other sopranos. How proud Mama and Daddy had been when she told them. Then the night of the show and that huge, nearly filled auditorium. Her voice quivered on the opening line, but she'd redeemed herself with a pitch-perfect ending so powerful she surprised even herself. It was one of the best nights of her life. It was also one of the last times she'd ever sang in public, and the night that she and Ray had driven to a subdivision still under construction, in his old Toyota pickup, and parked for an hour while her parents thought they were going for ice cream.

"That was a long time ago, Ray. And besides, a solo at a birthday party is a lot different than performing with a whole choir standing there behind you."

Missy headed to the family room to take control of the television. With the kids asleep, maybe she'd be able to watch something on the home and garden channel before she conked out.

Soon, Ray plopped into the recliner next to the couch. The mechanical clunk of the footrest made Missy jump.

"The kids missed you at dinner tonight."

"They didn't miss me enough to save me any spaghetti, did they?" He chuckled around another mouthful of bologna sandwich.

"Oh, Emma wants you to help with her science project this weekend. It has something to do with a motor, and she says you can help her better than I can."

"Fine, fine. I can help her. So, back to your daddy's party. You just nervous about singing in front of people, or what?"

Missy flipped through all the channels instead of punching the numbers on the remote to get to the right one, doing her best to ignore the candy residue that covered the device.

"Ray—" She stopped channel-surfing and turned toward him. "The party's kind of second on my list of worries right now." Back to the TV, she paused on a weight-loss reality show and considered it. Those always made her feel better about herself.

She landed on the home and garden channel as she felt Ray staring. She turned to him again to see his head tilted and one eyebrow raised.

"Well, are you gonna tell me what's number one or do you want me to guess? All you've talked about for months is that party and reaching the next Southern Kitchen sales goal."

She rolled her eyes and huffed. "It's just . . . well, it's Grandma. You would not believe how she snapped at me the other day."

"Annie? Snapped?" His mouth started for the last bite of sandwich but stopped. "Never seen her do that. Over what?"

"That's just it. It was over nothing. At least it seemed like nothing to me. I mean . . . we were moving her things and there was this folder full of papers that had gotten rained on, and I when I tried to dry them, she just . . . snapped. Took them from me and told me she didn't want anyone looking at 'em."

He swallowed the last bite of his sandwich. "Sounds pretty strange." He took off the gray ballcap that read *Ray's Automotive and Towing* and set it on the end table between them.

"It's like she's hiding something, and just knowing there's a secret, it hurts my feelings."

"Maybe you took her wrong. You can be a little sensitive." He licked an escaped dollop of mustard from his thumb. "It was probably a Christmas list or something. She probably didn't want you to find out what she's getting you."

"A little sensitive, huh? Well, I may be sensitive, but I'm not stupid. Except maybe stupid enough to try to talk to you about something that's bothering me and expect you to understand."

"Now, wait a second, I—"

Missy stood and dropped the remote onto the couch, then headed for the bedroom. "I'm going to bed."

"Well, thanks for proving me right," he whisper-yelled after her. Even with her back turned, she knew he spoke through gritted teeth.

Missy peeked into the girls' room, then the boys' one last time for the night, before she stepped into her own bedroom and shut the door gently behind her. She rested her forehead and one palm against the cool wood of the door.

Grandma never snaps. I'm not *just being sensitive.*

Missy swapped her lounge pants out for the sleep shorts that lay on the pillow before she climbed into the detestable old waterbed. She gripped the corner of the sheet and the comforter together and pulled them over herself with a wide sweep of the arm. As if the *swoosh* of the bedding had fanned the flame of frustration her husband had lighted, a fire began to burn in Missy's heart the moment she closed her eyes. A burning to learn exactly what was in that folder.

Whatever Grandma Annie's secret, she was going to find out.

Chapter Eight

July 1963

T HE HOLLYWOOD starlet on the giant screen turned to face her leading man, her bright red lips puckered in a sultry pout. From the last row of The Flamingo Drive-in, Annie studied the couple in larger-than-life detail. The male actor smiled at the pretty blonde as he brushed the back of his hand across her cheek.

Annie turned to look up at Julian. His chiseled jaw was parallel to and inches from her eyes. She breathed in the smell of him, her favorite in all the world—department store musk and shirt starch underneath a citrus aftershave. If only she could slow time, stay with him there forever. But she'd toyed with time already. There was none left with which to play. She turned back to the screen. The actors were so good, one might have thought they were really in love. The man's eyes spoke of admiration and desire that seemed impossible to fake.

Oh, Julian. Will you ever look at me like that again, after I tell you?

He put his arm around her, and she rested in the embrace until the credits rolled. That's when she would usually have let him kiss her, until the lights around the drive-in came back on. Instead, she buried her face in her hands.

"I've done a bad thing, Julian." Annie raised her head and forced herself to look him in the eye, to read his every movement as she broke the news. She'd come to know him so well. If he answered her quickly, he'd be mostly hurt. If he paused for a long time, he'd be angrier than hurt.

Why had she waited so long to tell him?

"Hey, now. What's wrong with my girl? You look so upset."

"I should have told you sooner, but . . ."

"You're not breaking up with me, are you, Annie?"

The deep hurt in his eyes made the weight on her chest multiply.

"Oh, no. No. Of course not. How could you imagine such a thing? I love you, Julian. That's why I feel so terrible that I've kept this from you."

Julian rubbed at his temples. "Are you in some kind of trouble? How can I help?"

His kind eyes gave her comfort. He would understand. She was sure of it now.

"I'm not in trouble, Julian. But I'm going to have to go away for a while. The last thing in the world I want to do is leave you, but I'm going to go stay with my Aunt Brenda in Georgia for a few months. Mama's sister. She's a widow, too. Has a little farm outside of Gainesville."

"Oh . . ." He looked down and his voice grew solemn. "But why? And why did you say you've done something bad?"

Annie relaxed back into the seat and looked ahead. The credits would be done soon, and they'd have to find somewhere else to talk.

"I just meant that I should have told you sooner. I've known for a while that I would be leaving, but I was afraid to tell you. I'm so sorry, Julian. I don't want to go, and I just kept putting it off."

"If you don't want to go, then why are you? Does your aunt need help?"

That's what Julian was supposed to believe. Mama hadn't told her to lie, but she'd also told her not to tell him the truth. Either way, she'd have to sin—let him believe a lie or disobey her mother. Was one worse than the other? No, the Bible said it was all the same. But an answer of "I can't tell you" didn't seem right, either. That kind of secrecy would destroy their relationship.

"No, my aunt is okay. It's R.C. She needs to go stay with our aunt, and she needs me to go with her." Before Julian could question her, she took one big breath and continued with the rest of the news. "I've lost the studio, too, Julian." She began to cry. "Miss Melinda is letting her niece take over instead of me. So, all my plans for school are worthless now. She'll let me stay on just to teach when I come back, but I'm not sure I can do that. Not when I had my heart set on— Oh, Julian, your girlfriend is a failure."

"Annie, listen to me. You are not a failure. I'm so sorry about the studio. I knew you seemed distracted, but I didn't know you had this on your shoulders. You should have told me." He wiped at her tears with gentle fingers. "But don't worry. You won't even need a job when we're married. I know it was important to you to finish your business classes and manage the dance studio, but I can take care of us."

The lights came up. Soon, the manager would start knocking on windows.

"And if you want to keep dancing," Julian went on, "we'll find a way. You know my father is on the conservatory committee. I'm sure we can get you some kind of position when the school opens."

For the first time since Miss Melinda had crushed her dreams and betrayed her trust, Annie felt hope for her dancing career. Of course, if God wanted her to be a housewife and mother, that would be fine, too. But it was hard to imagine a life without dancing.

"But it will probably be years before the school opens, Julian," Annie said.

"I know. But maybe we could help you open your own dance studio to teach little girls, then see how we can help you get involved with the arts school when the time is right. An intern, an assistant. Something. Like I said, maybe a student. You're still young."

Annie couldn't help herself. She grabbed the back of Julian's head and pulled him toward her, then kissed him with a grateful passion. She kissed away the sadness of leaving him soon and the fear of the future. She lost herself and her cares in the warmth of their closeness. Then the sound of knuckles on glass made her pull away.

The window was too fogged to see through clearly, and for that, Annie was thankful. Her cheeks must have been ten shades of red, even in the dark.

Julian cranked the engine and headed for the exit. As they pulled out into the road, the questions came. "So, tell me more about Georgia. What's this all about? How long do you plan to stay there? Why does R.C. need to go?"

There was no way to keep it from him. If Julian Lane was to be her husband soon, he'd have to know about their niece or nephew.

"Um, about four months, I guess. Maybe a little longer. It depends." She ran her hands down the length of her plaid twill skirt and rested them on her bare knees. "Why don't you turn there at Miller Park, so we can talk some more."

After Julian had parked the Ford Fairlane near an empty tennis court, he flipped the switch that retracted the roof of the car, revealing the night sky and the court lights above them. Annie took a deep breath of steamy summer air as Julian turned off the motor. She turned to him, wishing their moment alone could be more pleasant than revealing family secrets and painful decisions.

"Julian, you can't tell anyone . . . but the truth is, R.C. is going to have a baby. Around November. Mother doesn't want anyone to know, and we're going to Georgia until the baby is born."

Julian's eyes went wide, and he shifted in his seat.

"The ex-boyfriend?"

Annie nodded. "He wants no part."

"Wow." He drew a deep breath and let it out slowly, then he turned to her again and took her hand. "What is she going to do, Annie? I mean, is she going to keep it? Even if she were normal, she's only sixteen, and . . ."

Annie slid her hand slowly out of Julian's and sat up straight. Her jaw tightened. "I think she *could* be a wonderful mother, maybe with just a little help."

"Oh, Annie, I didn't mean—"

"But she's not keeping it anyway. I told you, Mama doesn't want anyone to know. She and I made arrangements with Aunt Brenda. There's an orphanage there that can take care of the child and make sure he or she gets good parents. I hate that it has to be this way, but it probably is for the best."

She'd repeated the line to herself over and over. *The baby would have good parents. The baby would have good parents.* A mother and a father who loved the little one and loved each other. That's what would be best. But it was still no easier to swallow.

"We'll go there, she'll have the baby, and it will be placed in the orphanage. Then, after R.C. heals up, we'll come back here like nothing ever happened." Annie stared up into the night sky. "Mama wants her to be able to go on with her life. Finish school. Not have to carry the shame."

"But . . ." Julian rubbed at the back of his neck. "But why do *you* have to go? R.C.'s the one having the baby. Can't you take her down there, then come back? I could even drive you. Or why doesn't your mother stay with her? Wouldn't it make more sense for *her* to be there?"

Annie opened her mouth then closed it again. She'd never considered *not* going. After a few moments, she found the words. "Well, Mama is in so much pain lately. And she gets so overwhelmed. I just think it's better if I go with R.C. I understand her better, anyway."

Julian looked straight ahead, toward the empty tennis court, his head tilted to the side. He swished his thumbs on the thighs of his jeans like windshield wipers, making a brushing sound. "It's pretty remarkable, Annie—putting your entire life on hold just to help your sister."

"You have a little sister, Julian. You know how important family is."

"Yeah, I love her and all, but . . ." He turned toward her again. "Is there anything I can do? Do you need money? Whatever you need, I can do it."

"Oh, Julian, I couldn't."

"Of course, you could. I told you, Annie, I plan to take care of you."

She swallowed hard. "A little money might help, I guess. For bus tickets."

Julian's expression brightened.

Annie swung her pointer finger and made it an arrow toward him. "And there are two things I need you to do while I'm gone."

"Anything. You name it."

"First of all, wait for me. Promise me you'll wait for me and remember that I'm coming home to you just as soon as I can. Promise me you won't so much as look at another female." She winked.

Julian flashed a smile that made her heart skip a beat then he pressed her hand against his chest.

"You know I will, Annie. Wait for you, that is." He laughed. "What else?"

"Can you look in on Mama sometimes? I know you haven't gotten to know her very well yet, but it would mean a lot to me. She has a few relatives, and church friends and old friends from the mill, but I'm worried about leaving her alone. It will help to know that someone I trust is checking on her."

Julian nodded. "I'll stop by and check on your mother at least once a week. Promise." He gave the Boy Scout salute.

"Oh, Julian, I don't deserve you."

She kissed him again, this time for longer.

"And can I come visit you in Georgia?" Julian asked when the kiss was over. He touched her lips with his fingertips. "I'm not sure how long I can go without one of those before I go completely crazy."

Annie smiled and looked down, cutting her eyes upward at him.

"Maybe on the weekends, I can visit," he said. "You think your aunt would be okay with that?"

The sadness Annie felt when they had arrived at Miller Park had melted under the tennis court lights with the reassurance of Julian's love.

"It might be all right for you to come sleep on the couch. I don't know my Aunt Brenda all that well. I mean I used to know her. We visited a few times before Daddy died, but I haven't seen her in so long. That's another reason I can't let R.C. go alone. But it's a long drive, Julian. Mama says probably eight hours. Do you think it would be worth the drive just to stay for a night or two?"

He gave her a quick, gentle kiss on the tip of her nose then stayed close to her face. In the most tender of whispers, he said, "You're worth everything, Annie Swaim. Everything."

One thing was for sure. The next four months couldn't go by fast enough.

Chapter Nine

October, Present Day

$\mathcal{T}$HE MINIVAN smelled of stale French fries and liniment. The former was a constant, no matter how often she vacuumed; the latter accompanied Grandma Annie. That sweet vanilla fragrance in Missy's memory—the smell of hello hugs and bedtime snuggles—had been long-replaced by the odor of pain-relief cream. So long now that Missy smiled whenever she smelled menthol, no matter the place.

The van bounced over the driveway—an inhomogeneous collection of dirt, clay, and fine granite gravel—then lurched when Missy pushed the gear selector into PARK too soon. Grandma Annie, in the passenger seat, rubbed at the small of her back.

Piper stood and leaned on the seats. "Gigi, you have to come see my room. I cleaned it up just so I could show you."

Grandma tilted the rearview mirror and gave Piper a smile. "Well, good girl."

"Nope. She's going to my room first," Joshua said. "I want to show her my racetrack."

"She's seen it, dummy. She's the one who gave it to you for your birthday."

"I know that, but I want her to see me play with it. Mom, Piper called me a dummy."

"Now, children," Grandma Annie said.

Missy leaned her forehead on the steering wheel. "Piper, don't call your brother names." She slowly leaned up again. "It's not—wait." Panic rose in Missy's chest until it arrived at her throat and clamped down with a painful grip. "Why is the front door open?"

Emma knew not to open the door when she was home alone. Not for any reason. That was rule number one, followed by not using the stove and keeping her phone close in case Missy called to check on her.

Missy swung the van door wide and jumped out in a sprinting stance then stopped short as she spotted the roof of Ray's pickup through the garage window. She bent slightly at the waist and pressed a hand against her chest.

What on earth was he doing home? She straightened and double-checked the time on her phone screen. The shop wasn't supposed to close for another hour and a half. But if he were sick, he would have texted.

As Missy stood there puzzling, Emma ran out of the house and onto the porch, waving and jumping. The Labrador retriever slipped through the open door and ran to Missy, his hind parts wiggling as he made circles around her.

"Hey, Mr. Peanut." Missy patted his moving target of a head and waved back to Emma.

"You got a surprise, Mama! You got a surprise!" Emma's long hair bounced as she did.

A surprise?

She turned her attention back to the van full of passengers, first unbuckling John Thomas, then helping her grandmother out of the seat. The kids ran toward the house, chased by a brisk wind and Mr. Peanut, as Missy linked arms with her grandmother to cross the uneven gravel.

Missy shivered.

"You need a jacket, honey. Or at least some long sleeves." Grandma Annie rubbed Missy's bare arm.

"I know. I just keep hoping summer will come back again, after those eighty-degree days we had last week. You know how up and down the temps are."

Emma stood at the top of the steps that were lined on each side with medium-sized pumpkins—one for each member of the family. Her face beamed as Missy and Grandma neared.

"Hi, Gigi. Come on, Mama." Emma opened the door for them. "He's working on it now."

"I don't know what Ray's up to, but it sure makes me nervous." Missy whispered in Grandma's ear then chuckled, though nothing was funny. She'd never liked surprises—the happy kind or otherwise—and especially not from Ray. Not after the way their marriage got its start.

"Sounds like I came at an exciting time," Grandma said.

Missy kept pace with her grandma as they entered the house and followed Emma down the narrow hallway to the bedroom. They found Ray there, dressed in his grease-stained coveralls and wearing his favorite NASCAR hat, stripping the sheets from their bed.

A new headboard, footboard, and mattress were propped against the dresser. Joshua used a bedrail in the floor as a balance beam while John Thomas attempted to scale the mattress, still wrapped in plastic, like a climbing wall without grips.

Missy propped her hands on her hips. "You bought a new bed?"

"Yes, ma'am." Ray's stubbly cheeks lifted as he grinned. "Actually, the bed was free. Roy at work was getting rid of it. I just bought a new mattress for it. Hey, Annie." He studied the valve on the waterbed. "Now I just gotta remember how to drain the water and take the frame apart. Emma, go grab my phone so I can look it up."

Emma did as her father asked.

"But you love that waterbed, Ray. We've had it our entire marriage."

"I know. But *you* hate it. You've been fussing about it for thirteen years."

"Well, mostly when I was pregnant out to here." She placed her hands as far out in front of her as they would reach. "Remember? When I couldn't get out of it on my own. I had to sleep in the recliner for the last trimester with all four pregnancies."

Piper Grace stood beside her, back arched, imitating the pose of Missy's arms. Ray looked at their daughter and chuckled.

"I know. I know. But now we have a new one, and you're gonna love it. I sprang for the memory foam."

Emma came back with the phone.

"But Christmas is almost here, Ray. These kids have wish lists a mile long, and you decide it's a good time to spend money on a mattress set?"

Grandma Annie slipped from the doorway and out of sight.

"C'mon. They've got more toys than they know what to do with." His hands went in the air and back down. "I was trying to do something nice for you, woman."

He may have been trying, but he still should have asked. She repeated the thought, this time aloud.

Ray stared. He didn't blink. He didn't speak. He just stared for the longest time, then walked by her and out of the room.

Great. Walk away like you always do. And in front of my grandma, too.

She suspected he'd gone out to the garage to tinker with something. Maybe even back to the shop. That was the joy of owning your own business. He could come and go as he pleased, as long as someone was at the body shop to do the work. In Missy's line of work, she was the only capable someone.

A sitcom laugh track blasted from the family room. The boys looked at each other then darted out, leaving their make-shift jungle gym. Missy stared at the pile of wadded-up bed-sheets on the floor. White with little pale green diamonds all over, they were outdated and worn thin, and they needed washing anyway. She gathered them off the floor and headed to the laundry room.

As she passed the family room, she paused. Grandma Annie sat with John Thomas snuggled next to her on the couch and the older ones huddled in the floor around her feet. It was an Instagram-worthy moment. The last time she'd shared a pic-ture of Grandma Annie and the kids, her phone dinged for hours with *likes*.

Missy pulled the phone from her pocket and snapped a pic-ture with her free hand. The scene was so precious, it tamped the frustration she fought to contain. But as she smiled at the photo on the screen, she noticed a scowl on her grandmother's face. She looked up to find the same sour expression as in the picture.

She put the phone away and stepped closer. Missy made her voice soft. "What's wrong?"

Grandma cut her eyes upward toward Missy as she stroked John Thomas's yellow hair. "You know you hurt that man, don't you? Men hurt easier than you think, Melissa."

"Well, I—"

"Don't you know an act of love when you see one?"

There was nothing to say. Maybe Grandma was right, but it couldn't be undone. And Ray still should have asked first.

"I'll talk to him later. I'm sure he'll be all right."

Missy turned and went through the kitchen to the laundry closet where she dropped the raggedy sheets into the washer. Scolded by Grandma for the second time in twenty years, and both times within less than a week. She ran her fingers through the tangly mess of curls on both sides of her head as she stared into the tub. Too bad she'd met her cigarette quota while the older kids were at school. One day she was just going to smoke as much as she wanted and not care what anybody else thought. Maybe when they were grown up and moved out.

The familiar blue liquid poured from the bottle and into the dispenser in a mesmerizing stream. As she closed the lid of the washer, an inkling of regret crept into her consciousness. Not about Ray, but about Grandma. She'd walked away, had shut down a conversation with her as if it didn't matter. She'd disrespected her elder.

Missy turned to head back, but Grandma Annie shuffled into the kitchen first. She stopped and plopped her hands on the butcher-block top of the island. "Little Bit wants a snack."

"He always wants a snack." Missy sighed and let out a phony laugh. "There's goldfish crackers in the pantry if you want to take him some. Or I can get it."

It was a balancing act—asking her grandmother to help so that she felt useful, but not so much that it risked her being in bed with a sore back the next day.

"I'll get it. And some for the others, too. They said they were fine, but you know how it goes. As soon as they see one with something . . ."

Missy gave her a knowing smile.

Grandma Annie seemed to have dropped the "Ray" conversation. Maybe it was best to not bring it up again. And maybe now was a good time to put her plan into action. For four days

Missy had plotted how to get her grandmother to talk about the mystery papers, but the only segue she could come up with was the ballet shoes that had shared the drawer with the folder and had brought such a tender smile to Grandma Annie's face.

"You know, I was thinking about signing the girls up for dance."

"Is that right?" Grandma looked up for only a second as she poured the orange fish-shaped crackers into a paper bowl, but it was long enough for Missy to see the glint in her eye.

"Yeah. Some of their school friends take lessons," Missy said, "and I thought they might enjoy it, too. Emma's a little old to just be starting, but . . ."

The older woman cleared her throat. "I think that would be good."

"And since we didn't get to talk about it the other day, I thought maybe you could tell them about you taking dance classes when you were younger. You know, get 'em excited to learn. And we'd all like to hear about it."

Grandma set the snacks down and came closer.

"I didn't just *study* dance, dear. I *taught* dance. To little girls like your precious daughters. During high school and for a couple years after. And I loved it."

The new detail pushed the folder conversation out of its priority spot.

"Wait. You used to be a dance *instructor*? That's incredible. Grandma. How have I never known this?"

Grandma moved a short sprig of white hair behind her ear and adjusted her glasses. "I—I just don't talk about it anymore."

"Well, why not? I mean, if I had ever been *that* good at something, I'd want everyone to know."

Grandma Annie stared, with her head to one side and her brow furrowed. Then, she spoke softly. "I happen to know that you are good at a right many things, Melissa Jo Hall Robbins." She drew a deep breath. "But since you asked . . . I don't talk about dance because, it's part of another life—the me of another time."

The last words rang out like the hammering of the last nail into a coffin.

Maybe the papers in the folder had something to do with her dancing career. But why was it a secret? She'd seemed so happy when she cradled the ballet slippers. Why had that part of her life ceased to exist?

They stood for a moment, neither saying a word. With the silence, Missy told Grandma that she wouldn't press her. And she wouldn't . . . today.

Missy studied her grandmother. Tall and lean. So much different than Missy's physique. She could see it now. Before time took its toll, a younger Annie would have had a dancer's body.

Missy's mind warred with itself as the older woman left the kitchen carrying the snacks. Not only did she *want* to know about the folder, now she *needed* to understand how her grandmother had been a good enough dancer to teach others, yet Missy had never heard about it.

As she pondered her next move, Grandma came back into the kitchen. She had a determined look.

"Your father told me he wants you to sing at his party."

"Well, uh . . . yeah. But it's a birthday party, not a concert. I'm not sure we really need a song."

"Of course, we don't *need* it. But it *would* be a special touch. I think you should do it. I know I'd like to hear it, and it sure would make your daddy happy." Grandma Annie had turned on the charm with a syrupy tone. How had the conversation gone from being about her grandmother to becoming about her?

"I don't know. That's more Erica's thing, don't you think?" Missy picked up a dish rag and started wiping at the counter she'd already cleaned that morning.

"Well, sure, she's a great singer, but you know she doesn't have a monopoly on talent in this family. Have you prayed about it, Missy?"

The screen door slammed and the sounds of Ray's work boots on the floor came from the hall. Missy froze and stayed quiet as he came into the kitchen, took a drink out of the refrigerator, and left again without looking at either of them.

"I said, have you prayed about it?" Grandma asked when Ray had gone.

Missy couldn't shut her down this time. She sighed. "Well, it's just that—I don't really do that anymore."

"I know you don't go to church anymore. But not even *praying?* I can't imagine. Why in the world not?"

Missy paused. Her chest tightened at the idea of heading down this path.

"It's just—" She remembered Grandma Annie's excuse. "It's just the me of another time."

"Oh, I see." Grandma pursed her lips and tapped the side of her fist on the island. "Okay, I'll make a deal with you, honeybee. If you agree to sing at your daddy's party, I'll tell you about my dancing career." Her grandma sighed. "The truth is, I don't know how much longer God will grant me to stay here on this earth, and I guess there are some things that should be known before I go."

The way Grandma talked about dancing, it seemed as big a secret as the folder. And Missy desperately wanted to know about both. She nodded. Not ready to commit just yet, but she wouldn't say no.

"And will you at least think about what I said about Ray? You *do* owe him an apology, Missy. Once upon a time, you loved him. And there was a reason you did. Please try to remember that."

"I'll think about that, too." Missy resumed wiping the stove with the rag.

John Thomas ran into the kitchen, his bare feet slapping the floor like flippers. "Gigi, you're missin' the show. C'mon."

Grandma Annie assured him she'd be there soon, and he left as fast as he'd come in.

"One last thing, Missy, then I'll go rest this aching back while I watch cartoons."

Missy tossed the rag into the sink and turned to face her grandmother who took a step forward and stroked Missy's cheek with the back of her hand, a safe and familiar feeling like the opening notes of a favorite song.

"I love you with all my heart, Melissa, and that's why I'm telling you this. You're not unhappy with your husband. You're unhappy with yourself."

Chapter Ten

Thursday, November 7, 1963

"*I*T's OKAY, R.C. It's gonna be okay. Just a little while longer, and it will all be over."

Annie looked at Aunt Brenda. The bony woman, who stood a head taller than Annie's five-foot-ten-inch frame and attended to R.C. from the end of the bed, shook her head.

"She still has quite a ways to go," Aunt Brenda whispered as she lowered the sheet. "Poor child."

If only R.C. would cry or scream, Annie wouldn't be so worried. If she'd just make a noise, any kind of noise. But she only stared at the ceiling, toward where the pullcord for the bare lightbulb swayed like a winding-down pendulum with the slight breeze from an electric fan, her jaw clenched and the breath coming out hard from her nostrils.

The delivery room was a back porch-turned-bedroom, closed in on all sides but with a screened door and tall screened windows that ran the lengths of the exterior walls. The single bed, with its antique frame, sat in the corner, opposite the door to the outside. From her seat next to R.C., Annie could see three of Aunt Brenda's chickens searching for grasshoppers in the yard—a nice, fleeting distraction.

From a wobbly nightstand, four quick-moving aluminum blades of the old Emerson fan pushed air toward R.C., and the sound helped steady Annie's worried mind, at least a small measure. Even with the fan, perspiration erupted on R.C.'s forehead. Tiny droplets peeked from all around her wispy, strawberry-blond hairline and ran toward her temples. The surprise heatwave made the November afternoon feel like July, but Annie knew it wasn't the temperature that caused R.C. to sweat. Pain and fear, compounded by the misfitting puzzle pieces of her mind, made R.C. "glow."

"Can I fix your pillow, Ruth Claire?" Annie spoke to her as if R.C. hadn't been silent for over an hour, ever since the first big contraction hit right after breakfast. "Is there something I can get you? Maybe you'd like me to read to you while we wait for the next one."

Annie had spent many evenings reading on the porch in the last four months—fashion magazines from the grocery store in town, books on pregnancy from the nearest library, and the Bible she'd brought from home, especially when the pain of missing Julian became too great, and she needed to be reminded that she wasn't alone. And she read Tolkien to R.C. when the discomfort of the girl's heavy, round belly made it hard to sleep.

Aside from the fan and Annie's voice, the only noise in the room was the incessant whining of Aunt Brenda's blue tick hound. Buster had taken to R.C. during their time in Georgia. She'd charmed him with gentle motions and whispered conversations, and in Annie's mind, a bit of magic, like she could charm almost any animal. Now he cried for her in a high-pitched repeating pattern that matched the rhythm of Annie's heartbeat, until Aunt Brenda bent down and spoke to the dog as if comforting a small child. He quieted and curled up at Annie's feet.

"Hey, R.C." Annie leaned within inches of her sister's face and whispered. "You remember the day you told me about the baby?"

R.C.'s gaze stayed fixed on the ceiling.

"You remember being at Hanging Rock with Julian, and that blasted snake, and how bad you scared me?" Annie forced a laughed, but still, R.C. didn't move. Annie ran a hand through her hair. "Ruth Claire, I bet Aunt Brenda would like to hear that story. Why don't you tell her? Tell her what kind of snake it was. I don't remember. *You* tell her, R.C. Come on."

"Oh, yes, R.C." Aunt Brenda nodded. "Tell me about it. I love a good story."

Annie's chest tightened as she continued her plea. "Was it a cottonmouth? Oh, I know. It was a copperhead. Something poisonous." From the inside out she ached to hear her sister's voice.

Please speak, R.C. Please correct me. Tell me I'm wrong; say that it was a timber rattler, and that it's venomous, not poisonous. Just say something.

But R.C. remained silent, though she squeezed her hand, with a constant pressure and a strength that rivaled a grown man's. And though she couldn't feel her fingers, and the color had drained from the tips of them, Annie wouldn't ask R.C. to let go, or even ease up. As long as R.C. held on, it meant she hadn't slipped away.

"Should we call an ambulance, Aunt Brenda? I mean, we don't even know her blood pressure. Ruth Claire could have a stroke or something."

"The child begged me not to take her to a hospital for the birth. You know what happened at her last appointment." She came closer and whispered in Annie's ear. "She was petrified, and even with the drugs they would give her, I'm afraid it would just make the whole experience even harder. She's so ...*fragile.* You know, it happens all the time that a baby comes before a woman can get to the hospital."

Annie nodded. Aunt Brenda was right. At the hospital, they'd be separated. R.C. would be with strangers. And it wasn't hard to see that Brenda wanted to be by R.C.'s side as much as Annie did.

With a thin, straight mouth and hair usually pulled back so tightly it drew her eyes into a fierce slant, Aunt Brenda had proven much kinder than her appearance suggested. To Annie's great relief, she had connected with Ruth Claire right away. She seemed to relate to the girl in a way that only Annie had done before.

Annie thought back to that day in late July when Aunt Brenda had come to pick them up at the bus station. She bore only a slight resemblance to the woman in the black-and-white photos that Mother kept tucked away in the back of her Bible. The effects of being widowed young were written on her face.

R.C. had hidden behind Annie as they stood outside the terminal, but Aunt Brenda had coached the child to come to her, with soft words and an understanding smile. Within only an hour, they were friends. All it had taken was Brenda giving her a tour of the farm and letting R.C. pet and name all the animals. A slice of fresh-baked pound cake had helped speed the bonding process, too. And Annie was forever indebted to Aunt Brenda for her kindness.

"I know you're worried, dear, but I'm keeping a close eye." She propped herself on the end of the bed near R.C.'s feet.

"But she hasn't had a contraction in a long time. She shouldn't be in any pain right now. That's what all the books said. Why is she ...*frozen?*"

"I don't know for sure. But it's as if those first ones put her into a kind of shock. Like she's traumatized."

"The not-talking . . . she's done that before. When Daddy died. Took about three days for her to speak again. But this is different."

"I've seen to quite a few births, child. I've not seen this, for sure, but I'm not ready to call for an ambulance yet."

She came near the head of the bed again and pressed two fingertips to R.C.'s neck as she looked at the tarnished silver watch on her wrist. Annie drew a breath and held it. Aunt Brenda's lips moved as she counted silently. *One. Two. Three. Four* . . . Every second felt like five.

"Her pulse is strong and steady, Annie."

Annie breathed again.

"And we must stay positive, for her sake. How we respond, how we speak, it will all make a difference. Have faith."

Brenda patted Annie on the shoulder and left the room. The dog followed, leaving Annie and R.C. alone with their unspoken fears. With her free hand, Annie touched her sister's cheek, feverish and the color of a ripe tomato. In contrast, the rest of her face around her pale blue eyes was stark white, resembling the faces of the geishas Annie had seen in a movie the year before. She began to tell R.C. the funny plot of the movie, making up what she couldn't remember. R.C.'s grip softened, but only a little. Just enough for Annie to regain feeling in her fingers. They hurt worse as the blood circulated again, but it was a good sign that R.C. had relaxed.

Aunt Brenda came back into the room and placed a folded wash rag on R.C.'s forehead, and Buster reclaimed his spot at Annie's feet. Then R.C. clamped down on Annie's hand again, with more force than before, and her whole body seemed to go completely rigid. The veins in her neck bulged, and her eyes protruded from their sockets, as if the entirety of R.C.'s insides was trying to come out along with the child.

If ever Annie had wanted to trade places with someone, it was now. To take her sister's pain until it was done.

"What can we do, Aunt Brenda?"

"You can pray, child. Just pray."

"Yes, Annie. Pray." The sound of R.C.'s voice—quiet, raspy, insistent—made Annie jump. "Pray for me. Pray for me."

Finally.

Annie scooted to the edge of the straight-backed wooden chair and the woven seat squeaked beneath her. She searched her brain for words as her free hand fluttered about in the air. For the better part of the last hour, she'd prayed silently, but now, when R.C. needed to hear the petition, the words didn't come. She looked at R.C., so pale and frightened. So small in the bed, save for the round mass of belly pointed toward the ceiling. "Um, okay, okay. I'll pray, R.C." Annie cleared her throat. She searched her brain until it landed on something familiar. "Yea, though I walk through the valley of the shadow of death, I will fear no evil, for thou art with me. Thy rod and thy staff—"

"No, Annie." Aunt Brenda's tone was firm and insistent, yet tender. "Speak life, not death. The power of both is in the tongue, and no one is going *anywhere* near that dark valley today. Just speak life for your sister. For this baby."

Only for a moment, it felt like a scolding. But Aunt Brenda was right, and her encouragement pulled out the words Annie had prayed silently before.

"Lord, thank you for this new life. Thank you that this baby *will* be born healthy. Thank you for making Ruth Claire strong and courageous." Annie went on with more of the same, asking for help and thanking God for it, even as the fear in R.C.'s eyes grew more intense with each second. Annie prayed even harder. The words came fast, and her volume grew as R.C. squeezed her hand.

R.C. soon let out a loud cry as her body finally relaxed. Another one was over.

"It hurts, Annie," she said. "It hurts so much."

"I know, baby sister. I know it does. But you're so brave."

With Ruth Claire talking again, Annie was sure she would be all right. But as the morning became afternoon, and then the sky turned from a bright pink and orange to an opaque black, Annie became less and less sure of their plan.

The adoption agency expected them to take Ruth Claire to the hospital when it was time for the baby. The doctor there had been made aware of the arrangements. There was a family picked out, and they would expect to be notified. But when the contractions started, and Ruth Claire became so afraid, Aunt Brenda had taken charge. She'd decided to rely on her background as a nurse during the war to bring the baby into the world.

"Ruth Claire," Aunt Brenda coached, "on the next one, you just bear down as hard as you can. But keep breathing. You can do this." She waited a breath before saying, "Okay, just one more push. The baby is almost out."

Finally, a shrill cry filled the small room, and R.C.'s head fell back on the pillow. Annie rushed to her side, nearly tripping over Buster. She leaned close to R.C.'s ear as a single tear rolled from R.C.'s left eye and fell onto the pillow.

"Oh, you did it. You did it, R.C." Annie kissed the wet track of R.C.'s tear.

Aunt Brenda let out a joyful gasp as she wrapped the wriggling, red baby in a towel and rubbed the child clean. "It's a boy." Then she held him on display, with one hand around the back of his neck and one under his backside.

Annie's breath hitched and her heart skipped at the sight of him. In her swirling thoughts, she became conscious of the notion that everything she'd thought she knew about life was now different, as though twenty years of living had all been leading up to this very moment, when on an unseasonably warm day in November 1963, a tiny person would take a first breath and she'd never be the same for having met him.

Aunt Brenda laid the squalling child between Ruth Claire's feet as she used sterilized scissors to separate him from his mother. Then she wrapped him again in a fresh towel and presented the baby like a bouquet of flowers, laying him into R.C.'s arms.

"Aunt Brenda, are you sure she should hold him?" Annie stood and whispered to her. "At the hospital, they would have just taken him. That's what the lady at the agency explained to us."

"Exactly, dear. But she needs this. Trust me. This is best, for R.C.'s healing. Maybe for yours, too."

R.C. smiled at the baby and kissed him on the nose. "Hello, little baby. You're so wrinkly." Then she lifted him away from her chest, the space the height of a matchbook. As Annie took the baby, R.C.'s shaky arms withered by her side, palms up and fingers splayed like the petals of a flower in the summer sun.

Annie tensed and shot a look toward Aunt Brenda, but her face still read only of joy and relief.

"She's fine, Annie. You just take care of the baby. I'm looking after R.C. They're both fine." Aunt Brenda stepped lightly to look down over Annie's shoulder. "He's beautiful, isn't he?"

"So beautiful. It's like—like a miracle."

"That's what children are, dear heart. Never had one of my own, but I'm sure your mother felt the same about you when she first saw you." She patted Annie's shoulder. "Once I get R.C.

cleaned up, I'll wash up myself and go make him his first bottle. We'll give him a proper bath soon, too."

"A bottle? Oh, I guess he does need—but I didn't know—how did you?"

"I have everything we need to keep him with us for at least a night or two." Brenda winked. "Don't worry."

Aunt Brenda went back to work at the foot of the bed.

To Annie's surprise, the child quieted quickly, and for five minutes or more, they sat in silence as R.C. rested and Annie studied him, mesmerized.

In a whisper, Annie spoke. "Ruth Claire, what will you name him?"

Ruth Claire opened her eyes halfway. "You mean I get to name him?"

"I think you should. Even if his adoptive parents change it, you can call him what you want to for now. And he'll always be that to you. Don't you think so?"

The moonlight came through the window and cast an angelic glow on Ruth Claire's glistening face. "I'll call him . . . Thomas."

Annie sat up straighter. "Oh, R.C., that's . . . are you . . . I mean . . ."

R.C. looked up at Annie expectantly, her tired face so innocent.

"That's a great name, Ruth Claire. Thomas is perfect."

Annie looked down at the perfect infant in her arms. If Tommy Jacobs never knew he had a namesake, it wouldn't matter in the end. It's what little Thomas's mother wanted.

"And for his middle name," Annie said, "I mean, if you want to give him one—what about Theodore? After Daddy?"

Ruth Claire gave a slight nod. "Thomas Theodore Swaim." And with the pronouncement, she closed her eyes again and turned her head toward the wall.

As Annie held Thomas, she couldn't help but wonder if she'd ever hold her own baby this way. Hopefully she and Julian would have a son as wonderful as this little one. Soon, she'd be able to go home to him, and pick back up where they'd left off. He'd never gotten around to visiting like they'd hoped, and the four months had seemed like four years apart. But it was worth it. Ruth Claire had needed her there. Annie had no regrets. And R.C. would need her even more in the next few days, to do the hard thing that needed to be done.

Annie pressed her lips to the sleeping child's forehead.

"It was all worth it to meet you, little one. And I'll love you forever. No matter what."

Chapter Eleven

Saturday, November 4, Present Day

Serving punch and cutting cake proved great distractions. And Daddy looked so happy mingling with his guests. The nerves Missy had choked on most of the morning were all but gone, and now it was all about him. Thomas Theodore Hall was the man of the hour. He more than deserved it.

"Thank you for coming." Missy poured another cup of red punch into the fancy kind of clear plastic cup and handed it to a lady she didn't know. Had to be a coworker. There were at least sixty people there, one for each year of her father's life. Missy recognized most. Aunts, uncles, long-lost cousins, church members. Even old high-school friends and a few former students had shown up. A good thing they'd rented the fellowship hall at the Moravian church down the street, instead of using the smaller one where her parents were members.

Missy looked to the corner of the fellowship hall for the fifteenth time. Ray seemed to be managing. He and the kids nearly filled up one of the round tables with the white linen tablecloths. John Thomas sat in Ray's lap, staring at his daddy's smartphone, and Joshua had a coloring book and a pack of crayons in front of him. Thank goodness the girls seemed to be getting along now after bickering most of the morning.

Mama, with her arm in a sling but looking sensational in a festive red dress, stood beside the next table over from Ray and the kids, entertaining a never-ending line of guests. Grandma Annie had been there earlier but disappeared some time ago.

Missy took a deep breath, smoothed out her dress with moist palms, and stepped to the dessert end of the table to slice another row in the sheet cake. Half of *Happy Birthday, Thomas* had been consumed, leaving a puzzle of letters behind in green icing, Daddy's favorite color. Head down, she started on one side and drew the knife across, drawing a clean line through the thick icing until it came out on the other side of the cake. Missy let out a quiet gasp. The neckline of her dress had dropped again. She laid the utensil down, looked around to make sure no one was watching, and turned her back to the crowd. She hitched the black dress up at the top and pulled it apart at the shoulders, checking to make sure her bra straps didn't show and cursing herself for not going with the blue dress she'd debated over. Then the nerves kicked in again. In just a few minutes, her father would address the guests, then introduce his daughter as their entertainment. Entertainment. She couldn't even serve cake without being self-conscious about her chest. How in the world was she gonna get up there and share her voice? She'd sooner show them her cleavage.

Since she and Ray were speaking again, she *could* go over and whisper to him that she needed to step outside. He'd know why. One cigarette behind the church might calm her down before she had to perform, and there was half a pack buried somewhere in the glove box of the minivan.

Perform. Who did she think she was? The great Erica Hall? Her sister was the performer, not her. Though she had given it her best effort. Once she had finally agreed to sing at the party, she'd managed to find a soundtrack for the perfect version of

"Amazing Grace" in just the right key and had rehearsed it over and over—washing dishes, folding laundry, in the car. But she wouldn't be fooling anyone. She was still just a stay-at-home mom, not a performer.

She scanned the room again. Where had Grandma gotten off to?

With a lull in the line for cake and punch, Missy left her station and slipped toward the door. Maybe she had gotten tired and gone to the car.

Like she'd predicted, the cold snap had given way to a pseudo-summer, and after the frigid temperatures of late, the mid-seventies felt like ninety. Or maybe it was nerves. Either way, beads of perspiration trailed down the back of Missy's neck as she rounded the corner of the building and stopped short of running into her grandma.

"Where've you been? I was starting to get worried."

Grandma Annie offered a smile. "No need to worry about me, sweetie. I was in the sanctuary praying for you."

Missy sighed. "Oh . . . well, thanks, I guess. I'm glad you're okay. It's time we get back inside." She turned to head for the black-framed double doors.

"What do you mean, *you guess?*" Grandma Annie asked. "Missy, there was a time when you had faith. What happened?"

An invisible wall stopped Missy in her tracks. She couldn't ignore Grandma Annie, but there was nothing she'd rather talk about less. She sighed as she pivoted in slow motion.

"Grandma," she said, "I promise I don't mean to be disrespectful, and I know you care about me, but I really can't have a discussion about religion right now."

Grandma Annie stepped closer. "I'm not talking about religion, baby. I'm talking about you and your relationship with God."

Missy shrugged. "People change."

"I know you have a lot on your mind, but honey, I love you, and I want to help. Tell me." Grandma looked deep into Missy's eyes. "What made you walk away?"

Pain flooded Missy's chest. Was this really happening? Here? Now?

"All right. I'll tell you." She took a deep breath. "It wasn't a *what*. It was a *who*. Mary Sue Montgomery."

Even after all these years, the name still left a bad taste in her mouth.

"What?"

"You asked, and I told you. Mary Sue Montgomery made me walk away from the church."

"Honey . . ." Grandma's voice wavered with confusion and sadness. She reached a shaky hand toward Missy and let it hover in the air for a time. "But she was your Sunday school teacher for years. She loved you."

"I thought she did. I know I loved her. But things changed. And it wasn't just her. There were others. They all . . ." Missy choked on the memories.

"Sweetheart, is this about—"

"We'll talk some other time, okay?" She patted Grandma Annie's shoulder. "I need to get back."

Missy's mind raced as she crossed the threshold and reentered the party. She tried to regroup, refocus, and recenter when everything in her said to retreat. The crippling anxiety she'd felt earlier seemed magnified by the painful memories to which she'd been reintroduced at the most inopportune time. Within seconds, Dad approached the microphone at the other side of the room. He used two fingers to tap on the round black casing, and a feedback squeal made every head in the room whip toward the front.

Missy turned back toward the door, but Grandma had come in behind her, blocking the way out. Even though she had become feebler in these last ten years, she remained a force to be reckoned with, reminding Missy of a defensive lineman.

"Thank you all again for coming, friends." Dad's gentle voice sounded rich and full through the system. "I am overwhelmed and humbled by your show of love, and I especially want to thank my family for hosting this wonderful party. Especially, my oldest daughter Melissa, who has agreed to bless me with the gift of her voice at my party, and who will be singing my favorite song for all of us today."

Dad stretched his arm toward her, palm up. People turned to look at her and began to clap. They watched as she made her way to the front of the room, probably thinking she walked like a penguin, trying to avoid losing traction on the shiny floor. The walk of a few yards felt like a football field, and as she traversed the room, a thought occurred to her. When Dad greeted the crowd, he hadn't mentioned that Erica was not present.

She hugged her father, and he took his seat next to Mama as the applause ended.

"Happy birthday, Daddy," she whispered it into the microphone, with her head down, as her stomach performed a somersault. She pushed at the nose piece of her glasses with a pointer finger as she raised her head. Ray and the kids all had wide eyes and straight backs. Even Little Bit was still for the moment.

Missy turned to her cousin, who stood in the corner, ready to hit the button on the sound system. She gave him a nod and soon the familiar opening chord of the song rang out from the speakers. There was no turning back.

She tried to look at the crowd. That's what Mr. Turner, the high school chorus teacher, had taught. "Draw your audience in," he'd said. "Reach them with your eyes first and then your voice." But there were so many people looking back. She couldn't get over the feeling of it. Eyeballs all over her. Everyone in the room looked at her, but what did they see? Did they see an overweight, not-so-young-anymore mother? A second-choice party singer? A high school-chorus dropout? For the first time in a long time, Missy felt like she was *really* being seen . . . and it wasn't a good thing. She closed her eyes.

She carefully counted out the beats of the introduction in her head, the way she'd learned from Mr. Turner. *One, two, three. Two, two, three. Three, two, three.* It was different than with live accompaniment. A good piano player could follow her. But if she missed a measure of the track and came in at the wrong time, they'd have to start the CD all over again. *Six, two, three. Seven, two, three.*

Then came the last beat of measure eight, and Missy opened her mouth at the right time, and the right notes along with the right words came out, and there was no one in the room but Missy and her father. She opened her eyes and zeroed in on his face. The power in her voice was fueled by the look in his eyes as she sang. Rich emotion poured forth in sound from a long-untapped well of talent. She could have gone on singing forever, but three minutes and forty-one seconds passed in a blink, and before the sustain of the final chord had ended, the room erupted with applause. Some stood, including Daddy and Mama, and Missy swallowed back tears as they made their way toward her.

Dad wrapped his arms around her and kissed her cheek. "I knew you were good, Melissa, but I couldn't have imagined anything that beautiful. It's been such a long time."

He released her, then Mama was there, grabbing Missy with her good arm. "I am so proud of you, baby. You were simply magnificent." Missy leaned into the warmth of Mama's cheek against hers.

Ray and the kids joined the swarm and sang her praises, too. Missy's face was hot, and her legs felt like noodles. Her mind tossed like a buoy in rough seas. She gave Ray a side hug and kissed each of the children on the top of the head, even Emma, who had grown to stand nearly shoulder-to-shoulder with her. "Thank you, all. Thank you. I think I need some air." She flapped her hand back and forth near her face and slipped away from the group.

As she made her way to the back, nodding and saying "thank you" over and over to all those smiling faces, still flapping her hand as a fan, a short man with fair skin and rosy cheeks approached. He wore a bowtie and fancy shoes and was the first man Missy had seen wearing cuff links in a very long time. Wispy locks of blond hair lay across his mostly bald head.

"I need you in my choir," the stranger said in a drawly, high-pitched voice. He pointed a stubby finger at Missy's chest.

Missy looked down to realize that her dress had slipped again. Had it been like that when she was singing? If so, wouldn't Ray have said something?

"Excuse me?" She hoisted the dress at the shoulders in the most obvious of ways. Discretion wasn't an option with his face so close to her exposed self. "I don't believe we've—"

"Now I'm not taking no for an answer. I don't mean to be rude, but this is important, so a little forcefulness is to be understood in the matter, you see." He took her by the elbow and maneuvered her a quarter turn this way and that, inspecting up and down. "I already have a robe that will fit just fine. Might be a little big. It belonged to Jeannie Wallace, God rest her soul. She was my soloist. Wonderful pipes, but terrible cholesterol. Now she's in the heavenly choir and I'm short a soprano. Until today. Two rehearsals with me, maybe one with the whole choir, you'll be good to go."

"I'm sorry, Mister . . ."

"Forgive me. It's Barker. Henry Barker. I teach music at the middle school where your father works. But I also direct the choir over at Bethabara Presbyterian. And I would be pleased as punch for you to join us for our Advent season."

"Oh," Missy said, taking in a short breath. "You meant a church choir."

Henry raised his hand and let it flop down at the wrist with his fingers pointed in Missy's direction.

"Why, yes, honey. With a gift like that, you would be a tremendous blessing to our congregation. Now, I understand you probably have your own church, and I wouldn't want to steal you away from there—that would be egregious—but maybe if we could simply borrow you, just for a few weeks."

"No, it's not that. I just—"

Grandma Annie approached, her face aglow and eyes misty behind glasses. She eased an arm around Missy's waist as Henry continued his plea.

"Here, let me give you my card, and you think about it and give me a call when you've made up your mind. But I've already told you I'm not taking no for an answer, now haven't I? Oh, me. I can come on a little strong at times, but most people love me for it. Just ask your daddy."

Missy stared at the card in her hand, at its raised silver script font.

"Okay, Mr. Barker."

"Henry."

"Yes, sir."

Henry gave Grandma Annie a smile and a slight bow, then headed over to where the rest of Missy's family was still congregated near the front of the hall.

"Well, what was that all about?"

Missy's mind swirled. "I'll tell you later. I—I think it's about time to start cleaning up."

"Missy, listen." She held both of Missy's elbows and looked at her squarely. "I'm as proud of you right now as I've ever been of anybody in my eighty years of life. You sang beautifully, and you made your daddy very proud, too. And I want you to know, I'm going to keep my end of the bargain. You come pick me up one day soon, and we'll have us a long talk. You do that, and I'll finally tell you about your grandma, the dancer."

Chapter Twelve

November 1963

*A*COOL BREEZE came through the window and seemed to give lift to Annie's sneakered feet as they glided over the wooden boards in perfect time with the music. Her body flitted around the room with ease, like one of the orange-colored leaves newly released from the giant poplar in the yard. The record player in the corner, turned down low, produced Elvis's cool, clear voice, and she pretended he was there, putting on a private concert for the two of them.

The waltz was simple. *Forward, pause. Right, pause. Backward, pause. Left, pause. Repeat.* And sometimes she'd add a careful spin. "This is the perfect dance for beginners, Thomas. And I'm so glad you don't mind that I lead." She cradled the peapod form, a tight bundle of green blanket and baby. That newborn person fit just so, head to toe, from the crook of her arm to the ends of her fingers, no doubt part of God's grand design for a woman's body.

Even as Annie's heart brimmed with joy, it ached for Julian, and over the decision at hand. The melody Elvis crooned only twisted the knife. The answer to "Are You Lonesome Tonight?" was a resounding *yes*. If only Julian were here to help her decide what to do.

Annie sat on the bed where Thomas had made his entrance into the world. With her feet flat on the floor, and her legs together, she placed his head on her knees with his feet pressed against her stomach. "I do wish your Uncle Julian could meet you, sweet boy. Somehow. But maybe he will, if . . ." Thomas gurgled. "He was in such a hurry when he called the last time, I didn't even get to tell him how adorable you are, only that you're finally here."

She leaned forward with her face above the baby's. "Things are very complicated, Thomas. I know I've told you already. But don't worry. We're going to make the best decision for you. I promise. I've been praying . . ."

She reached up and rubbed at the heart-shaped locket around her neck, feeling the tiny cross etched on the front. The gift from Julian, which he'd given her the night before she left, brought her comfort in more ways than one. It reminded her of him, of course, though she never really needed reminding. The handsome man she'd left in Winston-Salem was never very far from her thoughts. But also, since she hadn't found a photograph small enough to fit, she'd written a special Bible verse on a piece of paper, folded it very small, and placed it inside instead.

She looked down at the still-shiny silver and smiled. Julian didn't have to buy a necklace with a cross on it. She was sure there were others he could have chosen, and the fact that he'd picked this one gave her hope. It was a sign, for sure. The man she loved would come around to believing, as she did.

"What do *you* think of the necklace, Thomas?" She held up the chain and let the locket dangle and sway. "It's pretty, isn't it? I miss Julian so much. I miss him holding me, and I miss talking to him. But I'm glad you're here. You make an excellent confidante."

Four-day-old Thomas had wise eyes. Deep blue and so new they still held the mysteries of the ages. He probably understood every word she said to him. Her nephew was obviously a genius. Annie had been convinced of it since the first night, when she'd rocked him as R.C. slept and he'd waved his little arm in rhythm with the lullaby she sang, the one her mother had sung to her when she was small. She sang it to him again, though it was daytime and he'd just had a good nap.

> *"Sleep my child and peace attend thee,*
> *all through the night.*
> *Guardian angels God will send thee,*
> *all through the night."*

The phone rang from the front room just as Annie placed a kiss on the tip of Thomas's tiny nose. Her heart leapt. "Maybe it's Julian." She whispered close to the baby's face. "Let's go see."

Annie carried Thomas into the living room, toward the phone table that sat at the end of the couch. Aunt Brenda got there first and answered after wiping her hands on the apron tied around her waist.

"Yes, ma'am. Thank you for calling," her aunt said into the receiver. "Yes, things are going just fine. He's eating well. Took to the bottle fine."

Annie's heart sank. The caller wasn't Julian.

When would he call again? She'd only been able to speak to him for a couple of minutes the last time. For weeks, he had called every Sunday at 8:00, and they had said as much as could possibly be said in five minutes, almost talking at the same time. Julian's daddy paid the long-distance bill—for which she was grateful—but the time limit wasn't nearly long enough. Then he'd missed a call at the end of October, and on the last call—just as she was trying to tell him about her plans to come home soon now that the baby was here—his mother needed to use the phone and he'd had to go.

If only she could tell him more about the baby and about how frightening R.C.'s delivery had been, and if only she could ask him how Mama was really doing. Annie could only afford to call Mama every other week. Twice during her stay, she had made collect calls home, just to hear her voice before hanging up. Now she needed Julian and Mama as much as ever. She needed them both to help her decide—

Brenda held the olive-colored phone away from her mouth, placed a hand over the mouthpiece, and whispered to Annie. "It's the lady from the adoption agency, Annie. They need to know what's going on, what the plan is. Can you speak to her?"

"Oh, um . . . well . . ."

"We're going to have to finalize the arrangements soon."

Plans. Arrangements. They should have been made by now, but she'd been lost in a different world. A world of soft baby skin, first coos, and late-night snuggles. A world she never knew she would love so much.

"I'm just not sure R.C. is ready. Can you tell her we'll call tomorrow?"

Aunt Brenda tilted her head and raised an eyebrow. Her lips turned inward, and Annie looked away. She drew a breath then looked back at her aunt. "Please, ask them for one more day?"

*   *   *

"There you are." Annie stopped halfway between the house and the corral and shielded her eyes from the afternoon sun as she called to her sister. R.C. leaned against the fence rail with both forearms, her head turning slowly in the direction of the trio of horses as they pranced in circles in the afternoon sun. "You've been out here a while. Don't you think you should come inside to rest?"

R.C. shook her head but didn't turn around.

Annie studied Ruth Claire from a distance. She was barefooted, even though the air now held a proper feel of mid-autumn. The thin, button-up, floral-patterned house dress—one of two that had become R.C.s wardrobe during the last couple of months—hung loose around her quickly shrinking body. Her hair stood inches away from her head all around, in terrible need of brushing.

Annie came close to R.C. and spoke softly. "You still need to get plenty of rest, Ruth Claire. Your body's been through—well, it's been through a lot. Are you sure you don't want to come back inside?"

She shook her head again. "I want to stay out here with Shadow."

"That one?" Annie pointed to the gray horse that pranced between a solid sorrel and the palomino.

"Yes. He's my favorite."

"He's beautiful. They all are. And seeing them live and in color is even better than watching *Mr. Ed*. Even if they can't talk."

Annie laughed, but Ruth Claire turned to her with a solemn expression. "But they can. Not like the one on television, but it's still a way of talking."

Annie brushed a hand over R.C.'s unruly hair. "Only to people special enough to listen."

R.C. turned back to the horses. "How's Thomas Theodore?"

Annie giggled again. Ruth Claire always called him by both names, probably because that's how she'd always been known.

"He's fine. Do you want to come inside and play with him?"

"He's very little. He can't play, Annie. He likes to sleep a lot, though. And I like to look at him."

"Yes, yes, I know." Annie put her arm around R.C. "Say, little sister—um—it's going to be Christmas before you know it." She expected R.C. to look at her with wide eyes, the way she always did at the mention of the word. Instead, R.C. watched the horses.

"Just think about it. The parade downtown—that's always just the best. Oh, and the Candle Tea at Old Salem. We have to do that, of course. That's tradition. And we'll go caroling with the church choir. You liked that last year, didn't you?"

"We're missing putting the flowers on Daddy's grave today."

"Oh, goodness, R.C. You're right, it's Veterans Day." Annie patted her sister's hand. "I know Mama will leave a flower for both of us. I just hate she has to go alone."

"They'll be red, I bet. She does red roses most years. Sometimes white. Or carnations."

"You're right, as usual. Such a memory you have. I bet they will be red. Listen, R.C., I need to ask you something. Can you look at me?"

Her sister turned slowly and fixed her eyes. Annie took her by the shoulders. There was no other way to do it but to come out and ask. She had to know what was going through R.C.'s mind. And it was now or never.

"R.C., have you thought about keeping the baby?"

R.C. took a tiny step backward. "But Mama told me I *couldn't* keep him. That I had to finish school, and that people would say mean things about me if—if they knew that I—that Tommy Jacobs and I—"

"I *know* what Mama said, R.C. And she's definitely right that it wouldn't be easy to keep the baby. But there's a lot of things worth having in life that don't come easy." Annie jumped as the horses thundered past. "I just want to know first, have you *thought* about it?"

"I don't know if I've thought about it, Annie. I didn't think I could think about it." Her voice rose in pitch and volume. "He's my baby. I know he's my baby. But he has other parents already. That's what you told me."

Annie put her arm around R.C again.

"I didn't mean to upset you, sweetheart. You know I didn't. I'm just still thinking about what's best for you. And for Thomas."

"Annie, does it make me bad to give my baby away? I do think about that. If I'm a bad person."

"Of course, you're not bad. Don't ever think that. And I'm not bad, and Mama's not bad. We're just trying to do what's best. For everyone."

"Annie, he'll still be mine, won't he? Even though he's somebody else's, too?"

"Well . . . of course. He'll still be yours." Annie reached down and picked up R.C.'s hand and pushed it against R.C.'s heart. "In here, he'll always be yours."

R.C. smiled and nodded. She put her arm by her side again. "That's good."

"So, you're going to be okay with taking him to the agency? They'll be calling back tomorrow, and they need to know."

"Are *you* okay with it, Annie?"

"I—to tell you the truth, R.C., I'm not sure. I think you're doing a wonderful thing for him. And a very brave thing. And I'm so proud of you. But I'm going to miss him."

"But you're a grown-up, Annie. You can do what you want. You don't have to miss him. You can take care of him. If you want to."

Did R.C. want her to take him? Maybe it was confirmation. She'd been praying so hard. But there was much to consider.

"I—I don't know. I mean, there's Julian, and my schoolwork. And, grown-up or not, I still have to obey Mama, too. And we know what she thinks is best. There's a lot to think about."

The chill was more than Annie could stand since she didn't have to be out there. "Come on, R.C." She took her by the hand and pulled gently. After only a few steps, R.C. stopped.

"Annie, I don't want to go."

"Sweetie, I know you like watching Shadow and the others, but it's getting cold out, and you need to—"

"No. I don't want to go home, Annie. I don't want to go home for Christmas. I want to stay here."

"What on earth are you talking about? We have to go back. One way or another, with the baby or without him, we have to go back to Winston-Salem. We have to go home to Mama. She's missing us. That's our home."

R.C. stared down at her bare feet. "I miss Mama. But—but if I go home, I'm going to miss Shadow. And all the other animals." She looked up again. "Annie, I really like it here. It just feels better here. The animals understand me. They don't laugh at me."

"R.C., I don't know what to say, I—" Annie cupped her hands over her face and spoke into them. "I just don't know."

"And if I go back to school, *he'll* be there, and I . . ."

How could she not have understood it before? Whether Thomas was with them or not, life would be different for Ruth Claire. And her skills for handling *different* weren't the same as most people's. She'd already adjusted to life in Georgia. If she left, she'd have to adjust to being back home, with the added complications of seeing Tommy.

An unexpected baby had seemed like Annie's biggest concern, but the possibility of losing her sister suddenly surpassed it by far.

*   *   *

Annie and Aunt Brenda sat at the square kitchen table. The first rays of morning sun poured through the window over the sink and caught the wisps of steam that danced above their cups of coffee and cast lines of shadows on the marbled Formica tabletop.

"Your mother and I talked last night."

Annie sat up straight. "You talked to Mama? I didn't know. How is she? What did she say?"

"I didn't want you to know, dear. I needed to talk to my sister privately." Brenda placed her hand over Annie's and looked deep into her eyes. "I told Leeta that you're thinking of keeping the baby."

"What? But I never said—"

"You didn't have to say it, dear. I know you've been struggling with the plan to place Thomas for adoption. It's written all over your face every time we talk about it. And to be honest, the idea is hard for me, too, even though I have far less at stake."

"But I can't—"

"Tell me it's not been on your mind."

Annie eased out of the chair and sidled to the sink. The fields that stretched beyond her view outside the window—the land tended by a small army of hired hands to produce Aunt Brenda's livelihood—had just enough rise and fall to them to make Annie think of home.

"I can't tell you that. It *is* what I want. I'm just not sure it's what's best."

"Listen, Annie. You don't have to decide right away. I talked to the lady at the agency, too. She said things like this happen, and they have been praying for you, and for R.C., and for Thomas. They want what's best for all of you."

It was hard to believe. Someone she didn't even know had been praying for her to make the right decision.

"As his aunt, you can take guardianship for now," Brenda said, "and they'll work with you to help make it permanent, if that's what you decide."

Annie took a deep breath then sipped her coffee. She sat the cup down and immediately picked it up for another sip. She swallowed hard. "And what about Mama?"

"She's worried about you, for your future. But she's also worried about her grandson. Regardless of what she thought to begin with, I think she'd be more than happy to meet him." Brenda leaned in closer. "Things don't have to turn out the way we think they should, Annie. There's a God in heaven, you know. Do you trust Him?"

This woman, who had been mostly a stranger a few months ago, focused on Annie with the same look of care and concern that her mother might have given.

"Well, yes. Yes, I trust Him."

"Then you pray and do whatever it is you think He's telling you to do, whether or not it matches with any plan you had, and you can be sure that everything will work out all right."

"But what about Julian? I mean, we're not officially engaged, but he's said he wants to marry me. Shouldn't I talk to him about it first?"

"Maybe. But if you're supposed to raise this child, and if he's the one you're supposed to raise him with, it will work out."

"Well, there's something else we have to work out."

"I know. And I've told R.C. she is welcome to stay here. Surely, I wasn't expecting it, but by my way a-thinking, it's a—well, gracious, it's a lovely surprise."

Aunt Brenda seemed to have everything figured out one step ahead of Annie.

"I just don't know, Aunt Brenda. I mean the whole reason I came here and left Julian and Mama behind is that I didn't want Ruth Claire to be without me. And I didn't want to be without her. How can I possibly go back home and leave her here?"

"All I can tell you to do is to pray. He'll show you the way, Annie. But listen. When He does show you, that's His part now, you understand? Your part is walking it. You have to be willing to walk the path, no matter where it leads."

Chapter Thirteen

November, Present Day

$\mathcal{E}$VERY DAY since the party, and since Grandma Annie's promise to share about her strangely secret past, something had come up. A doctor appointment for Mama, a teacher conference concerning Emma, chaperoning a field trip for Joshua, and an orthodontist consultation for Piper Grace. Thank goodness, they said another year before braces. Finally, it was Friday, and Missy and Grandma rode alone.

"I hope Mama will be okay watching Little Bit for a while." Missy hit the radio button and turned the volume down.

"I'm sure she'll be fine. She's been getting around a lot better lately. Getting used to that sling, bless her heart."

Missy came to a stop sign and made a right turn. Two more turns until the cemetery.

"I think your mama was happy to see me leave the house for a little while," Grandma Annie said.

"Oh, don't be silly. She loves having you there."

"No, it's true. She's a gracious host, but two grown women in the same house isn't easy. I get on her nerves sometimes. I slip up and tell her how to cook something she's been cooking in that kitchen for years and years. Or she'll baby me a bit too much and I get snippity. We don't mean to. It just happens."

"But you love each other."

"Of course, we love each other. JoAnn has been good to my Thomas. And she's a good mama to my grandgirls. She's always been kind to me, too, and I think of her as a daughter. But sometimes, family fusses." She took a breath. "Like you and your sister."

"What do you mean? We're grown now. We don't fuss with one another."

"Uh-huh."

Her grandma obviously wasn't buying it.

"Anyway . . ." Grandma Annie's thumbs circled one another in her lap, "it will be a lot easier when your mama can drive again. After the surgery next week, she should be healed up by the new year."

"Oh, I hope so."

But what about your secrets, Grandma? That's what she really wanted to talk about.

Missy turned the wheel hand-over-hand and pulled into the gravel parking lot beside the cemetery where her grandfather and the great-grandfather she never knew, along with others in their family, had been laid to rest. Ten or so long rows of headstones and monuments faced a white church with a wide porch and large wooden double doors, each with a stained-glass window in the shape of a cross. How long had it been since she was here last? The familiar place that she'd made a stranger brought back strong emotions.

Missy's sneakered feet crunched the white gravel as she stepped out of the van. She retrieved the two reusable shopping bags filled with silk floral arrangements from the back of the van and came around to help Grandma Annie.

"Are you sure you feel up to this?" Missy extended the arm that wasn't laden with bags. "You can stay in the van, and I can do this by myself."

"I'll be fine." Grandma gripped Missy's arm and pulled herself up. "As long as you do all the squatting and bending. It won't take us long to get these flowers on the graves, honeybee . . . then you and I will have ourselves a little talk."

Missy nodded, nervous and hopeful at once.

Grandma Annie led the way, using a tripod cane to navigate the uneven ground, across the parking lot and into the cemetery. Missy stayed within a yard of her heels.

The air was back to normal for November—brisk, but tolerable.

Grandma Annie stopped at the earthly resting place of her parents—Theodore and Leeta Swaim. Missy hadn't seen these graves in years, but being there now, with her grandma, to place flowers for Veterans Day, felt right.

Missy placed the flowers as she was instructed—a small, patriotic bouquet of carnations, lilies, and delphinium for Grandma's father, and two red roses tied with a white ribbon for her mother. As she hovered close to the ground, she ran her fingers along the etched epitaph of Great-Grandpa's stone. *Husband, Father, Friend, World War II Veteran.*

She stood and traced the lines of each letter again with her eyes. What would be on her marker someday? Certainly nothing as important as Great-Grandpa's last title. "Any special meaning in two roses?" she asked.

Grandma Annie pointed at the simple offering. "One from me, and the other from R.C." She closed her eyes and whispered a few words Missy couldn't discern, then ambled two steps over to the stone that bore the name *Ruth Claire Swaim Johnson.* The great-aunt that Missy never got to meet.

"The white roses you've got in the bag there are for R.C."

Again, there were two long stems tied together. Missy laid them on the base of the stone, then looked up at Grandma Annie and asked the question with her eyes.

"One from me, the other from your daddy."

"Oh, that's nice."

Missy grunted as she stood. It would have been smart to have worn the bigger jeans for this kind of up-and-down.

Grandma smiled toward the headstone, then did a careful pivot and scanned the rows. She sighed. "Look at all those bare graves. I wonder how many of them are veterans." She turned back to Missy. "Listen, baby. You don't have to leave flowers like this for me when I'm gone. Don't you worry about it, 'cause I won't know one way or the other. But don't forget the veterans. It's a way we show the world that our soldiers were important. Whether they died fighting or not, they served. And we can't ever forget why."

Missy's throat tightened. "Yes, ma'am. I won't forget. I promise."

On the next row, they stopped at Missy's grandfather's grave, and the spot beside him reserved for Grandma Annie. It was troubling, seeing the name *Annie Swaim Hall* on a tombstone while her grandma was alive and mostly well. All that was left to add was the date of death. But Grandma Annie didn't seem the least bit fazed.

Missy kneeled again and placed the same red, white, and blue arrangement that she'd left for her great-grandpa on Grandpa David's stone as a flood of memories washed over her. She ran her hand along the base of the smooth, cool stone. *You were the absolute best grandpa I could have hoped for. Gentle, affectionate, fun* she whispered to him, knowing full well he wasn't there and disregarding the belief that he was no longer anywhere at all.

Grandma Annie touched her fingertips to her lips then transferred the kiss to the stone with a gentle touch. "Okay, my dear." She took a deep breath. "These old stones are dressed for Veterans Day tomorrow. That was step one. Now let's get to the hard work. Follow me."

*   *   *

Annie had yet to decide just how much to tell her granddaughter, but being there in that cemetery, surrounded by bodies that could no longer speak, made the truth bubble closer to the surface than expected.

Lord, I don't know how much time you'll let me stay here. Let me say what needs to be said. And help me point Missy to You . . . somehow. The solitude of the cemetery made it a good place to talk, though the cold wind grabbed at her joints and twisted. With each step, she willed the pain to go, but it wouldn't obey.

Annie led Missy to an ornate metal bench near a line of tall pines that separated the church's graveyard from the cow pasture on the other side. They sat, facing one another, and a different type of pain overtook her. Her heart hurt to see the tiredness in Melissa's eyes—way too much for someone so young. Missy carried burdens that she longed to understand.

"Melissa, I know you want to hear about my dancing. And I do want you to know about that. But first"—she placed her wrinkled hand on Missy's blue jeaned knee—"tell me more about Mary Sue Montgomery. I want to know how she hurt you."

Missy drew a deep breath and leaned against the back of the bench. She stuffed her hands into the pockets of her zipped-up hooded jacket. "I think you know, Grandma. I looked up to her. She was, like, the perfect Christian. Taught me most of what I ever learned about the Bible. But when I got pregnant with Emma . . . I mean, I know she was disappointed in me, but

I—I didn't expect her to completely turn her back on me. You didn't. And Mama and Daddy didn't. But Miss Mary Sue, and lots of others in that church over there, they acted as if . . ."

Annie's heart ached. She understood the shame Missy had endured, even more than Missy knew.

"Oh, honey. That was so hard for you at seventeen. But God made something good out of it. Didn't He?"

"Trust me, the only thing that gives me an ounce of faith in God now is seeing my babies' faces. I look at them and think, maybe He is there. But when the people I trusted to love me and be there for me wanted nothing to do with me anymore, just because I wasn't as good and decent and as holy as the rest of them, that's when I started having doubts about their God."

"Baby girl, listen. People are, well . . . people. But that's not God. He didn't turn his back on you. He loves you just as much now as He always has. And you can't let the mistakes of some church folks steal your joy in Him."

"I don't know, Grandma . . ."

"It's like this, Missy." Annie leaned closer. "You know in those action movies, when the good guy is running just as fast as he can, and all the while he's being shot at from every direction?"

Missy chuckled, and her mouth turned up on one side. "I guess so."

"Well, what happens when one of those bullets grazes the hero in the arm? Does he stop running?"

"No. He keeps going."

"Exactly. And sometimes in this life, we get some pretty bad flesh wounds. And they hurt. They can hurt a might bad. And, baby, it would be so much easier to stop. But the spiritual race, this race for eternity . . . it's a race for our lives. And Mary Sue Montgomery, and ones like her, they only dealt you a flesh wound. You can't give up on account of that."

"I—I didn't know you liked action movies, Grandma."

"Oh, that's just an analogy I heard somewhere. A sermon on the radio, I think. But I did enjoy *Rambo*. And the comparison is a good one."

"I'll think on it. But you know, we had a deal. I want to know more about you being a dance instructor once upon a time, and why I never heard about it before the other day. And . . ." Missy took a breath, then exhaled slowly. "I think I need to know about the folder. The one you didn't want me to see. I can't explain why, but I'd like to know. If you're willing to tell me."

"One thing at a time."

Annie used her cane to push herself up from the bench, then gripped at her wrist until the pain eased. She began to walk back across the graveyard with Missy by her side.

"Once upon a time, I lived and breathed ballet. And there was a studio, here in Winston-Salem, where I took classes as a child. When I graduated high school, I started taking classes at the business school, because the owner of the studio had promised to let me manage it when she retired. A degree in dance from a university was way out of reach. And I thought at least that way, I could keep dancing and could teach others to love it, too. And the little girls were so fun."

"What happened? Why did you quit?"

"It turned out that the owner—Miss Melinda—well, I guess you could say she was my Mary Sue Montgomery." By the time they'd reached the van, Annie had told Missy a big part of her story—how her dream of managing the studio had been ripped away from her. "But there was a reason, Missy. God's ways and thoughts are much higher than ours. We have to trust Him in all of it."

"And you never talked about it because it was too painful? The memories?"

"God took the pain away over time, but I had already buried the memories. I never considered you might like to know about that part of my life."

Missy clicked her seat belt in place. "And is there more you think I'd like to know?"

The truth sat on the tip of Annie's tongue, ready to be launched. It wouldn't be fair for them to find out after she was in the cold, hard parcel of ground in front of them. With just a few words, she could be free. But they wouldn't come.

"I think I've said enough for today."

*   *   *

John Thomas slid off his grandmother's lap and ran to Missy and Grandma Annie at the door.

"Were you a good boy for Grandma?" Missy picked him up around the waist and held him close, letting his blue-jeaned legs dangle toward the floor.

"I dunno. Ask Grandma."

"Oh, he was fine. He minded real good." Missy's mother eased herself out of the recliner, pushing up with the good arm. "We sat right here and read picture books for almost an hour. He's a great page turner. I only gave him my phone just a minute ago. Here, Annie, take the recliner and rest your back."

Grandma Annie made no argument. After their excursion, her discomfort was visible.

Missy set John Thomas down and hugged her mother. "Thank you for watching him."

"No trouble, baby. I'm glad I was able. I've missed it."

"Gigi, watch this video with me." John Thomas climbed back into the recliner and held the phone near his great-grandmother. "It's funny."

"Well, we've got to go soon, Little Bit. You watch the video with Gigi while I run to the bathroom, then we've got to hurry and get on home before your brother and sisters get there."

Two steps down the hallway, the beginnings of an unexpected idea took hold of Missy's brain. *Crazy. There's no way.* But the thought grew with each step. When she finished using the toilet, she didn't flush, to make them think she wasn't finished. She washed her hands under a small stream of water, then she tiptoed from the hallway bathroom into the tiny bedroom at the end of the hall that had been set up for Grandma Annie.

Little Bit laughed loudly from the front room.

"I told you it was funny." He cackled as the intro music of another video began.

Missy surveyed the space that had been her bedroom. The bed, the rocking chair, the nightstand, all the beautiful furniture she'd helped move into the house was there. And against the wall, the dresser. If the folder was still in the bottom drawer, she'd have to look inside. If Grandma had left it there, it would practically be *meant* for Missy to see it.

She sat on the edge of the bed with her knees wide apart, then she leaned forward and eased the drawer open. The contents looked the same—the ballet shoes, the framed pictures of Daddy, the Bible, and the picture of Great-Grandpa Theodore. The plain beige folder peeked from beneath all of it. Missy looked over her shoulder and back again. There was just enough room to pull the folder out without disturbing the rest of the drawer's contents, and she managed to do it without a sound.

A wave of guilt hit her racing heart as she held the folder in her hands. Just as much as she knew she shouldn't look inside, that she shouldn't snoop and break her grandmother's sacred trust, she knew she had to. A force drove her to know what had made Grandma so secretive.

Her hands shook as she opened the folder. The papers inside were yellowed. The faded words had been typed on a typewriter, and though legible, they made no sense. The paper on top had an official-looking heading that read Decree of Adoption, and her father's name typed on top of a blank line. The paper listed his birthdate of just over sixty years ago. But as the blood rushed in Missy's ears, another name on the page jumped out at her. The title was *Birth Mother*, but the entry was *Ruth Claire Swaim*.

Missy shut the folder and dropped it back into the drawer. She'd pretend she never saw it. It didn't exist. And there was certainly no need to talk to Grandma Annie about it. Because it wasn't real. She'd simply get John Thomas and go home, and life would continue on as it had for all of them before. She closed the drawer and turned to leave.

Grandma Annie stood in the doorway with a stunned expression. "Melissa, what are you doing in my room? Did you go into my drawer?"

"I—I'm sorry, Grandma. I have to get home."

She brushed past and made her way to the living room. "Let's go, John Thomas. The school bus is going to beat us home if we don't hurry."

"But I didn't say bye to Gigi."

"It's okay, Grandma will tell her bye for you."

Missy thanked her mother again and kissed her on the cheek, then she rushed out the door, pulling John Thomas along behind her.

*   *   *

Does Daddy know? Of course, he must know. But why didn't I know? This can't be real.

She focused on the road through narrow eyes, as the muscles in her brow and forehead tightened more and more. Her short breaths came quick, and there was a slight ringing in her ears, muffled only by the sound of John Thomas singing a cartoon theme song behind her.

Half-way home, her cell phone rang from the passenger seat.

Oh, go away. Whoever you are, just go away.

But it could be about the children. She couldn't let it go to voicemail. What if there was an emergency? She looked at the display. The number wasn't familiar.

"Hello?"

A twangy voice, unmistakable though she'd only heard it once before, came through the phone speaker.

"Hello, Mrs. Robbins. How you doing?"

Could there be a worse time . . . ?

"Oh, Mr. Barker. *Henry.* I'm—I'm fine."

"Good, good. Well, I bet you can guess the reason for my call. Time's a ticking, young lady. Have you considered the invitation to join my choir?"

Chapter Fourteen

November 1963

"**W**E HAVE a lot to be thankful for, don't we, baby sister?" Annie said.

Focusing on the positive wasn't easy. The whole country had experienced a long and trying week. But holidays were for celebration.

Ruth Claire nodded as she stuffed half a biscuit into her mouth. A piece crumbled and fell from her lip onto the ceramic plate. She quickly snatched it and added it to the bite. Annie smiled. Aunt Brenda's White Lily biscuits were every bit as good as Mama's—like biting into a piece of home—and the rest of their Thanksgiving meal for sure gave the biscuits a run for their money.

Annie looked down at her plate and made a track in the mashed potatoes with her fork as she thought of Mama. How was she managing on the first Thanksgiving without her girls? And how she would feel at Christmas, with only one of her daughters there?

"Girls, I can't tell you what it means to have you here with me." Aunt Brenda interrupted Annie's thoughts, repeating the sentiment she'd directed to God during the blessing. "This really is a special Thanksgiving, despite all the sadness around.

And I hope we'll be together again this time next year. All of us and Leeta, too."

"Mama's having lunch with Mrs. Douglas. Right, Annie?"

Annie nodded at R.C. "And one other widow from church, too, I think. Makes me happy to know she's having a meal like this back home. She's really shaken up about . . . well, we all are."

The television news had talked about nothing but President Kennedy's assassination for days, and rightly so. A cloud of uncertainty hung over the entire country, and, though Annie felt like the most selfish person alive for thinking it, it seemed that the center of that cloud was right over her own head.

Thomas attracted their attention with cooing from his spot on the floor atop a pile of blankets.

Aunt Brenda laughed. "I think he wants some of this good turkey."

R.C. half stood, peered over at the baby, then sat back down. "He can't have turkey. He doesn't have any teeth."

Annie and Brenda exchanged smiles and knowing looks.

"I know, sweetheart," Aunt Brenda said. "It's just a little joke."

"Oh." R.C. shrugged and took a big gulp of her milk.

"Annie, we're sure going to miss you and Thomas when you head home next week."

Every chance they got, Annie and Aunt Brenda spoke of their leaving in front of R.C., to make sure she understood, and that she hadn't changed her mind.

"We're going to miss you both, too," Annie said. "Bunches. But I'll call as often as I can. And we'll write, of course." *Oh, R.C. Tell me you're coming home, too. Tell me you don't want to stay here without me.*

R.C. looked up from her plate with a big grin. "Is it time for pie?"

*   *   *

"I think you should say your goodbyes here, Annie, then I'll take you and Thomas to the bus stop. It'll be best for R.C. not to go. Cleet will come in to look after her."

Annie ran her hand over the flour sack that held all the clothes and books she'd brought with her, save for the smart pencil skirt and jacket she sported now. A quilted bag of bright colors that held Thomas's clothes, diapers, and bottles lay beside the flour sack.

"Um, I'm not sure that's a good idea," Annie said. "I mean, I don't really like her being alone here with—"

Aunt Brenda held up her hand. "Cleet is a good, Christian man. I understand what you mean, and I won't make a habit of leaving them alone, but R.C. is perfectly safe with him."

Out of all the workers that had been part of her life on the farm—most of which wouldn't be back until planting time rolled around again in the spring—Cleet *was* her favorite. Soft-spoken, attentive. And he did seem like a good man. One of only a few farmhands that Aunt Brenda kept on year-round.

"Okay. I'm sure you're right." Annie filled her lungs with a courage-giving breath and whispered a prayer as she let it out. She scanned the room one more time. "Okay, I think we're ready."

She walked out of the bedroom and to the living room with Aunt Brenda following. R.C. sat on the green frieze couch, holding Thomas close to her chest, while her eyes were fixed on Captain Kangaroo and Mr. Moose on the television's screen.

As she took in the scene, their childhoods flashed in Annie's mind. Sitting on the wooden church pew between Daddy and

Mama, the picnics at Hanging Rock as a family, and their yearly visit to the Dixie Classic Fair, where R.C.'s favorite part had always been the petting zoo. Annie's heartache over leaving pulled out painful scenes, too, like the two of them huddled together in their room floor, the night Daddy lost his life in that terrible highway crash.

Annie shook off the thoughts and replaced them with the knowledge that she'd see Julian and Mama soon. And that she wasn't leaving Ruth Claire forever. After Aunt Brenda enrolled R.C. in high school there, and R.C. saw that she couldn't spend all her time with the horses, Annie was sure she'd decide to come home.

"Okay, baby sister. About time for us to get on the road." She sat on the edge of the couch beside R.C. "Mind if I turn off the set for a minute?"

Ruth Claire shook her head.

"I'll get it." Aunt Brenda bustled over to turn the knob then left the room.

R.C. handed the baby to Annie and hung her head. "I don't want you to go, Annie." Her voice was even and low.

"And you know I don't want you to stay here, Ruth Claire." Annie inched closer. "I want you to come home, to be with me and Mama and Thomas. It doesn't seem right leaving you here. But I know it's what you want."

"Aunt Brenda's alone, Annie. Mama will have you and the baby."

"Is that why you're wanting to stay? To keep her company?"

R.C. twirled a strand of hair—which she'd actually allowed Aunt Brenda to brush—tightly around her finger. "Just a part of the reason. Not the biggest part. I like it here. Just like I told you. I really like it here."

"But you like home, too, right?"

R.C. nodded and the corners of her mouth turned up the slightest bit. "*Yes, Ann-nniieee.*" She huffed and rolled her eyes then smiled again.

Annie grabbed R.C.'s hands and smiled back. That kind of joking and sarcasm were skills R.C. had only just begun to learn, and Annie hated to miss any of it.

"Okay. But it's not goodbye forever. Aunt Brenda says she's long overdue for a visit with Mama anyway. She'll be bringing you back to us very soon, okay? We don't have to say when right now, but soon."

Ruth Claire nodded.

Aunt Brenda poked her head around the door and whispered. "We need to be getting on in a couple a' minutes."

Annie let her know she'd heard her.

"R.C., do you want to say goodbye to Thomas? I know you're going to miss him." She held the newborn toward his mother.

R.C. rubbed one of his pinky toes, which stuck out from the bottom of the white dressing gown, between her thumb and forefinger. "I'm glad you're my baby, Thomas Theodore," she said. "And I'm glad you're gonna be Annie's baby, too. Annie's good at taking care of people." She leaned and placed a kiss on the baby's forehead.

Aunt Brenda entered, with Buster following behind. He could always tell when they were fixing to leave the house. "I took your stuff to the car, all except for our little man here. I'll wrap him up real good and get him ready to go out." She took Thomas from Annie's arms as she and R.C. both stood.

"R.C., I want to give you something before I leave." Annie reached up and fumbled with the clasp of her necklace until it came undone. She laid the pendant in her open palm and stared at it. "I think you need to keep this."

Ruth Claire's eyes went wide.

Annie held the necklace out for R.C. to see, then she opened the locket and removed the folded paper for the first time since she'd placed it there. She opened it into a matchbook-sized square. The tiny writing had been done with a well-sharpened pencil, and thankfully, the words hadn't smudged.

"Read it, R.C."

"The LORD bless thee, and keep thee: The LORD make his face shine upon thee, and be gracious unto thee: The LORD lift up his countenance upon thee, and give thee peace."

R.C. folded the paper, following the original creases, and placed it back inside the locket. She looked up with glistening eyes.

"It's from the book of Numbers. I wrote it as a prayer for Mama and Julian, to remember to pray for them while we were apart. But now that I'm going back home and leaving you here—just for a little while, mind you—it's my prayer for you. It's always been my prayer for you, Ruth Claire Swaim. Blessings and peace, the grace and safety of the Good Lord. And I know He'll do it, too."

R.C., who had never been one for hugs, stepped forward and laid her head on Annie's shoulder with her arms by her side. She nuzzled closer as Annie wrapped her arms around her and breathed in the scent of her. With a heart whisper she cried. *Goodbye, baby sister.*

Chapter Fifteen

Tuesday, November 28, Present Day

"**W**E NEED to talk, Melissa."

Over and over, the words Grandma Annie had left on her voicemail that morning played in Missy's mind. Hurt, angry, sad, scared—every one of these emotions were in Grandma's shaky voice.

After the miserable Thanksgiving they'd had the week before, Missy was almost ready to talk. She couldn't very well go on forever saying things like "Please pass the gravy," when she really wanted to scream, *Are you my real grandmother or not?*

Missy dunked another plate in the hot, sudsy water, wiped it clean, then ran it under the faucet for two seconds, front and back. Then she plunked it into the blue strainer beside the sink and moved on to the next one.

Ray just had to get that dishwasher fixed like he'd promised. With six people in this house . . .

At least washing dishes was a mindless task and it afforded her time to think.

She'd managed to avoid her grandmother for the most part. That is until they were seated across the dining room table from each other at Mama and Daddy's house for Thanksgiving dinner. Everyone had been there, minus Erica. How Missy had wished her sister *could* have been there. Erica would have told stories and laughed at her own jokes until everyone was infected with laughter whether what she'd said was funny or not, diluting the tension between Missy and their grandmother—if she was, in fact, that. But Erica was celebrating Thanksgiving in Nashville for the first time. Probably at some catered party. And Missy had done most of the cooking alone, in Mama and Daddy's kitchen, since Mama couldn't do much more than set something in the microwave and stir a pot on the stove.

Missy had eaten her feelings that day, doubling up on the macaroni and cheese and having a full-size piece of both the pecan and pumpkin pies, not to mention turkey and all the other trimmings. And every time Grandma Annie made eye contact, Missy had raised her glass and took a nervous gulp of sweet tea. Her mouth had been full of drink when Daddy, from the head of the table, brought up Henry Barker, and Missy had to fight to swallow it down.

"He told me at work that he called you a couple weeks ago. He really, I mean *really*, wants you to help his choir for Christmas. Have you decided about it yet?"

Ray had looked at her with a puzzled expression since she'd failed to even mention the invitation.

"Um—not yet. I have to tell him soon, though," Missy told her father.

"After the performance you gave at my party, it's no wonder he's so excited to have you join them."

Oh, how she enjoyed the proud look on Daddy's face when he talked about the party. The praise from her parents—which they'd given nearly every time she'd talked to them since—was about the only thing that had made Thanksgiving dinner bearable.

But she couldn't keep on like this. There'd be a time, possibly soon, when she'd have to face Grandma Annie. She wanted to. Not today, but soon. Deep in her soul, Missy longed to be able to hug her, and talk to her, and laugh with her like normal. Even if it meant confirming things she didn't want to know.

Maybe she could call her, just to tell her she loved her. Maybe nothing else would have to be said. Maybe they could pretend nothing was wrong.

Missy balanced a pot on top of the mountain of dishes in the strainer, then dried her hands on a kitchen towel. As soon as she dropped the towel back on the counter, the doorbell rang, and Mr. Peanut began to bark.

"Shhh." She gave the dog's collar a gentle tug. "If the doorbell didn't wake Little Bit, you're going to."

The delivery drivers had been there with presents for Christmas every day that week so far. Piper's new tablet and clothes for Emma were scheduled to arrive. More of the boys' toys were coming tomorrow.

Missy stood on her tiptoes and looked through the half-circle pane in the top of the door to be sure. Even in the rural part of the city, a body couldn't be too careful.

It was not a delivery.

She put on a smile and opened the door. "Well, hey. Y'all surprised me. Come on in." Missy opened the door wider.

Daddy stood holding the storm door. Grandma Annie stood beside him, leaning on her cane, her hair and clothes neat as usual and with a modestly made-up face that bore no expression.

"I wish I could stay, but it's just your grandma visiting today," Daddy said. "She wanted to come see you, and I had the afternoon off to take your mama to an appointment, so I told her I'd bring her by." He offered an apologetic nod to

Missy. "Now I gotta run." He kissed his mother on the cheek. "Bye, Mama. I'll be back in a couple hours unless Missy wants to bring you home sooner."

"That's fine." Grandma Annie nodded at him. "Love you."

"Love you, too, Mama."

Daddy leaned and gave Missy a kiss then turned and headed down the porch steps. Missy held the storm door for Grandma as she entered. A cold wind came into the foyer with her, and Missy shivered.

"Is anyone else here?"

"Little Bit's taking a nap."

"Good, that's good." Grandma Annie patted Mr. Peanut's head as he rubbed his muzzle on her pant leg.

The weight of Missy's guilt grew heavier, pressing at her heart like floodwaters against a dam. There was no way to hold back the words. "I know that I owe you an apology, Grandma. It was wrong to go through your things, and I'm so—"

Grandma held up her hand like a crossing guard. "Yes, it *was* wrong. And I accept. I've had time to get over that, and I'm not here to get an apology." Her eyes found Missy's and held. "I'm here to talk about what you saw."

Missy turned, took a deep breath as she bit her bottom lip, then turned back in slow motion. "Okay."

Grandma led her to the living room where they sat on opposite ends of the couch. Missy stared at the carpet, trying to make sense of things—how she'd gone from washing dishes to confronting a family secret that could change her identity, in just a matter of minutes.

"I knew this day would come eventually . . . when someone would find out." Grandma Annie's gaze traveled to the window and whatever she found to focus on beyond it. "I just didn't know who, or how, or when."

Missy's stomach muscles tensed. She'd tried to tell herself that she hadn't really seen what she thought she'd seen. That it was a mistake of some kind.

"I suppose I could have burned the papers, but it never felt right. They were too important to me."

"It's okay. Just—just tell me."

Facing reality often felt like razor blades to the soul, but the distress in Grandma Annie's voice cut deepest. "Missy, no. No, I didn't give birth to your father. My sister did. I know it's hard to understand, but I hope you will let me explain the best I can—for both our sakes."

"So, it's true—you're not my grandmother?"

"Of course I am." Grandma Annie's remorse exploded into indignation. "Don't be silly. Didn't I cook Sunday lunch for you most every week of your life until you were grown? Didn't I talk you down from the edge of calamity after your first heartbreak? Who waited for you on the front porch to get off the school bus? And who took you on picnics to Hanging Rock?"

"You know what I mean. You're my *grandma*, I know, but you're not my *real* grandmother." Saying the words out loud cemented them into existence, and Missy wished she could swallow them back again.

"I'm your grandma, just as real today as yesterday. Nothing has changed, Melissa."

"I'm sorry, Grandma. I need to . . . I just need to go to the garage for a minute. I'll be back."

Missy hurried out the kitchen door, through the short breezeway, and into the garage. She found the old army-green tackle box in the corner, where she kept her cigarettes and lighter. John Thomas should stay asleep for at least a few more minutes. The news was just too hard to handle. She lit the cigarette with a shaky hand and rested her forehead on one fist as she took a deep draw.

Missy's eyes grew moist, but no tears spilled. There'd been too many already. For over two weeks, as she'd pondered the discovery of adoption papers in her grandmother's dresser drawer, the tears had come often—in the shower, in the car, there in the garage. And now that the truth had been confirmed, there were no more tears left.

"Melissa Jo, what on earth are you doing?"

Missy spun around at the sound of Grandma Annie's voice in the doorway of the garage.

"Don't you know how bad that is for you?"

The thin cloud that hung in the air did not conceal her, but to Missy's surprise, her guilt dissipated more quickly than the smoke. If anyone should feel guilty about something, it was Grandma Annie, not her.

"I guess you're not the only one with secrets, Grandma." Missy shrugged. "I just needed to take the edge off."

Missy bent down and crushed the end of the cigarette into the coffee can that sat next to the tackle box on the concrete floor behind the wheelbarrow.

They stared at each other; Grandma's eyes filled with bewilderment. Without another word she shuffled in a slow three-point-turn and headed back inside the house, more hunched than when she first got there. Missy followed at a distance. With any luck, she'd be able to handle the rest of the conversation without another nicotine break.

"I'm ready to listen." Missy spoke barely above a whisper. "Again."

Grandma Annie returned to her place on the couch, letting out a grunt as she sat. She bit down on her bottom lip and squeezed her eyes closed as she slid the heart-shaped locket that she always wore, back and forth along its chain.

"I want you to understand that my sister, Ruth Claire, was a smart girl. Very smart. But she was different from most girls . . . in a way that's hard to explain. Amazing with information and facts, and especially with animals. All kinds. But with certain emotions and some things that might seem like common sense to me and you, she struggled." Grandma Annie paused and tilted her head forward. Missy nodded in response. Daddy had mentioned R.C. and her quirks a few times.

"When R.C. started dating, she didn't know what she was getting herself into exactly."

"How old was she?"

"Sixteen. And I was twenty. I always felt like it was my job to look after R.C., and back in those days . . . well, the plan was to put the baby up for adoption."

"So, why didn't you?"

Listening to the story was like listening to a soap opera, a melodrama about someone else's life. She had to remind herself, time and again, the baby her grandma talked about was Missy's own father.

"I fell in love with him the moment I saw him, Missy. And even though he could have had a good life with another family—maybe even better than the one he had with me—I couldn't stand the thought of not knowing him. He was my nephew, and I wanted him with me. Not someone else."

"And R.C.?"

"She agreed to it, of course. It had to be her choice, too. But I always wondered if I pushed her, if she felt like she had to give him to me. Was I guilty somehow for taking him? It's always haunted me, Melissa."

Missy's brain raced in circles. There must have been a thousand questions that needed to be asked, but none would form on her tongue. She clasped her hands and rested her forearms on her knees, teetering on the edge of the couch. For the moment of awkward silence, she rocked back and forth with short movements.

"There were some who knew, of course," Grandma said. "Friends and family that we had to tell. If I believed in luck, I'd say that's the reason no one let the truth slip out in front of Thomas when he was older. Just luck." She fixed her eyes on the window and sighed. "But lots of people assumed I'd had him out of wedlock. And some were really ugly to me about it."

"Like they were to me, when I . . . when Emma came along."

"Yes, baby. I knew your pain all too well back then, though I couldn't share it with you. Mine was different, but I still knew what you were going through."

The muscles in Missy's forehead tightened as she let another new truth soak in.

"Your grandpa and I married when Thomas was three, and all that changed."

Grandpa. The name stung Missy's heart. At least she and the woman she had always known as her grandmother were blood relatives. She couldn't say the same about the man she had idolized all her childhood.

Missy checked her watch. The big kids wouldn't be home for another hour and a half, but Little Bit would likely wake up any minute. What time had her daddy said he was coming back?

"*Wait.* Daddy." The question finally found its way to her lips. "Daddy knows, right? He's kept this from me, too, right? He has to know."

The look on Grandma's face gave her the answer.

"He doesn't know he's adopted? But how . . .?"

It seemed impossible. Daddy had always been there to give Missy the answers. Complicated things about life, the kind of wisdom that couldn't be found with an Internet search. But all along, he'd been in the dark about something so fundamental as who had birthed him. And now Missy had that answer.

She stood and paced the room. On the return trip from near the window, John Thomas stood there in front of her. He seemed not to notice Gigi as he walked to his mama. He raised his short arms in the air, and she bent down and picked him up, hugging him tightly and kissing his hair.

"Do you have a good nap, Little Bit? It was a long one today."

He nodded and laid his head on her shoulder. "Mama, you smell like burnt popcorn again."

"I know I do, baby. It's okay. I'll take a shower later." Missy caught Grandma Annie's knowing look as she carried the boy to the rocker recliner next to the couch and sat down.

When he raised his head and saw his great-grandmother, John Thomas scrambled out of Missy's lap. After he'd had a moment to visit with Gigi, Missy offered him her phone and he took off to another room to watch a video.

"Okay, Grandma." Missy kept her voice low. "Why did you never tell him?"

"I don't know." Grandma Annie wrung her hands. "If his real mother had been a stranger, I think I could have done it. But I just never found a way. I thought it would be too confusing. But I also did it for R.C. I thought it was easier for her to handle that way. After a while, it seemed best if we all just pretended that I *was* his birth mother."

The mama heart in Missy ached for R.C. *and* for Grandma, and for the first time since she'd found the folder, she was able to see beyond her own hurt. Grandma Annie had sacrificed for her sister. She had sacrificed to raise Missy's father. And the impact of those choices on Missy's life could only be imagined.

"Missy, I need you to promise me you won't tell him. Not now, after all this time. It would only hurt. Think of how you felt when you found out. It would be even worse for my Thomas. Please don't do that to him."

"Grandma, don't you feel like you've been living a lie? Isn't it wrong? Maybe it would be best for the truth to come out."

"Missy, I would never want you to lie. And I can tell you that I have never lied to Thomas about being his mother. I *am* his mother. And as far as I can remember, the Good Lord help me, I have *never* told him that I gave birth to him. That's different. He *does* think his daddy and I were married the year before he was born, which was a lie, but I couldn't . . ."

Missy leaned over and buried her face in her hands. How could she possibly keep such a secret from her father? "Grandma, I understand you not wanting him to know, but it—it does seem like—what is it that y'all call it—a *false witness*. You may not have misled him with your words, but you've let him believe something that isn't true."

Grandma Annie's long face contorted into a pained expression.

"Missy, I've spent the better part of sixty years dreading the day that Thomas would find out. Please don't make me. Please keep this between us, Missy. For me. *For your father*."

Chapter Sixteen

November 1963

*T*HE SQUARE faded-yellow house, with its low-hanging roof and peeled-paint shutters, had been concealed behind the bushy limbs of two short flowering dogwood trees when Annie left. Now it stood exposed behind naked branches, and the burnt red remnants of their foliage littered the narrow patch of yard.

Home. Home. Home.

The hours on the bus with a fussy baby, then the short drive from the station in the Studebaker—even after a joyous reunion with Mama—had felt like days. Now Annie was *home*, at the only house she'd ever known, save for the four months at Aunt Brenda's. She was finally home to . . .

Annie paused with one foot in the car and one on the ground. Home to what? Home to raise her nephew? Home to be Thomas's mother? To finish school and find a job that had nothing to do with dancing? Marry Julian and settle down as an instant family of three?

Julian had said he supported the decision when she'd spoken to him of it on the telephone. He'd said he understood why she was bringing Thomas home instead of giving him to the couple the agency had chosen. But his tone had betrayed him.

Annie sighed as she exited the car with Thomas in her arms. All of it would be sorted out soon enough. For now, she'd just enjoy being here, amid the wonderful familiarity of her surroundings—the tiny walkway to the front door, the row of old houses as far as she could see, all similar in size and shape—and the *God Bless This Home* sign that Daddy had painted, hanging to the right of the front door.

"We're home, Thomas. This is going to be your home," she whispered to the sleeping infant.

In a moment, Annie's kitten heels tapped at the three concrete front steps, echoing like the sound of a ball-peen hammer on the head of a tack. She reached for the doorknob, then turned back. Though Mama somehow seemed younger than when Annie left, she still took much longer than Annie to get from the car to the house. Annie waited on the top step.

When she felt the gentle nudge of Mama's hand at her back, Annie went inside.

A lived-in smell greeted her—one she'd always described in her mind as old wooden floorboards and cabinets that had absorbed years of bacon-frying and had been given a lick and a promise with Murphy Oil Soap on the regular. From the small living room, she saw across the half wall into the kitchen to the small table where so many meals had been shared.

She looked down, then scanned the room left to right and back again as she cradled the baby. Walking through that door with Thomas, but without Ruth Claire, had been like walking into an episode of *The Twilight Zone*. Never could Annie have ever imagined this deviation from the plan. But she remembered Aunt Brenda's words. *Things don't have to turn out the way we think they should, Annie.* That wisdom from her memory was immediately followed by more. *He'll show you the way, Annie. You just have to be willing to walk it.*

"Annie, go on over and sit down on the couch. You've had a long day." Mama gave her a nudge. "Here, let me take Thomas."

Annie didn't object. The couch called to her, and she'd held Thomas in her arms for most of the day. Mostly, Annie was relieved that Mama seemed to be dealing with the baby so well. Though her movements were jittery and her eyes worried, she wore a big smile, and she looked at Thomas with such love.

Mama left the flour sack of clothes and the baby's bag on the floor near the door, and she took a seat with Thomas in the chair across from the couch.

"I'll only sit for a minute, Mama. I'll need to put my things away and then go call Julian. Then I'll need to freshen up before he gets here." She hadn't worn makeup the entire time in Georgia. No need. But seeing Julian after so long called for getting dolled up.

"I'm surprised he didn't meet you at the bus station."

"I know, but he's been busy helping his father at the law office. Apparently, they're redoing their filing system, or something like that. He said it's been keeping him busy all fall break." Annie chuckled. "I think he's ready for classes to start back."

"And you're sure he's okay with . . . ?" Mama motioned her head toward the baby.

"Well . . . "

"You're taking a big risk with that man, Annie. I'd hate to see this decision come between the two of you."

Annie thought of Aunt Brenda again. She'd seemed so confident when she told Annie that things with Julian would work out if it was meant to be. Annie had no choice but to believe her.

"It will work out, Mama. However it's supposed to."

Mama nodded, then looked down at baby Thomas with equal parts love and disbelief. Annie understood.

"I think he's due for a bottle soon, Mama. Maybe you can feed him while I use the phone?"

Mama's eyes lit up. "Oh, of course. Do you have plenty of powdered milk, or do we need to go to the store?"

"I have plenty, but it's not milk. It's infant formula. The one the doctor in Georgia recommended."

"Oh. That's right. *Formula.*" Mama wagged her head.

Annie forced herself to leave the comfort of the age-worn couch. With a slow bend and a grunt, she picked up Thomas's bag and headed to the kitchen.

As she prepared the bottle—a routine she finally had down pat—tears formed in the corners of her eyes. Every detail of the room begged for attention. The dark oak cabinets with narrow black iron handles. The scalloped wooden valance over the window at the sink. The worn linoleum with rectangles of different sizes and shades of brown pointed in different directions. It seemed funny how a place that was nothing special could be something so wonderful, only because it was the place you knew. The only thing that could make the homecoming better would be if R.C. were there, too.

Annie took the bottle to Mama and returned to the kitchen where the phone sat on the counter against the wall. She picked up the handset. Thank goodness long distance charges wouldn't apply any more.

PA 2-51295. She knew both the office number and the house number by heart.

After the tenth ring, Annie hung up. No answer at his father's office meant Julian must have gone home already. She put her pointer finger into the round hole again and circled the dial around for each number.

Please be there. Please be there.

"Hello," a woman's voice answered.

"Hi, Mrs. Lane. It's Annie. How are—"

"Oh. Annie—um—how are you dear?"

"I'm fine, thank you. Is Julian home?"

His mother's voice was filled with regret as she told her that Julian was out, that she wasn't sure where and didn't know when he'd be back. Filled with regret and a tone of something else that multiplied Annie's sadness. What was it in her voice? After she hung up, Annie leaned over and pressed her forehead into the phone. Her chest tightened. Annie knew what it was. It was sympathy.

*   *   *

"Don't worry, sweetheart. I'm sure he has a good reason." Mama patted her on the back.

She'd muted her crying in the night so as not to wake up the baby, who slept next to her—next to her in R.C.'s place. Now the morning sun cast its light across the bed and forced her to face the day.

"I just don't understand, Mama."

"I know, sweetie."

Thomas began to cry. Diaper changes and bottles couldn't wait on heartbreak.

Mama took Annie by the hand. "I'm sure he'll call soon. Remember what you said yesterday? It will work out."

After Thomas was cleaned and fed, Mama sat beside the two of them on the couch in the living room again. "He's a little young for Saturday morning cartoons, isn't he?"

"I thought a little Mighty Mouse might cheer me up."

"R.C. likes this one, too."

Both women breathed in at the same time and released the air in the same solemn sigh.

Mama reached and took Thomas from Annie's arms, and Annie relaxed into the couch.

"Annie, I didn't tell you while you were gone, but... Melinda Bennett called more than once to ask about you. Not in a prying way, but she seemed concerned."

Annie tilted her head toward Mama. "Is that all?"

"Well, she asked me to tell you something when you got back. She wants you to know that you still have a job there if you want it, as an instructor."

Annie closed her eyes for a moment. Four months had eased the wound, but not enough.

"I guess I'm going to have to swallow my pride, aren't I?" Annie sat up straight. "We need the money, and I have to do right by Thomas." She squeezed her eyes tight again. "I'll have to tell her that I'll work for Alexandra. And at least I'll still get to dance."

"I know how much you love it, Annie. Maybe it would be best to go back."

"I could go today to see her. Keep myself busy until I hear from Julian."

Mama touched her nose to Thomas's, then drew back with a wisp of a smile. "And I can stay here and love on this precious baby."

The look on Mama's face melted Annie's heart. She leaned over, laid her head on Mama's shoulder, and looked down at Thomas. He would be in good hands while she was away, doing what she had to do.

*   *   *

Annie smacked at the wheel of the Studebaker as she drove, alternating hands to play along with the drum solo in "Wipe Out". *Thank you, WTOB.* The driving percussion and that far-out guitar helped Annie get her mind off her troubles. But the next song made her think of R.C. Ray Charles and "Georgia on My Mind" had a whole new meaning now.

She pulled into the parking lot and brought the car to a stop near the corner of the building with *Melinda's School of Dance* in white lettering on the window. With a shaky hand, Annie put the gear selector into PARK, but she kept her hand there. Maybe this was a bad idea. Maybe it would be too painful.

Through the window, she saw a woman's form in the lobby, slenderer than Miss Melinda's and without the beehive. Annie prayed for strength. It wasn't Alexandra's fault she'd lost her job—Miss Melinda had made the choice—and it wasn't right to hold ill will toward either of them. More than not right, it was sinful, and not who Annie wanted to be at all. But heartbreak was hard of hearing and could not always be reasoned with. She would simply have to do her best.

She whispered another prayer, took a steadying breath, then got out. The toes of her saddle oxfords ground loose gravels on the black asphalt as she rounded the front of the car. Three steps from the front door, she stopped as a familiar Ford turned into the parking lot. She called his name as soon as the car door opened.

"Julian! Oh, Julian!"

Annie ran to him as he exited the car, and though Julian looked as if he'd had a sudden shock, he reciprocated her embrace. "Annie, I didn't expect—"

"Oh, Julian, I've missed you so much." The side of her face pressed into his chest, making her words garbled.

He placed a gentle hand atop her head and stroked her hair. With the other arm, he held her. "Annie, it's nice to see you. It's been a very long time."

She pressed into him harder, and they stood there for several moments. Tears of joy pooled in her closed eyes. The feel of his arms, the smell of his aftershave, the sound of his heart beating—all of it was a dream come true. And she never wanted it to end.

"Hey, Annie, I'm sorry I didn't call—"

"Are you here to pick up Gina? Is she taking the Saturday class now?"

"Oh, yeah—yeah." He scratched his head, and Annie ached at the absence of his arm across her back.

"I thought you'd come over as soon as you could. What happened? I cried myself to sleep last night, Julian." She looked up at him as she wiped tears of happiness from her face.

Julian stepped back and bumped into the car. "Annie, I have to tell you something, and, well—the truth is"—He looked down and shuffled his feet—"I started seeing someone while you were gone. I'm really sorry, Annie. I didn't mean to. It just happened."

A cold wind whipped up out of nowhere and blasted against Annie's flaming cheeks. The whole world suddenly felt like a motion picture, and hers was not a role she wanted. "What? You can't be serious."

"Listen, Annie, you're a swell girl, *really*, but—"

She took a step backward. "But you said you wanted to marry me."

"I did, but I also want to run for office someday, Annie. I told you that a long time ago. I can't be a politician and raise someone's, you know, illegitimate child."

"I know things are different now, Julian, but if you'd only meet him, you'd see—"

"Look, this isn't easy for me either. I promise it's not. But it's not just about the baby. I mean, you were gone for so long, and I met somebody, and we kinda hit it off, so . . . "

She felt dizzy and all at once like she might vomit. Annie took another step backward and almost lost her balance. She looked at him squarely then turned and ran for the car. From the driver's seat, she could see him in her peripheral, standing like a deer in headlights, and she wished one of them could vanish into thin air. Disappear off the face of the earth.

Annie's pain spilled out in a loud, breathless sob as she started the engine, but she was too stunned to drive. Her lungs begged for air, and Annie startled herself with the mournful sound that came out of her as she filled them.

You have to leave now. Just drive the car. Get out of this parking lot. That's what you need to do first. The job doesn't matter. Nothing matters. Just get out of here. The voice in her head, muffled by her panting, sounded like someone else.

Julian headed for the door of the dance studio as Annie backed the car to turn around in the parking lot. She paused and rubbed the tears away from her eyes with her fingers then the backs of her hands. Annie gave one last look toward the building before she pulled away, and her stomach twisted harder. On the other side of the window, Julian walked toward the form Annie had seen earlier. The woman wrapped her arms around his neck and kissed his cheek. Now it was obvious. The *somebody else* was the same person who had taken her place at the studio. The other woman was Alexandra.

Chapter Seventeen

Saturday, December 2, Present Day

A SMALL, RECTANGULAR placard on the opened door read "Pastor's Study" in black, blocked letters. For all the turmoil in Missy's heart, it would have made sense for her to be there for counseling, instead of voice lessons, or rehearsal, or whatever she was there to do.

After meeting her at the front doors of the church, Henry had led her to the end of a basement hallway, to the room furnished with bookshelves, a desk and chair, a couch with a green-and-gold Seventies print, a coffee table, and an electric keyboard on a stand.

"I like to do one-on-one rehearsals down here. Pastor doesn't mind, and I think people relax more outside of that big sanctuary." Henry motioned for her to sit on the couch as he took his place behind the keyboard.

She obeyed, placing her patterned tote bag on the floor as she sat.

"I'm just pleased as punch that you agreed to meet me today, Melissa." His face beamed, and his elbows took turns resting in alternate palms as he perched his chin on his knuckles. Missy couldn't help but feel like the prizewinning heifer at the county fair as Henry eyeballed her.

"Um—you can call me Missy if you like. Most people do."
She looked around. The room had a single window to the outside, and the polish of the furniture glimmered in a beam of
afternoon sun that came through the frosted pane. The light
cast a yellow glow on Henry's eager face.

"Well, Missy, before we get to practicing your songs, tell
me." He played a run on the keyboard. "Did you have a nice
Thanksgiving?"

Missy pushed a curl behind her ear and adjusted her
glasses. "Oh, yes, it was great. What about you?"

Henry's eyes narrowed. "You're not very good at telling
fibs, now are you? Maybe outside of church you'd do better."

He let out a short cackle, and Missy felt her face grow hot.
This person worked with her father. She couldn't so much as
hint at a problem in her family.

"Well, you know how holidays can be. A little stressful
sometimes."

"I'm just going on at you, sweetheart. No worries." He
waved her off. "And mine was fine, thanks for asking. Had a
nice dinner with the pastor's family. Now let's get those vocal
cords warmed up, shall we? Stand up. You need maximum lung
capacity for the best sound."

The man changed subjects so fast, it was hard to keep up.
Missy stood and tugged at the waist of her jeans. Vocal warm-
ups. She could do this. It was all starting to come back to her—
the choir of teenagers matching the pitch of the piano while
chanting. *Me, may, ma, mo, moo.* Before each rehearsal and every
performance. Then it was, "Many mumbling mice go marching
in the night, mighty nice"—the same pitch for each word of the
line—modulating each time until they'd completed the scale
and their lips were loose.

Henry played a four-chord pattern. The rhythm was familiar.

"Okay, here we go. Ha-le-lu-jah." He demonstrated in falsetto, then changed keys and repeated the run. "Ha-le-lu-jah. Like that—you ready?"

She nodded, but was she really? Here in this church building with this insistent little man? It all suddenly seemed so bizarre. But Missy opened her mouth when the keyboard prompted, and the sound that spilled out gave her the answer. Singing was like breathing. It just came naturally.

After an octave and a half of progression, Henry stopped playing.

"Nice job. Very nice. Had you ever done Handel's *Messiah* as a warm-up?" He grinned.

Missy shook her head and focused on catching her breath.

"It's my favorite. Okay then, for our Advent performances, we'll be doing 'O Holy Night.' That'll be your big solo. We'll also do a medley of Christmas hymns that I've arranged—standard stuff, you'll catch on quick—and here"—he handed her a stack of sheet music—"these are some more contemporary pieces. You'll probably recognize them. But don't worry. The standards come earlier in the season, so you have more time to learn the others."

For the next forty minutes, she sang, pouring her heart into each song Henry asked her to try and enjoying each moment more than the last. Far more than she had imagined she would. Music took her to a place where there were no family secrets or tough decisions, and where even the little decisions, like what to cook for dinner, were erased. Through the power of her voice, which had too long been silent, Missy transcended problems. Singing again felt right, even if she had to be part of a church choir to do it.

The last refrain of "I Heard the Bells on Christmas Day" ended. Henry flipped the power switch on the keyboard.

"Okay. Time for a break. You've done great with these."

When the music stopped, so did her joy. "Oh, okay. And what about the solo?" She would have gone on singing for hours if he'd wanted.

He clapped his hands and took a seat behind the pastor's desk. "We'll get to that next time. I'm sure you have to be getting home soon, and I want to get to know *you* a little better now."

Missy sat on the couch again, teetering on the edge. What could he possibly want to know, apart from what she hoped she'd already proven? Was this an interview to find out if she was moral enough to sing in church? If he found out that her first child had been conceived when she was seventeen, before she and Ray were married, would he tell her "thanks, but no thanks"?

"So, you really think I did okay?"

"Oh, absolutely. I'm very pleased. Still, there's just something . . ." Henry placed his pointer fingers together and pressed them against his lips.

"What is it?"

"I feel like there's something holding you back, but I'm not quite sure. There's a lot of psychology involved with being an artist, you know. Maybe just a touch of nerves?"

Great. She'd somehow wound up in a pastor's office being psychoanalyzed by a choir director.

"Maybe."

Henry leaned back and propped his pristine canvas tennis shoes on the desk, ankles crossed. "So, your sister Erica is a professional singer, huh?"

The first question would be about her famous baby sister. "Yeah. Well, she's a back-up singer for a country music artist who's getting pretty popular."

Henry's mouth pulled to one side. "Does she get paid to sing?"

"Of course."

"Then she's a professional. No matter where she stands on stage." He got a far-off look in his eye. "Boy, I'd sure love to have her in my choir."

Missy slumped back against the couch. "As your new soloist, I bet."

"Oh, no, honey. I've found my soloist. I knew it before the end of your first stanza. But a few more powerful voices surely wouldn't hurt." He sat up and took his feet off the desk. "My altos overpower my sopranos by a ratio of about double, and they need help. H-E-L-P. Help. Let me tell you."

The phone vibrated in Missy's pocket. She looked at the screen, then held up a pointer finger. "Excuse me for a sec. It's my daughter." She swiped at the phone's face. "Hello."

Emma's greeting matched the pitch of a fire alarm and was quickly followed by a complaint that Piper had worn her favorite sweater—the light blue one she'd gotten for her birthday—without asking and had dropped ketchup on it.

"Yes, I know she didn't ask." Missy balanced keeping her voice down in front of Henry with being loud enough to be heard over Emma's sobs. "Listen, I'll talk to her when I get home." Missy glanced over her shoulder at Henry, whose eyes were fixed on the ceiling. "Emma, I know you're upset, but—" From the sound of things, there was no getting through to her. "Put your Daddy on the phone. I mean it."

Within a moment, Ray's voice came on the line.

"Ray, I'm trying to finish up here at my rehearsal, and Emma is hysterical. Now, I need you to separate the girls until I can get home and sort out what happened. And get the pretreat in the laundry room—it's the skinny bottle behind the dryer sheets—and spray some of that on the ketchup stain and leave it sitting on top of the washing machine. Don't try to wash it; I'll put it in when I get home."

She took a breath as she put the phone back in her pocket. Ray hadn't argued, so she hoped that meant he would do what she'd told him.

"I'm sorry about that. Where were we?"

"Well, after hearing that phone call"—Henry cleared his throat—"I think I was about to tell you that—and forgive me for butting in—that you oughta let your husband take care of his own children. I mean, he's a grown man, for crying out loud."

"Oh. Well," Missy chittered, "most of the time, he acts like a child himself."

Henry stood, came around the desk, and sat on the end of the couch opposite Missy. His scowl showed no hint of a joke. "That's probably because you act like his mother. Doesn't he already have a mother?"

Henry's directness startled her.

"Well, yes, but she lives in Florida, and she was never really around much when—why am I telling you this?"

"I have that effect on people." The smirk on Henry's face was an odd combination of endearing and annoying. "I'm just trying to be helpful," he said. "If you'll change your tack with him—try lifting him up instead of putting him down—I think you'll see a big difference in how the two of you get along."

"Oh, is that right?"

He smiled and nodded, either oblivious to, or in defiance of, her sarcasm.

"Well, you sure do have a lot of relationship advice for someone who's never been married."

She should have known better. Henry sat up straight. His face was solemn, but something in his soft blue eyes said that he'd be gracious.

"Well, my dear," he said, "sometimes there are sacrifices to be made for righteousness' sake. I'll be the first to admit that.

In the end, eternity matters more than anything that happens. Or doesn't happen here." He cleared his throat. "Now let's get back to the matter at hand."

Henry leaned forward with his forearms on his knees, his palms together and fingers pointed toward her. "You are going to do *great* with the choir tomorrow. I have no doubt."

"Thank you, Henry. I really—wait. *What?*"

"You're going to do great with the choir tomorrow."

"Tomorrow?"

"Yes, it *is* the start of Advent." His eyes rolled in a near three-sixty. "The church is expecting some beautiful Christmas music, and I need you here to help us."

"But I haven't even practiced with the choir yet. I didn't know you wanted me to start tomorrow."

"I have faith in you. You can do it."

She leaned back and studied him. Such an unusual man. If only she could channel his optimism and suave persuasion, she'd be at bronze level in no time. Henry would make a great Southern Living consultant.

That's it.

"I have a proposition for you, Henry."

It was just the kind of leverage she needed. Missy pulled a Southern Kitchen catalog from the bag at her feet. "Let's make a deal. Any single item on pages four or five will get me to the next sales tier. You need a new choir member, and I need to get my name on the big screen on awards night at regional conference."

Henry's mouth turned up on one side and he slowly nodded. Then came a wink.

With a little effort, Missy kept her poker face. "I recommend the full cookware set. It's on special this month."

*   *   *

"I'm real happy you're singing again. I mean, if it makes you happy, but ... I thought we decided we were done with church." Ray pulled the covers up to his underarms. "It hasn't been part of our lives since we were first married. Easter, Mother's Day, Father's Day, Christmas. To make your parents happy. But that's it."

Missy placed her glasses on the nightstand. "Nothing has changed, Ray. I just like the idea of singing in a group again. Doing something different. And it's just through Christmas. Like a seasonal job at Walmart, 'cept I'm not getting paid."

He rolled over on his side, facing her.

Missy switched off the lamp then stared into the darkness toward the ceiling as her body relaxed into the firmness of the mattress. She had to admit, it was so much better than the waterbed.

"I'm not even going to tell Daddy and Mama," she said. "And I asked Henry not to tell Daddy at work. I just didn't tell him why not. I'm sure Daddy will ask again eventually, but, for now, I don't want my parents to get their hopes up about something that isn't going to happen."

"Well, do you want us to come with you? Like, for moral support or something? We will if you want."

"Maybe next week."

He wriggled closer to her. Close enough to smell toothpaste. "You tired?"

"Very."

A long silence passed, then his hand rested on her shoulder. He fiddled with the wide strap of her night shirt, and his rough fingers tickled her skin. She flinched and turned to face the wall, pulling the covers close to her chin. "Goodnight, Ray."

Chapter Eighteen

February 1964

$\mathcal{J}$N THREE months' time, any doubts Annie had, big or small, had melted away like a winter snow. She was Thomas's mother. The legal papers in the folder that she kept in her dresser drawer said so, and the love in her heart screamed it. Having Thomas in her life was worth everything, though the costs had been higher than she could have imagined—Julian, dancing, her job at the studio, business school. Mama's disability check kept the lights on, and they never went hungry—for those things she was grateful—but starting classes again in January hadn't been possible. Still, where there was a will, there was a way.

Annie straightened the large floppy bow that fell from the neck of her white blouse. She ran her hands down the silky front and adjusted her skirt before picking up the spray bottle. She spritzed blue liquid onto the glass countertop and rubbed it with a white cloth, back and forth until it gleamed. The new job would at least help with diapers and formula. Eventually, she'd save enough for school. It would just take time. She only needed time for her heart to heal, too. The pain had lessened, she supposed—there was no tool for measuring heartbreak like degrees on a thermometer or inches on a ruler—but not a day went by that she didn't cry over Julian, at least a little.

"He was a wolf in sheep's clothing, Annie. That's all there is to it," Mama reminded her of the same thing over and over. "The Good Lord done you a favor, showing you how Julian really is, before it was too late."

Mama might have been right. Only the Lord knew for sure. But Mama's words didn't do a thing for the heartache. They didn't make Annie stop missing him. Didn't make her stop wondering what might have been. But Thomas helped—his brand-new lopsided smile, his cheeks starting to fill out, his wisps of caramel-colored hair, the smell of baby lotion on his freshly bathed skin, and the sound of his breathing as he slept on her chest with his head under her chin.

The thought of him made her smile and want to cry at the same time. Only the first hour of her first shift and she missed him already. As she stood behind the candy counter in the basement of Thalhimers Department Store, the hiring manager's words rang in her mind. "You seem like a very sweet girl, Annie, and we're happy to have you on board, but an unwed mother *could* be bad for business. Please make sure not to mention the baby here at work. Okay?"

At least it would be easier today than most, not talking about the baby. The only thing any of her new coworkers wanted to talk about was the Beatles's appearance on Ed Sullivan the night before. And the customers, too, for that matter. She had to admit, it was nice being around other young women for a change and having grown-up conversations.

After Annie had made the display cases shine, a redhaired salesclerk named Roberta trained her how to stock them and chattered between instructions.

"Did you watch last night, Annie?" Roberta said.

Annie smiled and nodded. "Oh, yeah. I watched. They were really outta sight, but I'm still an Elvis girl. They'll never touch him, as far as I'm concerned."

"Oh, c'mon." Roberta waved a hand at Annie then leaned in close. "Who's your favorite Beatle?"

Annie shrugged. None of them held a candle to Elvis. Or Julian. "I guess Ringo. I kinda like his goofy smile. You?"

"Oh, John *would* be my favorite if he wasn't married. I almost cried when that message flashed across the screen. 'Sorry girls, he's married.'" Roberta rolled her eyes then giggled. "So since I can't have John, I'll say George. But the way those girls screamed and carried on. I think I would have had more dignity, but then again, I wasn't there. Who knows?" Roberta laughed again. "Here, you'll have to pay attention to the order of the inventory. The different types of candies have to go back to the same spot every time. Real simple, though." She pointed to the trays lined up on the counter, then to the labels on the shelving inside the cases.

Annie nodded and began helping her refill the case.

"What was your favorite song the Beatles did last night?" Roberta said. "I loved all of them."

Annie took another tray from the counter. "I think the first one. "All My Loving." I didn't see the second set, though."

"You're kidding. You turned it off?"

"Well, I had to take care of—I, I had things to do."

Annie slid the last yellow plastic tray of specialty chocolates onto the glass shelf, taking in their tempting smell as she closed the door of the case. Not spending her whole paycheck on inventory might be a challenge. That, on top of missing Thomas.

She stood as a customer approached.

"*Annie Swaim?* Oh, my, how nice to see you again." The New Hampshire accent registered before the face did.

"Alexandra." Annie felt the blood drain from her head. She patted at the sides of her hair pulled back with an elastic. "It's nice to see you, too. What can I help you with?"

Alexandra turned to the left and made a come-here motion with her hand. Then Annie saw him.

"My fiancé is taking me on a shopping spree for Valentine's Day. He's promised to buy me something from every floor of the store, starting with a box of my favorite chocolates. Since I've been in town, I've just fallen in love with these. And with him, too, I guess." Her phony laughed echoed through the room. "Isn't that right, honey?" Alexandra wrapped an arm around Julian's waist and put her hand on his chest, the diamond on her finger nearly blinding.

Julian nodded, but he didn't look at Annie.

For a moment, Annie thought of Doris Day in *Move Over, Darling*. Face to face with the man she'd expected to spend her life with and the other woman, who obviously didn't expect to run into her. But that was a comedy film, and this was real life, and there was nothing funny about it.

Annie struggled to find words.

"Roberta, can you please help this customer, I need to . . ."

Her new coworker seemed to understand. Roberta took over as Annie made her way around the counter. She walked across the salesfloor, picking up pace as she neared the door that led to the parking lot. The brisk February air shocked her senses, affording her a moment to reset.

Annie walked several yards down the sidewalk and stood with her back to the door of the store, willing herself not to cry. Tears were *not* an option. She had no choice but to pull herself together and go back inside. Julian had already cost her one job, and she would *not* break down now and lose this one.

"Annie, can I talk to you?"

Her whole body tensed at the sound of his voice so close behind her. She turned slowly and looked at him but refused to answer.

"Annie, I know you're upset, but—" He squinted in the afternoon sun.

"Upset? Why would I be upset?" She tried to fake a laugh. "You and I are old news."

"C'mon, Annie. I know you better." He shoved his hands into the pockets of his slacks. "Alexandra, well—she's a nice girl and all. But the truth is, she's not you."

Annie's stomach muscles clenched even tighter.

"Are you—are you still keeping R.C.'s baby?" he said.

Fury began to bubble inside her. "What is that to you?"

Voices came from nearby as customers exited the store. Julian turned fast. Two older ladies clad from shoulder to knee in mink headed toward the parking lot, loaded down with shopping bags.

He turned back to her and took a step closer—close enough that she could smell his aftershave and the starch of his shirt. Then he took another step forward. Annie's mind screamed *retreat*, but her heart melted as his fingers circled her upper arm. A cold wind whipped around her body as the fire that had started in her chest radiated to the rest of her. The fury had dissipated.

Julian took another tiny step forward without letting go then ran his hand down her arm and back up again. "I like your blouse. Silky." He lowered his head and raised his eyebrows. One side of his perfect mouth turned upward. "Annie, when you were in Georgia, you still hadn't decided for sure—I mean, about the baby. I thought that maybe since then, you mighta made other arrangements for Ruth Claire's son. And maybe you and I could have another chance?"

Annie stepped backward and wrapped her arms around herself. "Aren't you engaged to someone else now? And isn't she right inside that store? Waiting on you?"

"Yes, but I would call it off right now if I knew you'd take me back. I mean it, Annie. We had a good thing."

Mama's voice rang in her mind. *He's a wolf in sheep's clothing, Annie.*

She focused on the door, planning her steps before she knew if she'd be strong enough to take them. "No, Julian. I can't abandon people as easily as you can. And you need to understand something. Thomas *isn't* Ruth Claire's son. He's *mine*."

Annie left him standing there, his mouth half-opened. No doubt she'd cry herself to sleep later, remembering the warmth of his touch, but for now, she had a job to do.

Chapter Nineteen

Sunday, December 3, Present Day

MEMORIES FLOODED her, being there in the front row of that choir box—ones that she fought against, though they were fundamentally good. It was the loss of place and people, and maybe even of belief, of which Missy didn't want to be reminded. She'd never been so callous as to *not* miss the God of her childhood.

The expanse of sanctuary before her was a brilliant sea of faces. She recognized none of them except Henry's. He flitted about in a light-gray suit with a red-and-green-plaid bow tie and matching pocket square, shaking hands, and smiling and waving like a politician.

Henry had been right about Jeannie Wallace's choir robe. It fit just fine. Roomy, even. Silky and dark blue. While the parishioners continued to file in and the pianist played "O Come Let Us Adore Him," Missy couldn't help but wonder how Jeannie would feel if she knew that a stranger was there in *her* choir, sweating through *her* old robe.

A round-faced woman side-stepped between Missy's feet and the half wall that separated the choir from the pulpit, flashing a full-tooth smile. She took the seat to Missy's left. "Henry's told us so much about you. We're glad to have you with us." Her voice was all cotton candy, sweet and airy. "I'm Carolyn." The blonde extended a soft hand that left the scent of cherry blossom lotion behind.

"Hello." Missy forced a smiled. "Thank you. It's—it's nice to be here."

Missy could tell what Carolyn was thinking. Anyone with half a brain would wonder why someone who didn't go to their church and had never even rehearsed with the choir was help-ing them mark the start of the Christmas season.

Missy shrunk away from the lady and looked out at the grow-ing crowd again. It seemed the people would never stop coming through those double doors. So many starched shirts and neck-ties and long skirts. Singles, couples, families. Old and young.

"Good morning, Miss Carolyn. You doing good today?" A broad-shouldered woman with the same painted-on smile as Carolyn sat down on Missy's right and spoke across her.

"Hey, Wanda. We missed you last week."

Carolyn and Wanda chatted about Wanda's visit to the Outer Banks, while Missy stared straight ahead at the clock on the back wall. Ten-fifty-three. She was content to be left out of the conversation, but when she and Carolyn were all caught up, Wanda introduced herself and spent the next few minutes asking Missy questions about her family. She seemed set on finding a connection.

"You have such familiar features. I'm bound to know some of your people." Wanda put her forefinger over her lip and her thumb under her chin. Her forehead crinkled. "Hmm—do you know any Jacobses? You remind me a good bit of some Jacobses I know."

"I don't believe so. No, ma'am."

Wanda settled back in her chair finally. "Okay, then." She wagged her head. "I was sure that was it."

It was all about good breeding with these people. What family you came from, and how much you could contribute to the collection plate. But what if Wanda was right? What if she did look like the Jacobs Wanda mentioned. Missy hadn't thought to ask Grandma Annie about her real grandfather, the part of her biology she'd never known. Not that she had time to think about it now. In fact, she didn't want to think about it at all.

The minute hand on the clock now showed 10:59. At least the chitchat had distracted her from the nervousness, though she shouldn't have been nervous at all. Her solo wasn't for two more weeks. Most anybody could sing the old standards.

Missy released her grip on the red music binder and welcomed the air that dried her palms as Henry approached the music stand in front of the choir box. He motioned for the choir to stand, then signaled the piano player with a nod. A realization hit her as she stood. There was probably lipstick on her teeth. It almost always wound up on her teeth, though she'd never figured out how. She ran her tongue over them in hopes of capturing any stains.

With his hands poised in the air and his head in an upward tilt, Henry mouthed the count of the introduction. The piano and organ produced the familiar notes of "Hark the Herald Angels Sing."

With the first word, the nerves vanished, just like at Daddy's birthday party. The congregation wasn't there. Tone, melody, vibrato, crescendo, rhythms, bridge, pitch—Missy focused on all things singing. The lyrics and their meaning were only secondary.

After three songs, she sat with the rest of the choir, and the applause from the congregation made the world shift into focus. Satisfaction. Her job was done. She took a deep breath.

So then now what? Oh, no. How had she not realized that sing-ing in the choir also meant sitting through a sermon? There was no way of getting out of it.

The elderly minister walked to the pulpit. He wore a dark suit and a tie, just like all the preachers of Missy's memory. He opened the Bible on the lectern and adjusted the microphone, then a voice more powerful than his body represented rang out through the sanctuary. "And the Word was made flesh, and dwelt among us, and we beheld his glory, the glory as of the only begotten of the Father, full of grace and truth."

Missy's mind drifted. *Truth.* The truth had plagued her for days. She'd discovered the truth about her bloodline, and in exchange for truth she had accepted a secret heavier than she wanted to carry. And the one question she kept asking herself: Would she change it if she could? Would she take back know-ing, so that she wouldn't have to decide whether to tell her father?

Missy focused on the clock on the wall again and pushed away everything except the Christmas-shopping list in her head. She passed the time that way, making a mental note of what was left to buy. Emma's main gift was more expensive than Piper Grace's, but Piper's looked like more. Maybe Emma needed something to go with it. The boys' gifts were pretty even. She hadn't thought of Ray's yet, but a gift card to the sporting-goods store would work if she couldn't come up with something else.

Movement from the other end of the choir box caught her attention. A young woman slipped out of her seat, made her way down the steps of the platform and vanished on the other side of the organ. Missy turned toward the piano. There was probably a door on that side, too. The young woman had made it look easy to excuse herself in the middle of the sermon, and it was perfectly normal to need to go the restroom during church.

She stood, slightly hunched, looking at the pairs of dress pumps she had to maneuver across. *Don't trip and don't step on any.* Her pep talk worked. The three red-carpeted stairs were the next obstacle. No incident there. Around the piano, and . . .

There was no door, no exit matching the organ side of the choir. And she couldn't cross in front of the congregation after the production she'd already made. Missy walked double-time down the side aisle and toward the back of the sanctuary. Halfway to the door her heel caught on a floor vent. Her body lurched but righted after two awkward steps. With one foot across the threshold, she let out a relieved sigh.

In the lobby bathroom, Missy flattened her palms against the white marble counter, locked her elbows, and stared herself down in the mirror. *That could have gone better, Melissa.* Good news, at least. There was no lipstick on her teeth.

*   *   *

A tall, artificial ficus made for good cover as parishioners filed out, and Missy had a great vantage point for keeping watch on the door. She'd talked herself into staying until service was over. Henry deserved to hear in person that she wouldn't be coming back.

"There you are. Everything okay?"

She turned to see him coming from a hallway behind her. This place was like a maze.

"Yeah, I just needed some air, and I didn't want to disturb the service by coming back inside."

"Well, I—"

"You have an amazing voice." The exclamation came from her choirmate, Carolyn, as she exited the sanctuary.

Wanda followed close behind. "Yes, that was terrific."

The women cornered Missy and grabbed her hands at the same time, showering her with praise.

"Oh, thank you. I—I do love to sing. I haven't done it in a while, and it was nice to—"

"Henry, we need her for the concert." Carolyn made a face at Henry that said it was not a request.

"Definitely," Wanda said.

"Ladies, I was just getting ready to discuss that with Missy. If you'll excuse us."

Missy nodded at the two women as Henry took her by the arm and led her to the stairs. She followed him to the basement and back to the pastor's study. He motioned for her to sit on the couch. *Déjà vu.*

"Carolyn and Wanda seem to agree that you passed the test with flying colors." Henry sat at the other end.

Missy smiled with her top teeth rested evenly on the bottom.

"Of course, I knew you would," he said, "but I had to be sure."

"Henry, what is that you need to tell me. What concert? What is this about?"

"Tell me, how did you feel up there?"

Ugh. He always answered a question with a question.

"Well, the singing was great. I enjoyed that part—"

"You carried my sopranos today. They sounded twice as good with you there. The pastor even said so. And now, I'm *sure* you will do fantastic at the Twin City Church Choir Christmas Showcase."

"Come again?" Her eyebrows must have reached her hairline.

"My choir—*our* choir—has been invited to perform at the first annual Christmas concert being held at Reynolds Auditorium, two weeks from yesterday."

"Two weeks. And you want me to join you?"

His eyes grew large, and his head moved like a woodpecker on caffeine as he flashed a toothy smile.

"Henry, this is exactly what you did to me yesterday when you told me I'd be singing *today*. I'm starting to wonder if there's more you're not telling me. Maybe after the concert you'll say I'm scheduled to sing the National Anthem at the Super Bowl. Or maybe you've signed me up for *Singing with the Stars*."

Henry's fingertips covered his mouth as he snickered. "But you'll do it, right? You'll be my soloist for the concert?"

Missy sighed. All this because Erica hadn't shown up to sing for their daddy's party. All this. "Don't you have other good singers? I mean, somebody is bound to get a little miffed at you for letting a stranger come in and—"

"I have plenty of good singers. But I want a great one for this concert. My choir knows I love them, and they understand. Didn't you like singing with us today?"

Missy wrung her hands. Being on stage had felt wonderful, but everything else . . . "Actually, I'm not sure this is going to work out. I'm real grateful that you asked me, but there's something I should have already told you about—"

"Listen, I need you at this concert, and if I have to buy another set of cookware to get you to do it, I will. Whatever the problem is, we can handle it. Just tell me."

She took a deep breath and held it until it hurt. What she'd planned to say wouldn't come out—that she was a phony singing about holy things, a pretender. She swallowed the words down and capped the lid on one of her bottled-up secrets.

"You liked being up there, right? Weren't too nervous? You sure did look like a natural."

Missy smiled, remembering it. She couldn't deny how nice it was to be appreciated for her talent, to feel important, worthwhile, noticed. But mostly how powerful she felt using her voice. And Henry's transparent blue eyes were so incredibly kind, almost hypnotizing. Maybe he could be trusted with secrets.

"You know, when my oldest babies were little, I used to dream of being on a stage. I sang to them all the time, and in my daydreams, I sang in front of this big crowd, like in a coliseum with a spotlight."

Henry smiled like a kid with a triple-scoop ice cream cone.

"I even use to think I'd like to learn to play guitar, maybe even write my own songs."

"How nice. And what kind of music would you play?"

"I'm not even sure. Any kind."

"Well, I'd say you're off to a pretty good start on chasing your dreams."

Missy smirked and tilted her head.

"A week ago, you weren't part of a choir, were you?"

She shook her head.

"And a day ago, you weren't the main soloist for the headlining choir at a concert to be held in an auditorium that seats almost two thousand people, were you?"

Missy's lips slowly curled into a smile.

"I'd say that's a pretty good start on your dreams," Henry said.

Maybe he was right. The concert was an opportunity. But when she took her eyes off Henry's smiling face, the same ugly truths bounced around in her mind. No matter how many local concerts she sang in, she'd never catch up to Erica. Her

175

sister had made her dream a priority. Erica hadn't let herself get pregnant in high school. Erica had more ambition in her pinky finger than Missy had in her whole body. Erica had gone to college. She had done something besides just staying home, washing dishes, doing the laundry by the loads, and making beds. Wiping sticky from the counters and floors and the refrigerator handles.

Then again, maybe it wasn't about her sister.

Missy turned toward him again. While she'd been debating, that slaphappy grin hadn't gone anywhere. What was it about this man? There was no way to tell Henry "no."

Chapter Twenty

September 1965

*G*ENERAL HOUSEKEEPING. *No heavy lifting. $1.55 per hour.*

The job description sounded promising. Almost too good to be true.

Annie folded the classifieds section after double-checking the address in the ad circled in blue ink and laid it on the kitchen table. One last sip of coffee and she'd be ready to leave for the interview.

"I really like your hair that way." Mama came closer and patted at a flipped-out curl with the tips of her fingers.

"Do you, Mama?"

It certainly hadn't been as easy as Annie thought it would be to straighten and curl. And she was sure she had used too much hairspray.

Mama nodded. "It's the style. Not that I know much about style. But I've seen it in all the shows, and in magazines. It makes you look like a younger Mary Tyler Moore."

"Oh, really?" Annie liked the sound of that. "I thought it might look more, you know, professional. Even if it is just for a housekeeping job. I really want them to like me. Twenty cents more an hour than the department store. Can you imagine?" She took a big breath and let it out slowly, her eyes squeezed shut.

School wasn't the priority. Not anymore. She'd saved enough to pay for the rest of her classes months ago, but it never seemed like the right time. And having a little extra stashed away, just in case, was more important. Eventually. . . .

Thomas pushed himself up from the floor and toddled toward her. His toy telephone came along behind him, pulled by a string in his chubby fist and making a *wocka-wocka* sound as the wheels turned.

"He sure loves that thing, Mama. But you could have saved it for Christmas, you know."

"Oh, that's too far away. I couldn't wait to give it to him. I found some things for your sister at the thrift store, too, but I guess those will have to wait for Christmas." Mama sighed. Then her face brightened. "I'm so glad she's coming home then, even for a little while. Two whole weeks of having her here. Like old times. And Brenda and Cleet, too. I just can't wait to hug all of 'em."

"I know, Mama." Annie put her arm around Mama's shoulder. "I miss R.C. something fierce, but there's no doubt in my mind she's where she's supposed to be. Cleet is so good to her. So kind and patient."

Mama nodded, and a peace settled in her tired eyes. Annie stood, picked Thomas up, and planted him on her hip. He reached for her hair, and she grabbed his little fist and held it.

"Do you like Mama's hair, too? We can't mess it up now." She crinkled her nose and rubbed the tip of it across Thomas's nose. He let out a giggle, and she did it again. Annie sighed. "I never would have imagined R.C. would get married before me—not in a million years—but it was just meant to be. There's no doubt about it." Annie looked at her son. "All of it was just meant to be."

"She's done good for herself."

"That's 'cause you did a good job raising her, Mama." Annie put Thomas back on the floor and sat again at the table with Mama as he toddled into the living room, the pull-string toy *wocka-wocka*ing behind him.

"Oh, Annie, we both know you raised R.C. as much as I did. I'm not afraid to share the credit." She patted Annie's hand. "But I'm sorry you had to. I'm sorry I wasn't strong enough after your daddy died to be what you both needed me to be all the time."

"Mama, you took us to church every week, whether you felt like it or not. You made sure we had a roof over our heads, and clothes to wear, and food to eat. And you told us you loved us every single day. What more does a body need?"

Mama's eyes shined. "And now you're doing the same for your child. Our unexpected miracle." She pointed at Thomas in the next room. "That's just how much God loves us, Annie. All the time giving us good things we don't even know we need. Like your job interview." She sighed and leaned back in the chair with a smile on her face. "How could anybody *not* love a God like that?"

*   *   *

The woman's glasses sat perched on the tip of a long, thin nose. She peered over them at Annie.

"Hall. Annie Hall. Are you by chance one of the Ardmore Halls?"

"No, ma'am. I don't believe they're any relation." Annie shifted in the hard plastic seat. *Should* she be one of them? Maybe the lady would give her the job if—

"I didn't think so."

The employment agency was little more than a stark white room with a row of chairs and a long table with two typewriters.

The lady's desk sat in the middle of the room and was flanked by filing cabinets.

"I don't see anything on your application that would prevent you from being selected"—she cast a glance up and down the paper in her hand—"so I'm happy to refer you for this position, Miss Hall."

"Oh, that's wonderful. Thank you."

"There will be some weekend work, but not every weekend."

"That's fine. And you said it's for an office building here in town?"

"Oh, that's right. I didn't mention where. Silly me." She placed the index card back in the file box on the corner of the desk. "It's the old Gray High School campus. Now it's the new conservatory, the North Carolina School of the Arts. Doesn't that sound interesting? The first public arts conservatory in the nation."

Annie felt a gnawing in her stomach. The School of the Arts. The dream that Julian had almost convinced her could be hers. The opening had finally arrived. Would Julian really have helped her be a part of it?

"Classes start this month, and between the high school and the college, there's quite a number of students enrolled, I hear. Facilities need to be kept in tip-top shape, and that's where you come in."

"And—and when would I start?"

"You could start next week."

She swallowed hard. "Thank you again, Mrs. Greenly. I promise to do a good job."

From choreographing, or even starring in, *Swan Lake* to playing the role of Hazel, the pendulum had swung from fantasy to fantasy and come to a stop dead center on reality. This is how it was going to be. Not what she wanted. Not what she'd hoped. But worth it for Thomas.

Annie took the card Mrs. Greenly handed her and turned to go. She forced herself to keep her head held high as she left the office and walked out into the heat of the late summer sun and toward the Studebaker.

Mama had operated a loom. Daddy had been a mechanic at the mill and could fix any machine in the whole place. Those were good jobs. She was proud of them. And housekeeping was a good job, too. An honest, decent job. Nothing to be ashamed of. She wouldn't cry. She wouldn't even think about it.

Inside the car, she wrapped her fingers around the steering wheel and squeezed, letting the vinyl burn her skin. *But I'm supposed to be a dancer. I am a dancer.* Still, no tears.

Annie flexed her foot, and the pointy toe of her shoe met the gas pedal. The tires spun on loose gravel as she left the parking lot and headed for home.

Soon, the scenery changed from shops and office buildings to rows of houses and neighborhoods she'd known all her life. At the stop sign where she should have turned left, a line of yellow cones blocked her way. A rectangular wooden sign, painted orange with black letters, pointed to the right. *Detour.* Thank goodness there was more than one way to get where she needed to go.

At the end of the street, it hit her. She turned off The Chiffons who sang their tune from the radio and raised her eyes toward the car ceiling.

"Thank you, Lord. I trust You."

Chapter Twenty-one

Monday, December 4, Present Day

MISSY PERCHED on the arm of her parents' couch. The blue and white plaid gave the furniture away as a holdover from days gone by, but the shiny flat screen on the wall was fresh out of the box. It was Daddy's birthday present from the whole family, which he'd requested, in part, to watch his youngest daughter on a nationally broadcasted television show. Sunday football came in second.

Daddy had taken the morning off, just first and second periods. And even Ray was going to the shop late.

Daddy, Mama, and Ray sat on the couch. Grandma Annie sat in the microfiber recliner with a bolster pillow at her lower back. Emma perched on a stool that had been brought in from the kitchen, and the younger kids rolled about or sat on the floor. Being tardy for school wouldn't hurt. This was a special occasion.

"It's almost time," Mama said. "Tom, did you set the DVR?"

"Honey, for the third time, it's recording."

Missy took out her phone. A video of the whole family watching her sister's television debut would make a *great* post. All her old high school classmates loved learning about Erica's Nashville goings-on—the ones she'd been friends with, and even the ones who wouldn't give her the time of day back then. Missy might even gain followers with a carefully crafted post about the band, too. If it had the right hashtags.

Grandma looked up from her knitting. "I wonder if she'll get to talk to that new anchor."

"There's a new one?" Daddy said.

"You know, the blonde that used to be on my soap opera. She's such a cute girl. And so much energy. She's perfect for morning TV, but I do miss her on my show."

"You and your soap operas." Daddy chuckled and waved a hand in his mama's direction. "Those stories are so far-fetched. So unbelievable. Everybody's got a secret love interest or a secret identity or a secret baby. Or they've got a baby with a secret identity."

Ray laughed, and Dad's eyes smiled over the top of the mug as he sipped his coffee.

Missy tensed, and she and Grandma Annie exchanged a quick, knowing glance. What must she be feeling? How had she handled the real-life drama for all these years?

"Oh, I know they are. But wanting to learn those secrets helps me get out of bed some days, mister. Let an old woman have her make-believe."

The way Grandma played it off made Missy queasy. Her grandma said she had never lied about being Daddy's mother, and Missy believed her. But how many times had she done that—skirted the truth, tiptoed around it like a landmine—and no one noticed? Missy might never be able to do it. Any second, her train of thought could take a detour and she'd spit out something about the secret by mistake.

It was still so hard to believe.

"I wonder if it's cold in New York City," Emma said.

The change of subject pulled Missy away from her worrying.

Daddy smiled at Emma. "Not that much colder than here, I don't think."

The air was electric as they waited. Erica had done concerts for a couple years, but morning TV was on a different level. No one in Missy's family had ever been on television, except for Cousin Jeff who was interviewed by the local cable news network after a massive oak tree fell on his house during a hurricane. Then there was her great uncle Wendell, on her mother's side, and the unwanted publicity around the still on his property that he "forgot to tear down" years ago.

The theme music queued up, a bright ensemble of brass and strings, as an icon of a sun in several shades of yellow and orange appeared on the screen behind the title of the show.

"*Shhhh.* Quiet kids, it's on. You'll get to see Aunt Erica soon," Missy said.

Little Bit let out a delighted squeal.

Darn it. She'd missed recording the intro. Missy hit the round, red button on the phone screen and held the device in front of her for the first minute. She put it down when the hosts started reading the news, such as it was. Celebrity gossip and political dribble. Then some serious stuff about snowstorms in different parts of the country—something they hardly ever had to worry about there.

"Do we have to watch all this?" Joshua spread out on the floor on his stomach. "I want to see Aunt Erica."

Emma cocked her head and looked at Missy. "When will she be on, Mama?"

"All we know is that it will be sometime in the first hour of the show. Probably a while yet. Y'all just relax."

But none of them could *just relax.* The anticipation was too great, akin to the first day of school or Christmas morning.

They kept watching, though Daddy looked down at his wristwatch every couple of minutes and Missy checked her phone just as much. Ray handed his phone to John Thomas to keep him quiet. Mama kept asking if anybody wanted something else to eat, though they'd finished breakfast not half an hour ago and everybody was too excited to eat anyway, except for the boys who accepted her offer of another blueberry muffin. Grandma's rocker kept a steady rhythm as she sat with her hands folded over her stomach, her knitting beside her.

"And after the break," the anchor said," we'll have a live performance by rising country music sensation Justin Trent."

"Oh, it's coming up soon," Grandma said.

They were quiet through the commercials, and Missy had her camera ready. The opening shot after the break was of the band, all smiling, before the camera panned to the anchor. The kids screamed.

"There she is! It's Aunt Erica," Piper said.

Mama slapped at Daddy's knee. "There's our baby, Tom."

Missy focused on keeping the phone steady. So far, the reactions had been social media *gold*. She'd tag Erica and maybe even the band page when she uploaded the video later.

The whole family knew the song as soon as it began. They knew *all* the twangy, she-done-me-wrong songs that Justin sang. This one was about someone being done wrong at Christmastime, and Erica looked gorgeous as she crooned in harmony with him, just off to the left. The back-up trio wore matching black sequin tops and shiny black pants. Their Santa hats were cliché, but cute, nonetheless. The white of the brim popped against the black of Erica's long, gorgeous curls.

Missy caught herself humming along then remembered she was recording. She took her eyes off the television to gets shots of the family. Mama and Daddy were on the edge of their seats. Ray bobbed his head with the music. Grandma wore a wide smile. John Thomas danced behind her chair while the rest of the kids were fixated on the set.

The television camera went in for a close-up of Justin. Then, for a brief moment, it zoomed in on the back-up singers and a funny feeling stirred in Missy's chest. Being proud of her sister was nothing new, but this time it was different. Less jealousy than normal seasoned the emotional soup. Still enough to taste, but less.

When the song was over, they all clapped, and Missy put the phone away.

"Look, she's doing the sign," Emma said. There was a quick shot of Erica and the girls, just before an advertisement for another prescription medication came on the screen. Emma turned to all of them, her eyes gleaming. "She told me that after the song, she'd put her hand over her heart to say she loves us all."

A collective *aww* sounded from the grown-ups and Piper.

"Do we have to go to school now?" Joshua said.

"Yes," Piper said. "I want to go tell my friends that my aunt was on TV."

"You could tell them tomorrow." Joshua made a face at his sister.

"You're all going to school, and I got to get to work." Ray pulled himself up off the couch, and Missy slid into the vacant spot.

"Hey, since we're all here . . ." She hadn't planned to do it. But in her excitement, the words just came out. "I guess I'll tell you *my* news." Missy took a deep breath and leaned forward with her forearms on her knees, then back just enough to keep the metal button on her jeans from pressing hard against her stomach.

Mama's jaw lowered, though her mouth remained closed, and she asked the question with her eyes, in that way that only a mama could.

Missy shook her head back and forth like a garden flag in a strong wind. "No, Mama. I assure you, I'm not pregnant again."

Mama's breath came out in a whoosh, and she wrapped her good arm around John Thomas, who had wriggled his little body in between both grandparents on the couch.

The look on Ray's face was a mix of relief and curiosity. She hadn't told him yet, either.

"Well, what is the news, honey? Let's hear it," Daddy said.

"I guess it's not that big of a deal, but I thought you'd like to know, and it should be fun for all of us. I mean, it's a way to celebrate the holidays, you know, all together—"

"Melissa, what *is* it?" Daddy's hint of a grin canceled out the harsh tone.

"Okay." She stood up next to Ray and held her arms out in front of her. "I'm going to be singing in a concert with Henry Barker's choir at Reynolds Auditorium. He's asked me to do a solo for a Christmas concert there."

Daddy stood and hugged her. "Honey, that's amazing."

Mama's hand went to her mouth and a glimmer of moisture glistened in the corners of her eyes. "The Twin City Church Choir Christmas Showcase?"

"Yeah, I think that's what he called it."

"They've been advertising that concert on the radio for weeks. My station is sponsoring it. It's one of the biggest Christmas events in town this year."

Mama loved her southern gospel radio. Preset number one had been her station for as long as Missy could remember. It seemed the concert was an even bigger deal than Henry had made it out to be. Maybe he hadn't wanted to make her nervous.

"My wife, the superstar. Y'all get a load a' that." The dimple in Ray's left cheek shined under a two-day-old beard.

"And we get to come hear you sing again?" Emma jumped up and threw her arms around her mama's neck.

She returned the hug, but before Missy could answer, Piper hugged her, too, at the waist. "Mama, hearing you sing again will be even better than seeing Aunt Erica on television."

The girls argued about which of them was most looking forward to hearing her perform as they held onto her. Missy didn't stop them. Everyone else prattled on about how proud they were and how exciting the news was.

Heat rose in Missy's cheeks as the jumble of voices continued around her. Her mind folded into itself, retreating toward the vertex of the cone of noise in the room. It was like a dream. Some topsy-turvy dream where routine became remarkable and the mundane somehow miraculous. All talk of *Good Morning, USA* had suddenly come to an end.

*   *   *

With all the big kids dropped off at school, and John Thomas staying with Mama, Missy drove Grandma Annie to her hair appointment. Every six weeks, like clockwork, Grandma got her trim with a wash and set.

Missy kept her arms straight and hands at ten and two. Her eyes were fixed on the road. In her peripheral, Grandma seemed as tense as she was. Would things ever go back to normal? Having all the family around was one thing. The two of them alone was different.

"I know I said it at the house, but I'm proud of you, honey. You using your talent again." Grandma's voice was tender, sincere.

Finally, the silence had been broken.

"Thanks, Grandma."

"Have you been okay since we talked the other day?" Grandma Annie fidgeted with the long faux-leather strap of the purse that sat between her feet.

Missy eased the brake to the floor as they came to a stoplight. A giant snowflake hung from the post on the corner. It reflected the midday sun and Missy shielded her eyes with her hand as she turned to her grandma. "Not really, if I'm being honest. I wish I could tell you that I'm fine. That it isn't constantly on my mind."

Grandma Annie's brow furrowed, and her mouth turned downward. "I'm so sorry, honey. I was hoping after a few days . . ."

The light changed just as Missy turned her head. "I still haven't figured out what I should do. I don't want to hurt you or disobey you." She raised her voice over the sound of the road. "But I'm not sure that I can carry this secret the way you have."

"And I don't want you to, Missy." Grandma was resolute.

"What? But I thought—"

"I *don't* want to hurt your father. But I realized I can't sacrifice your feelings to spare his."

A burning sensation attacked Missy's throat. It always happened when she held back tears. She turned the car into the parking lot of the salon and found a space. "What are you saying, Grandma?" She twisted toward her and read the pain written on Grandma Annie's face.

If only she hadn't snooped in that stupid dresser drawer. If only the furniture hadn't been left out in the rain. If only Grandma's bad back hadn't required that she move in with Daddy and Mama. Then all would be right. Neither of them would be faced with this impossible choice.

"I'm saying that if the burden gets too heavy for you to carry, then you just say the word, and I'll tell your father the truth. Lord knows I don't want to. But if I'm still living when he has to find out, I want it to be from me. Fair enough?"

The dashboard clock read 12:57. Three minutes until Grandma's appointment.

Missy sighed. "I guess so. But I'm sorry to be putting you through this."

Grandma patted her arm. "Same here, baby girl. But listen. After I'm gone, if you feel like you need to tell him, well, you just do what you think is right."

"I hope that's a very, very long time from now, Grandma."

Grandma Annie pulled her purse into her lap and reached for the door handle. "I've already had so much longer than my mama had. You just never can tell. The only thing we can do is to be ready when He calls us."

The numbers on the dashboard clock changed just as Grandma Annie opened the car door. Time for her appointment.

Chapter Twenty-two

December 1965

$\mathcal{F}$OR THE second time Annie could remember, a dead body was set up to view in the living room of her home. With the couch moved out and presently filling up the back porch, and with her casket in its place, Mama seemed right where she was supposed to be. At least her body did. In her little home, near the front window where she so often waited for Annie when she was out or watched Ruth Claire on the swing that hung from the tree out front. Mama's soul was where it was supposed to be, too, Annie reasoned. The Good Lord made that decision.

The funeral parlor lamps at either end of the casket, with their amber-colored globes pointed toward the ceiling, cast an ethereal glow on the whole room. That yellow haze soaked into everything in sight and softened up the edges. It smoothed over the edges of grief the smallest measure, too, though Annie wasn't sure how.

Aunt Brenda stood behind Annie and whispered into her ear as they looked at Mama in the casket, "They did a really good job with her."

Mama lay there, in the blue dress Annie had picked out from her closet, looking more youthful than Annie could remember ever seeing her. Not tired at all. And as long as Annie didn't think about not being able to hear the sound of her voice or feel her embrace again, she was able to hold back the tears. Mama was still there with them for now.

"There's hardly room in here for enough chairs, but I know she would have wanted us to bring her home."

"You're doing great, Annie. You've done right by your mama. She would be proud." Aunt Brenda's voice cracked.

"Two pages of the register are nearly full. And there are so many cakes on that kitchen counter, I'm not sure what we'll do with all of them."

"Don't worry about that right now. Most of 'em will freeze. And we'll be here to help you."

Headlights flashed through the window.

"There's somebody else coming in. Can you greet them for me, Aunt Brenda?"

"Of course. You go on and be with your sister."

Annie nodded at a bald man wearing a suit and his heavy-set wife in the corner as she left the room. Distant relations and plenty of church folk had come throughout the day and occupied the chairs that lined the walls of the room, brought in by the funeral parlor.

Ruth Claire sat at the kitchen table, so grown-up looking with her new bobbed haircut and Thomas on her lap. Cleet was there, too, and the picture of the three of them brought a brief smile to Annie's face.

"Everybody okay in here?" Annie sat at the table across from R.C., both in their old dinnertime spots.

"Yeah. Thomas Theodore likes the book I brought for him. He's going to be a good reader."

When Daddy died, R.C. hadn't spoken for days. Now, she could communicate and make eye contact and interact with Thomas. It was amazing how far she'd come.

Cleet smiled at Annie as he patted Thomas on the head. "We've been enjoying our time with the little feller."

Annie looked to the living room as more friends from church came through the door. Brenda introduced herself to them and directed them to the register.

The kindest blue eyes shined from beneath the mop of Cleet's dark blond hair. "Annie, I know you and R.C. are gonna miss your mama something terrible. And I'm real sorry. Forty-seven sure is young for a heart attack like that." He put a hand on R.C.'s knee, and R.C. smiled at him. Such a unique bond they shared. *Genuine. Honest.*

Cleet was the same age as Annie, though he looked older. An easygoing man and a hard worker with no other family to speak of. She'd sat him down four months ago and asked, "Why do you want to marry my sister?" Plain and simple, he loved Ruth Claire. He wanted to be with her always. That's all Annie had needed to know.

"Yes, it was young." Annie sniffed. "I thought for sure she'd be with us until Thomas was grown." She stood and went to the cupboard, brought out a stack of small plates, and carried them to the table. The new guests might want cake. "I think her heart got weaker every year since Daddy died. She missed him so much, it just finally gave up." No doubt R.C.'s pregnancy, then the whispers and questions about Thomas's parentage, hadn't helped. But Annie would never say those words out loud.

"I wish I had been here to see her. I hadn't seen her since the wedding." Ruth Claire wore a solemn expression—without tears—and tiredness mixed in with the sad in those crystal blue eyes. They'd driven overnight to be there, Brenda and Cleet taking turns.

"You know what I think?" R.C. said. "Jesus wanted Mama to celebrate His birthday with Him."

Thomas wriggled from R.C.'s lap and brought the book to Annie. She picked him up and flipped through the pages, laying the side of her face on his hair. "I like that thought, R.C. Christmas with Jesus." Annie sat up and pulled Thomas tighter to her. "And we have even more reason to celebrate Christmas now. Without Jesus' birth, we wouldn't have the promise of seeing Mama again one day."

"I believe it, Annie. I do." R.C. nodded like a child promising to be good.

Annie had often wondered about Ruth Claire's soul. If she hadn't chosen to believe, would the limitations of her mind mean that God would somehow waive the requirement of faith? With someone who was obviously handicapped, the answer was clear. They were innocent. But R.C.'s mind was strong. Strong, but different.

"That makes me very happy, baby sister." Annie reached and put her hand over Ruth Claire's. "God will take care of us. We just have to keep trusting."

"Want me to put on some more coffee, Annie?" Cleet said.

She'd forgotten to do it when she got the plates. "Yes, thank you, Cleet. I need to speak to the people who came in a minute ago."

She put Thomas on her hip and took a step toward the living room.

"I brought you a Christmas present, Annie," R.C. said.

Annie turned back.

"It's still in the car. Cleet says we'll bring all the gifts in tomorrow."

Christmas presents. It was so hard to think about. The Christmas tree had been moved to the corner of Annie's bedroom, which she and Thomas would be sharing with Aunt Brenda while R.C. and Cleet would stay in Mama's room.

"I can't wait, R.C." Annie looked at Thomas and pressed her forehead against his. She closed her eyes and whispered. "Mama would want us all to celebrate."

*   *   *

The couch was back in the living room, and Annie and Aunt Brenda sat in a pair of aluminum lawn chairs with green and white striped webbing on the concrete back porch. R.C. and Cleet threw a ball to Thomas in the patch of yard. The grass crunched under Thomas's little tie-up shoes as he ran, calling for them to toss the ball to him.

"It was a lovely service." Aunt Brenda crossed one leg over the other and pulled her sweater tighter. The temperature had risen to fifty-five degrees and the day had bloomed sunny, but every so often a breeze caused a shiver. In the glow of winter's light, Aunt Brenda looked as if she had a small coin purse strapped underneath each eye. No wonder. She'd cried all night. Not much above a whimper, but incessant.

"It really was, Aunt Brenda."

For as long as Annie lived, she'd never forget how the church had been decorated. So beautiful. Poinsettias had always been one of Mama's favorites.

"And so many people," Brenda said.

More than Annie had expected. Old coworkers from the mill and friends from church. Melinda Bennett had been there, too. Annie couldn't help but smile remembering. Thank goodness there had been no mention of Melinda's niece and her niece's fiancé, or whatever he was now. Annie didn't know and she didn't want to know. But her presence there, and the way she wrapped Annie in her arms and didn't let go for the longest time, had healed a deep wound.

"Are you sure I can't get you at least a piece of cake, Annie? That coconut in there is some of the best I've ever had."

Aunt Brenda was so much like Mama.

"No, thanks. I'm okay for now." Even as Annie said it, her stomach gurgled. But food just didn't taste right anymore. Not since four days ago when Mama started having chest pains during dinner.

"Aunt Brenda, I want to thank you again, for all your help."

"That's what family is for, dear." Brenda shifted in her chair. "But have you thought about after Christmas when we go back? I know it's hard to know now, but . . . who will look after Thomas while you're working?"

Annie sighed. "I have a few friends I can call on. Our neighbor next door has been very kind, and she's offered to help look after Thomas before." Annie pointed over a row of short boxwoods at the house to their right. "He seems to like her."

"You know the two of you are welcome to come live with us."

She had considered that alternative already, and her mind warred with itself. Needing independence and wanting family were hard realities when you couldn't have both. "House is paid for, and I can afford what we need, I guess." Her hands were like sandpaper as she wrung them. "But if we ever do need a place to go, it's a comfort to know we have you."

Thomas ran toward the porch with Cleet and R.C. following behind.

"Mama, Mama." He climbed the two steps.

"What is it, baby?"

In his two-year-old speak, Thomas told Annie that he wanted to go inside and show R.C. his toy phone, the one *Ga-ma* had bought for him.

The breath fell from her lungs and she covered her mouth. *Mama meant the world to Thomas.* Tears formed in the corners of her eyes, and she held them there.

"Okay, Thomas," Annie said. "Y'all go play inside."

Ruth Claire patted Annie's shoulder as she passed. *Empathy.* R.C. was learning more all the time.

The metal latch on the door clicked, but still Annie whispered. "R.C. and Thomas have really bonded in the last couple of days."

"Well, they should," Brenda said. "She's his aunt."

Annie picked up the lawn chair by the arms and moved a few inches closer to Brenda. She checked the door again.

"I wouldn't change my decision for the world," Annie said, "but sometimes I wonder what things would have been like if, instead of me raising Thomas, I had tried to teach R.C. how to be his mother."

"Oh, Annie . . ."

"I just worry if it was the right thing."

"Annie, listen. You probably could have taught her *what* to do. But some things aren't so easily learned, and I know for a fact that R.C. is *happy* with this arrangement. She knows you are taking good care of Thomas. She's mother enough to be concerned for him, and it means everything that she don't have to wonder if he's loved and treated well."

"She told you all that?"

"In her own way."

Annie rubbed at the headache in her temples. "But she's married now, and Thomas could have had a father. Cleet would have been a good father to him."

"And he'll be a very special uncle. Honey, you've done the right thing."

As awkward as it must have been, Annie was grateful that Aunt Brenda had discussed family planning with Cleet and R.C. They'd decided for themselves not to have children. Unless there was another surprise, they'd just have the one nephew, until . . .

"Sometimes I worry that I took him away from her, and I hate feeling like that. It doesn't happen often, but sometimes."

Brenda leaned forward and put her hand on Annie's knee. "The sacrifices you've made to take care of that baby, that was a blessing to your sister. I wish I could have been half as good a sister to your mother as you are to Ruth Claire." She let out a muffled sob as she leaned back in the chair.

"What do you mean?"

"I was so selfish, Annie. Your mama and I didn't talk for the longest time. I was mad that she moved up here when she married your daddy, because I wanted her to stay close to me. And if it hadn't been for R.C. getting pregnant with Thomas, I mighta went on being bitter, all on account of missing her so much. Isn't that the silliest thing?"

"Love makes us do silly things sometimes, I guess. Even hurt each other."

"No, sweetheart. Love is what *you* did, letting R.C. go. Doing what was best for her even though it was hard. Now *that's* love."

"But the Lord worked it all out, didn't he? I can't imagine you not being here now."

Aunt Brenda nodded with a grateful smile. Even through the pain, all things worked together for good.

*　　　*　　　*

Joy and grief lived side-by-side through Christmas. When Aunt Brenda, Ruth Claire, and Cleet left the Monday morning after, much of the joy left with them. Three pieces of her heart were probably crossing into Georgia about now, and with Thomas napping, the house was much too quiet.

Annie carried the record player from the bedroom to the living room. She found the outlet behind the end table and plugged it in. Then, on her hands and knees, she inched the coffee table across the floor, stopping and restarting when the feet squeaked too loudly. With the table out of the way, Annie sprawled onto her belly in the middle of the room, her arms and legs like a starfish, with the side of her face pressed into the cool wood. After a moment, she tried to push herself up, but her body fought to stay. Maybe the floor could soak up some of the grief, and when she stood again, it wouldn't be so heavy.

Her eyes closed, and from somewhere inside her brain, the quiet changed to music. It wasn't piano or guitar. The instruments couldn't be named. Unlike anything she'd ever heard, but she wasn't actually *hearing*. Maybe Mama had sent her some of heaven's music. It stirred her to life, and she opened her eyes. She'd come into that room with a purpose, and it wasn't to just lay there.

Annie stood and brushed off her dress. The afternoon sun poured in through the window, creating the perfect rectangular boundary for her dance floor. She reached for the silky scarf that was wrapped underneath her hair and tied in a knot on top of her head, then she pulled it down the length of her hair, untied the knot, pulled her hair into a low ponytail and tied the scarf around it. At the record player, Annie set the needle onto the black vinyl.

How long had it been? The longest it had ever been, since the very first time.

As the music started, she took her spot in the middle of the room and pushed herself into *en pointe*, her arms curved above her head. She stumbled and resumed the position.

That deep, familiar voice whispered to her from the record player as she bent into an arabesque then returned her feet to fifth position and began a slow pirouette. Oh, how she loved that voice. She'd been fourteen when she'd sat in front of the television in that same room with Daddy, Mama, and R.C. and watched him perform the song on Ed Sullivan. That was the moment she really fell in love. It had been the moment she realized that Elvis loved Jesus.

She needed him now, to remind her of the peace in the valley his song told of. She needed God to speak through the music and in the tensing and flexing of the muscles He had formed with His own hands.

In her indescribable grief, Annie needed to dance.

Chapter Twenty-three

Tuesday, December 12, Present Day

*I*T HAD to be a record. More than two whole weeks left until Christmas and the tree was up and decorated, *and* almost every present wrapped and placed underneath. Way too many of them, to be sure, but the kids would be so happy. Missy could hardly wait to see their faces.

Now she could relax—or attempt to—and focus on the upcoming performance. There were only four more days until the concert. And thirteen until Christmas, which meant at least that many days of being part of the same family she'd grown up with. The heart-wrenching decision could wait that long. After Christmas, and not a moment sooner. After Christmas she'd resume the great debate within her soul—whether Daddy should know the truth.

The cushiony couch absorbed the weight of Missy's body, the steam from her cup of coffee bathed her face in warmth, and her favorite seasonal song—the orchestra version, where the instruments imitate horses' hooves and a whip cracking—played from the smart speaker on the end table as she tapped her foot on the carpet.

The three youngest kids inspected the presents tucked around the base of the tree, with the lights from the tree casting multi-colored dots in their expectant eyes.

Joshua picked up a box wrapped in green-and-silver-plaid foil.

"This one has to be Legos." A loud rattle came from the box as he shook it. "I bet it's the astronaut set I asked for."

"You'll have to wait and find out."

John Thomas crawled around giving each one a tiny shake then putting it back. He giggled at the perfectly round package that made no noise. A kickball had been near the top of his list.

"Oh, I bet this one's mine." Piper pointed to a long, skinny box in solid red paper.

"Well, read the tag, stupid, and you'll find out," Emma called from across the room.

"Mama, Emma called me stupid."

"Emma . . ." Missy said.

"But she can't even read a tag," Emma said. "And she thinks every present under there is hers. She's so greedy."

"I am not greedy. I'm just excited about Christmas." Piper stomped. "At least I'm not an old Grinch like you."

"Girls. Stop it. Come here." She'd had all she could take for one day. Enough was enough.

Missy took them both by a shoulder and made them stand in front of her, side-by-side. Emma was a head taller than her younger sister, but Piper would be catching up soon. Both pretty girls, both smart. But so different from one another. If one was hot, the other was cold. If one was happy, the other was sad. And their relationship was a constant struggle.

"Girls, what have I told you over and over about having a sister?"

Emma looked at the floor. Piper huffed.

"Say it."

In unison they droned, "She's the only sister I'm ever gonna have and I should appreciate her."

"Good, that's right. Now, learn to get along, because if you don't stop fussin', you're both gonna be grounded."

When had she turned into her mother?

The girls nodded. Emma plopped onto the couch, phone in hand. Piper went back to the Christmas tree in the corner. On her hands and knees, she moved toward the far side of the tree until she met the wall, then she dove beneath the bottom branches. In a moment, Piper army-crawled out backwards, holding a small box.

"How about this one, Mama? It doesn't have a tag. *Is it for me?*"

"No, sweetie. That one's for Aunt Erica." Missy set her coffee mug on the end table. She stood, took the box from Piper, and placed it on the mantel. "It's fragile."

"*Ooh,* what is it, Mama?" Emma said from the couch, her dark eyes round. She *did* care about Christmas after all.

Missy reached to fluff the ribbon on top. She scanned the room and ducked her head. In a whisper she said, "If you promise not to tell her, it's a music box. It plays an old song that Justin Trent does a cover of, and Aunt Erica sang it on the last album with him. I think she'll like it."

Piper grinned. "I think she will, too, Mama."

"Okay, kids," Missy said. "Time to get started."

She herded the kids into the kitchen for their planned afternoon of Christmas baking. Hashtag *memories*. Since Mama couldn't mix and stir, they'd make twice as many freezer cookies, to share. Maybe even some chocolate no-bake cookies or peanut clusters. Missy could already taste them.

Jeannie Wallace's choir robe wouldn't be all that loose after these holiday binges.

"Emma, get the wax paper from the cabinet, and Joshua, the cookie cutters are in that drawer there."

She brought down an armful of mixing bowls from the cupboard as the phone rang from her back pocket. Missy set down the bowls and answered, holding an upright pointer finger to signal the kids. They'd have to wait a minute.

"Hey, we were talking about you just a little while ago," Missy said.

"Yeah?" Erica chuckled. "Hope it was good."

"It was. Just Christmas stuff. The kids are getting really excited. Still coming in on the twentieth? All your gigs are done by then, right?"

The line went quiet for a moment. "Well, sis, that's why I called. I'm—I'm actually not coming on the twentieth."

Missy walked to the patio door. The stillness of the backyard under a thick blanket of clouds hit the pause button on her tongue. She breathed out hard, then drew a long breath through her nose. *Steady, steady. There must be a good reason.*

Two black-and-white chickadees landed on the square patio table just as her palm met the glass door in a hard slap. Amidst the roiling of an angry sea inside, a wave of sadness hit. She didn't want the birds to go. And there was no good reason for her sister to disappoint her again.

"You've got to be kidding," Missy said.

She turned toward the kitchen. The kids' eyes had followed her, their ears hanging on her every word. Missy turned back again.

"Well, there's just been a change of plans, and I'm not going to—"

"Erica, you better not tell me you're not coming home for Christmas. After Dad's party and Thanksgiving. I mean, I know you're a grown woman and you have a career, or *whatever*, out there, but you still have a family back here. And I think you owe it to the family that loves you—"

"Missy, will you listen to me? I—"

"It feels like you've forgotten all about us sometimes. Like the only thing in the world that's important to you is the Nashville scene and being on a stage somewhere. And your family is just an afterthought—people that you *might* decide to spend time with if nothing better comes along."

"I can't believe this, Missy. You're not being fair."

She ignored the hurt in Erica's voice.

"What's not fair is never being important enough to you for you to put us first."

"Missy, the reason I'm not coming on the twentieth, is that I decided to come home *sooner*. So I could be there for your concert. I wanted to hear you sing and give you my support."

Missy moved the phone away from her ear. She held her breath for a long time. *I'm such a fool.* She slid her palm across her forehead and down the side of her face then looked around. The kids had disappeared. Probably afraid she'd yell at them, too.

"Erica, I shouldn't have flown off the handle like that. I was way outta line."

"You're only saying that because you finally let me explain I was coming home early. It doesn't change the fact that you meant what you said. You think I'm selfish for doing what I love to do. But what you don't know is that Justin got booked on *another* morning show, for two sets. On a major network. And I told him he could do it without me because I wanted to be with my *family*, and especially my big sister on an important day."

"Oh, Erica, you didn't—"

"Of course, I did. I mean, two back-up singers are plenty anyway. Right?"

"I don't know what to say."

"Well, don't worry about it. I gotta go. Call me sometime when you're not so angry and bitter about my life choices. Okay?"

The line went quiet.

Missy growled. At her sister. At herself. At the world. She growled again, this time louder, and slammed the phone—screen-down—on the table, hard. She picked it back up and inspected it. *No cracks.*

The top half of Piper's head poked from the doorway to the living room. "Mama, is everything okay?"

"Yes, but I want you kids to go out back for a while. At least thirty minutes. There's still enough daylight."

"But what about the cookies, Mama? You promised."

"The cookies will have to wait. Now don't backtalk me." The twang in her voice rang inside her head. There she was, sounding like her own mama again. "We'll do it later."

Piper slinked away, and Missy ran toward the garage. She couldn't get there fast enough.

The coffee can and tackle box were hidden under an old bedsheet, the one with the little green diamonds on it that she'd decided to get rid of, alongside all the Santa presents. Those gifts would stay unwrapped and would show up around the tree while the kids were sleeping on Christmas Eve.

Missy raised the hem of the sheet and slid the necessary accoutrements across the concrete floor to the blue five-gallon bucket that she used as a seat.

Pack in hand, Missy pinched a spongy filter and pulled out the cigarette. She must have completely lost it. First with

Grandma there, now with all the kids. It was risky, but worth it. The flame of the lighter danced between her eyes as she drew fire into the cigarette by inhaling.

She leaned forward and ran her fingers through her hair, starting from the middle of her forehead and running to the nape of her neck, breaking up tangles as she went. Maybe she needed a vacation. Just to get away from everything. Maybe a day or two at the beach could cure her short fuse. It had been at least two years since she'd seen the ocean. Even in December, it would be nice.

Her hands shook, and she felt herself spiraling. She leaned forward with her forearms pressed into her knees and fought not to hyperventilate. Being mad at herself made Missy ten times more jittery than being angry with someone else.

In no time, she'd sucked down the first cigarette. She tossed the glowing stub toward the coffee can and lit another.

"I should call her back," she said to the second cigarette. "Tell her I want her to come to the concert, and that I'm sorry I was such a jerk." She inhaled on her crutch. "She probably won't answer."

Missy's face hovered parallel to the floor, and her hair hung beside her eyes and brushed her cheeks. With the pointer finger of her free hand, she swiped underneath her glasses, one eye then the other. She sniffed then shivered. Chill bumps covered her bare arms. The uninsulated garage was not a place to hang out for very long.

In her peripheral, a small orange flame sprang up without warning, out of the cold slab of floor, inches from where she sat. Missy let out a curse as she pushed off with her feet and sent the bucket screeching backward on the concrete. One side of the bucket lifted off the floor, tipping Missy onto her backside. She scrambled to stand.

The fire that had startled her was only the size of her phone, and it didn't burn from the floor as it had seemed. The cigarette butt had landed on one of Ray's shop rags instead of in the can. The light gray cloth was almost used up already, and the fire dwindled on its own.

A loud noise from the backside of the garage made Missy jump. Mr. Peanut's bark continued in a loud, monotonous yap. Maybe he smelled smoke from the backyard. Or maybe something else was wrong. She needed to check on the children, but not with a fire smoldering in the garage. And she'd never be able to explain it away if they ran in and caught her.

She lunged forward to stomp out the remnants, but the fire whooshed, tripling in size. In an instant, the flame leaped to the edge of the sheet and claimed its new territory. *The presents.* A horrible vision flashed in her mind, of Christmas morning and trying to explain to the kids why Santa hadn't come. And she'd be the Grinch responsible.

She sprang into an unplanned hip-hop routine and smothered the fire from the rag and the edge of the sheet with the bottom of her tennis shoes. Finally, there was none of it left. Her heart raced as she lifted the sheet. Missy let out a relieved sigh. The presents hadn't ignited, and none of the packaging was even melted or singed.

Missy shoved the can and tackle box back under the sheet then ran into the house, to the glass door in the kitchen. All four of the kids were busy at play as the sun sank quickly. They'd be inside soon, and she still had to make dinner. Missy sprinted down the hall and into the bathroom in her room. Avoiding the mirror, she pulled off all her clothes in a frenzy then hopped into the shower. Immediately, she retreated to the farthest wall. She hadn't given the water time to warm up.

Missy, you need to think about your life choices. She smacked at her forehead.

The water gradually became a tolerable temperature and then a welcome relief to her tense muscles.

What a day. A fight with her sister and almost burning down the garage.

The hurt tone in Erica's voice replayed in Missy's memory. She had no clue how to make it better. As far as the garage, she'd need to replace the burned sheet before anyone saw it. And she had to admit that maybe her vice wasn't worth the trouble it had caused. She'd given it up through all four pregnancies anyway. No problem. Not to mention that smoking was terrible for her skin *and* her singing voice.

One less secret to carry.

Chapter Twenty-four

April 1966

"Thomas, please be a good boy for Mommy. This job is very important for us, and I need to be able to do my best. Do you understand?"

Whether two-year-old Thomas understood or not, he nodded. Annie squatted in front of him and pressed his cheeks with both hands, squeezing his lips into a pucker. His eyes danced. She laughed and kissed him on the nose.

"Here you go. I brought this whole bag of toys for you to play with." She lifted Thomas off his feet and sat him on the floor on his bottom, then dumped the contents of the bag beside him. "And while you play, I'm going to clean the room. See?"

She held up the cleaning rag.

Thomas looked up at her as he rolled a firetruck beside him. "Mama clean up."

"That's right. Good boy."

She stood and surveyed the job at hand. Wipe down the desks, clean the blackboard and windows, vacuum the floor. Just classrooms today. And hopefully Barb would feel better tomorrow. Her next-door-neighbor was one of the few people she trusted to take care of Thomas while she worked, and Barb had been so kind to her since Mama died.

Annie gave each desk in the front row a squirt of cleaner, her Mary Janes sidestepping from right to left like a dance. Then she wiped each one, moving from left to right down the row.

"Thomas, sing the twinkle, twinkle song for Mama, okay?" If she moved to a part of the room where she couldn't see him, Annie would know he was okay as long as she could hear him.

Thomas began the song like she'd asked as Annie started on the second row of desks. His voice was soft but steady, and the sweetest sound in the world. She often wondered if Tommy Jacobs was a good singer. Thomas had been able to carry a tune since before he could form a sentence.

"That's a good job, Thomas. Keep singing." She came to the end of the third row and moved on to the next. "Your song helps Mama with her cleaning. You're being a great helper."

"I believe there are laws against child labor."

Annie spun around at the sound of the man's voice and nearly tripped over her own feet. A stranger stood between the doorway and her son.

"Oh." She moved closer to Thomas with the cleaning rag pressed against her chest. She pulled it away and looked down at her dress front as the dampness reached her skin.

The man took a step forward. "I didn't mean to startle you." He wore a tweed jacket with wooden buttons, and it had leather patches on the elbows. Surely, he wasn't a teacher. He definitely wasn't a student, but he was too young and too handsome to be a teacher, with his brown eyes, narrow sideburns, and a subtle cleft in his chin. "I'm David Hall."

"You mean *Dr.* David Hall? Like the name on the classroom door?" She pointed toward it with a nod.

He only grinned, revealing the whitest teeth she'd ever seen. Thomas ran toward the teacher and grabbed at his pant leg.

"You certainly do have an adorable helper."

Annie rushed and scooped Thomas up, apologizing as she did. "My babysitter is sick. And since I have a short shift today, I thought it would be okay for him to tag along."

"I admire that. You could have called in, but you're here doing what needs to be done. No harm in that. Very admirable."

"I'm glad you think so. I wouldn't want to get in any trouble . . ."

"I wouldn't worry about that, Mrs. . . . ?"

"Actually it's *Miss*, and my name is Annie. Annie Swaim."

The same war raged in Annie's mind as it always did when she met someone new. Most of the time, she let people believe whatever their brains concocted—that she was an unwed mother, or maybe if they were of the more charitable sort, that she was a young widow. She rarely used the word that would classify her son as anything other than simply her son. But with this man, it seemed needed. With this man, she cared about whether he assumed she was chaste.

"This is my son, Thomas. He's my adopted son."

She steadied herself for the logical questions, but none came. "Oh, well, it's nice to meet you both," he said.

His eyes held such sincerity. But then again, she'd thought that about someone before.

"What do you teach, Dr. Hall?" she asked as Thomas went back to his pile of toys on the floor.

"Please call me David." He smiled again. "And I teach English."

She chuckled. "I forget that students have *regular* classes here."

"Oh, yes. Can't forget the basics now, can we? Actors and musicians, and even dancers like you, need English and Math."

"But I'm not—why do you think—"

"Oh, the way you've been shuffling your feet. You've been doing a change step, and the position of your feet perfectly matched each other."

She looked down. "I *used* to be a dancer."

"You certainly look like a dancer. I guess I could tell because I'm around a lot of them."

Annie's face grew warm as his eyes scanned her.

"But why is it *used to be*?" he said.

"It's a long story and—" She held the rag over one of the nearby desks, "I should really get back to my cleaning."

His dark eyes filled with disappointment.

"Perhaps when your babysitter is feeling better, you'd like to go out to dinner with me? And you can tell me about it then."

Did this man just ask her to go on a date? This stranger?

"Um—I don't know—I—"

"Do you like Staley's? My colleagues say I need to try it, but I don't want to go by myself."

"Oh, yes. It's very nice."

Julian had taken her there once, but Annie wasn't sure she'd know how to act in a nice restaurant now—or out anywhere—without Thomas, for that matter. Especially with a sophisticated man like David. It had been a long time since Julian.

"I only moved here a couple months ago. From Wilmington. You're welcome to suggest something else."

"Oh, no, no. Staley's is a great restaurant."

His eyes smiled toward her. "So, you'll join me there for dinner? May I call you to schedule it?"

He walked to his desk, pulled out paper and pencil from the drawer, and held them toward her. She looked down at the cleaning rag still in her hand and hurriedly set it on the nearest student desk, then she used the same desk to write her phone number on the paper he'd handed her. She could always say no when he called if she made up her mind not to go.

He smiled and tucked the paper into his jacket pocket.

"I just came back in to get my grade book, so I'll leave you to your work. I look forward to speaking with you again, Annie."

The way he said her name sent a tingle down Annie's back. All she could do was smile and nod.

"It was nice to meet you, Thomas. Bye-bye, buddy." David bent near Thomas's face and smiled at him. His fingers folded over and flapped up and back down. "Bye-bye."

Thomas copied the hand motion. "Bye-bye."

With David out of the room, Annie hurried to Thomas on her tiptoes. She kneeled and whispered. "He seemed like a very nice man, didn't he?" He smiled up at her and she tussled his hair. "What do you think? Should Mama have dinner with him?"

Thomas laughed and shook his head wildly. No was his new favorite word, and the answer to almost everything.

Annie stood and stared at the doorway. An English teacher and a housekeeper. Such a strange thought, but maybe a new friend was exactly what she needed.

*   *   *

"What a novelty." David pointed at the eleven-feet-tall bull statue that stood in front of the steakhouse.

"It definitely gets your attention, doesn't it? Some people call him Winston."

"Ah, of course." He grinned as he held the door open for her, following her with his eyes as she passed him. "I'm finding a lot of fun and interesting things about my new city."

Annie felt herself blushing. Dr. David Hall was proving to be quiet the charmer. But she worried. Charming men could be deceiving. She knew. From experience she knew.

The hostess led them to an empty booth, and David motioned for her to pick a side. Annie smoothed the seat of her straight, sheath dress and held the hem against the back of her leg as she slid into the bench. Only a few other tables and booths in the room were occupied, and it made her glad it was a Tuesday night instead of the busy weekend.

Exactly one week ago, she'd seen him for the first time, and those days in between their meeting and when he'd called the night before had helped make up her mind about saying yes to a dinner date. Every time the phone rang, she caught herself hoping it was him, disappointed when it wasn't.

"I'm glad your babysitter is feeling better. Not that Thomas wouldn't have been welcome to join us, but I'm happy to get to know you, just the two of us."

"Me too. Although after we talked on the phone so late last night, I'm not sure what else there is for either one of us to know."

"Oh, I think we're only getting started." He smiled at her from above the menu.

She hoped he was right. She already knew that he was the son of a pastor, that at twenty-seven he was the youngest teacher on staff at his school, that he was the oldest of five children, and that he wanted to have a large family of his own someday.

And she'd shared more about herself than she imagined she ever could during a first real conversation with someone. She'd even told him about her dancing and why it had come to an end. She'd told all about Julian and her past heartache, and about Mama and how much she missed her and Ruth Claire and Aunt Brenda.

Throughout the meal, the conversation was light and easy. The steak, salad, and baked potato—her first extravagant meal in a very long time—was delectable, and the whole atmosphere made Annie feel like she had begun to live someone else's life.

When their dessert arrived, David's expression grew serious. He reached for her hand across the table.

"Annie, I hope me saying this isn't bizarre, and that it doesn't scare you. But I feel like tonight was the start of something very meaningful for both of us."

Her breath hitched at those wonderful words, so like a prize to her soul. "It doesn't sound bizarre, David. It sounds lovely."

"It's just that, I believe God guides us through this life, if we let Him, and—I can't help but feel that, for some reason, He's led me to you."

Warmth started at the top of Annie's head and coursed down her shoulders and arms. "Well, the Bible does say, in all thy ways acknowledge Him—"

"And He shall direct thy paths."

She smiled and leaned in closer. David leaned, too, until their faces were less than a foot apart.

"A man's heart deviseth his way . . ." She paused, testing him.

"But the Lord directeth his steps."

"You know your Proverbs."

"And you do, as well."

In that moment she knew, this man was not like Julian. Still . . . "I need to ask you something, David."

His eyes invited her to continue.

"Does it bother you that I'm just a housekeeper? I mean, you're a teacher while I haven't even finished my business certificate like I'd planned and I'm almost twenty-four."

He looked at her with an earnestness and a tenderness she'd never seen before. "Annie, you are not *just* anything. And you are certainly not *just* a housekeeper. You are an amazing woman who loves God and puts others before herself, and I would be blessed to know you no matter what kind of job you had."

Chapter Twenty-five

Friday, December 15, Present Day

"*I*'VE FIGURED it out, Missy."

The warm breath of Henry's whispers brushed Missy's cheek and tickled her ear as the stares of the whole choir burned into the back of her head. They stood there waiting, all of them in their street clothes instead of the Sunday robes. Grandma Annie sat watching from a pew, the only person in the sanctuary other than the singers. She offered Missy a timid smile, and Missy nodded.

"I know what the *something missing* is," Henry said. "The thing that's holding you back."

"That's great, Henry, but did you really have to call me out in the middle of rehearsal? In the middle of the song?" Missy matched his whisper. "I'm nervous enough about this solo as it is, and I'm doing my best up there."

He took a step back, sized her up and down, furrowed his brow, then leaned close to her ear again.

"Do you want to be a better singer or don't you?"

"Well, of course. It's just, I didn't think—"

"You're not buying what you're selling."

A huff escaped her lips. "Can you just say what you mean, please?" The strain of the rehearsal, mixed with the emotion of the moment, came out in her scratchy voice.

"These hymns. The Christmas story. All of it. You know it here"—He tapped his index finger on her forehead like a reflex hammer to the knee—"but you don't really know it here." Henry pointed to somewhere around Missy's heart. "I sense that you don't have the *real* faith to back up what you're singing. Do you?"

Missy's chest tightened and the heat rose in her cheeks. She looked to Grandma again, then back at the choir. What must they all be thinking? He'd kept his voice down. No one else had heard what he said, she was sure. But it was such odd timing.

In the corners of her eyes, the sensation like alcohol on a papercut intensified.

"Henry, I'm not sure what you want me to say. I respect the stories and the songs. They're part of my heritage, and that's important. But what if I don't believe them? Would you want me to quit the choir? Would you find another soloist who can sell it better?"

Henry reached for her arm but stopped short. He walked to the choir box. "Everybody, you did a great job tonight. I think we've rehearsed enough, and I thank you for putting in one last practice before our special performance. Remember to bring your robes and be there at five-thirty. You're going to do great."

The choir began to disband.

Did that mean she should leave, too? Maybe she should slip out the door with Grandma Annie while his back was turned and pretend the conversation never happened. But her feet were cemented to the floor. It made absolutely no sense to stay after he'd ambushed her, but she couldn't go.

The nervousness and twinge of guilt she felt reminded her of eleventh grade and the one time she'd had to visit the principal's office. They'd accused her of skipping first period when really, she'd been in the bathroom throwing up from morning sickness and couldn't tell them the truth. Why did Henry seem so much like her high school principal now?

He returned and motioned for her to sit on the cushiony red pew, while the rest of the choir filed out of the sanctuary chattering, now free for the remainder of their Friday evening.

"Missy, to be fair, I reckon I really should have asked about your faith before I invited you to join my choir." He chuckled then his face turned solemn again. "It seems I made an incorrect assumption. But no, I'm not going to replace you. I wouldn't dream of it."

"It's the reason I was doubtful about it in the beginning. I wanted to sing, but I didn't want to act like something I'm not."

She looked over her shoulder at Grandma Annie, who sat on the other side of the church a few rows back, clutching the black purse in her lap with concern. She probably hadn't expected tagging along for rehearsal to turn out like this.

"I respect that," Henry said. "But I want you to know, darlin', these songs . . . they aren't just songs for a Sunday or some special concert. These are songs for *life*. About life. About the *Life Giver*."

The sincerity in Henry's voice overwhelmed her. She felt in her soul how badly he wanted her to believe. Then a new thought crossed her mind. What if Henry had known about her lack of faith all along? From the very beginning?

"Are you sure that's not why you invited me to sing in your choir?" Missy scanned the room. Everyone else had gone, so she let her volume match her emotion. "I'm sure Daddy has talked to you about me at work, right? He must have mentioned how I've strayed. I bet this whole thing was a project, to bring Missy back into the fold."

"Missy, your daddy never said—"

"Grandma, were you in on this?" Missy called over her shoulder before she turned. Grandma Annie eased into a standing position and strode toward them.

Missy turned back and searched Henry's eyes. The look on his face matched her own hurt.

"Missy, please listen to me. This was not any sort of project. We're not trying to trick you into changing what you believe. It doesn't work that way."

Missy felt the warmth of her grandma's hand on her shoulder, but the older woman stayed quiet.

"Let's leave it at this," Henry said. "I care about you. I haven't known you long, but I've grown very fond of you, Missy. What I said, I said out of concern. But we won't discuss it anymore if you don't want to. Just sing at the concert tomorrow night, finish our Advent series—if you want—and then, well, I'll be here if you ever want to hang out and sing vocal exercises to Handel's *Messiah* for the fun of it. How's that?"

Relief washed over her. "Okay. And I'm really sorry that I—"

Henry raised his hand, signaling her to stop. "We'll speak no more of it. Now go home and rest your voice for tomorrow night."

With hardly a thought, Missy lunged with her arms opened and grabbed Henry in a hug.

He returned the embrace and patted her on the back as she fought back tears that she didn't understand. "Thank you, Henry."

She leaned back to see him smiling. His concern for her was so real, almost tangible. Once she'd taken the gloves off, she could see it. But he was right—they hadn't known each other long. So how could what she felt from him feel so much like love?

*   *   *

Missy cut her stride in half to keep pace with Grandma Annie, taking baby steps down the well-lit walkway in front of the church to where she'd pulled the van next to the curb. The cold December air must have taken a toll on her grandma's joints, because even with the cane and the support of Missy's arm, her movements were impossibly slow.

"Almost there, Grandma. The van's just over there."

As Missy helped her into the passenger seat, a woman approached them.

She wore a silky, white button-up blouse and a straight, black skirt, and she hadn't changed at all in thirteen years. Same broad smile, same red lips, and same big, white hairdo.

"Missy Hall? I thought that was you I spied in the choir the other week. I go to church here now. I'm just meeting some ladies to discuss a fundraiser for the youth group." Mary Sue put a hand on Missy's shoulder. "I can't believe it. You're all grown up. Well, hey there, Miss Annie. I haven't seen you in ages."

Grandma grimaced and waved as she lifted her leg from the curb and into the van.

"Hello, Mary Sue." Missy turned to face her. "Actually, it's Missy Robbins." The pit of her stomach roiled like a lava hot spring. *Maintain, Missy. Just maintain. Everything is okay.*

"Oh, that's right, *Robbins*. And how is that beautiful little girl. Emma, is that it?"

How on earth did she remember Emma's name? It had been so long ago, and she'd acted like she'd wanted nothing to do with either of them when Emma was born.

"Um—she's good. But now I have four beautiful children."

"Four? Well, my, my. How blessed you are."

How could she act so nice, and like nothing had happened?

"And I bet you are just the *best* mama. You were always such a sweetheart. And *smart*. One of my favorites in Sunday school. Has your family started coming to church here?"

"Um—no, I'm just helping out with the Advent music and the Christmas concert tomorrow night."

"Oh, good. I have tickets to that. And I think it's wonderful that you're sharing your talent with the world. Just like your little sister. Last I heard she was out in Nashville. Is that right?"

"Yes, ma'am. But she's coming home tonight to spend Christmas with us."

Missy glanced at Grandma Annie. Her face said *you're doing good* and *keep it up.*

"That's nice. I hope y'all have a great Christmas, and I'm so glad I ran into you today. I hope I get to see you again soon." Mary Sue looked directly at her, so intently it made Missy want to look away. "Missy, can I give you a hug?"

She couldn't say no. That would be beyond rude.

"Well, of course."

Mary Sue wrapped one arm around Missy's middle and the other over her shoulder. She pulled her close and squeezed, the way someone might hug a long-lost friend or a dear relative. And she stayed there for the longest time while Missy wanted to scream, *"But you hurt me. You made me feel like you didn't love me anymore."* Then Missy tightened her hold on Mary Sue and let her seventeen-year-old-self enjoy the comfort and affirmation for which she'd longed. Her face rested against Mary Sue's and created a warmth that drove the chill around her away.

Mary Sue stepped back, said goodbye, and walked away toward the entrance of the church. Missy's heart cried after her: *Don't go. Don't go.* Still feeling their embrace and smelling Mary Sue's strong perfume, Missy's hurt began to melt, and it ran down her cheek as a single tear. So many emotions jumbled together. It was like finding a treasure that had been missing for years but still mourning for the time it had been gone. Mostly, she ached for the *why*. Not understanding *why* Mary Sue hurt her was the hardest.

"Are you okay?" With the door of the van was still open, Grandma Annie sat there shivering.

"Yes, Grandma. I'm okay."

Missy closed the door. From the driver side of the van, she looked to the sprawling church campus again, determining in her heart to somehow focus on what had been restored—no matter how small—instead of the part left unresolved.

I'm okay, Grandma. Maybe even better than okay.

* * *

Missy's mind tumbled over itself like the churn of the motor as she drove. So much had happened, and there was so much to process. If only she could go home, veg out in front of the TV with a giant bowl of ice cream, and forget everything. That's what she needed.

Grandma Annie, in her tender way, didn't press. She always seemed to know when Missy needed silence. The back and forth, the leaning into conversation or pulling back into her own mind, was like a dance, and her grandma was a good partner.

Missy turned onto the road that would lead them to Daddy and Mama's house through the dips and rises of the piedmont landscape. Her mind continued to spin until it landed on something that had to come out. "Have you talked to Erica?"

"Only for a minute, when she called to tell your daddy what time her flight would be in."

Missy shifted in the seat, easing off the gas pedal.

"Did she tell you I yelled at her the other day?"

Grandma Annie let out a long sigh. "No, baby girl, she didn't mention it. What on earth for?"

"It was a misunderstanding. I thought she was fixing to tell me she wouldn't be home for Christmas, like she wasn't here for Daddy's party, and I kinda lost it. Then I found out that she gave up being on another television program just to be here for my concert. Long story short, I feel like dirt, and we haven't spoken since."

Grandma produced a long, airy whistle that started on a high note and slid down. "Boy, you've really been put through the wringer lately, haven't you?"

"You can say that again."

"Did you tell her you're sorry? That's usually the first step."

"I did, but I know she's still hurt."

Grandma Annie tapped the radio button to shut off the country music station that had been barely loud enough to hear anyway, and she went into a thinking pose, her chin resting on her hand. Even in the dark, Missy knew that Grandma's brow was furrowed until the wrinkles in her forehead doubled. She could expect extra good advice whenever Grandma did that, and Missy welcomed it.

After a moment, Grandma Annie spoke. "Listen, Melissa. Your sister *will* forgive you. She must have already because she's still coming."

"I was so horrible to her, Grandma, but to tell you the truth, part of me is still mad at her for missing the party, and for not being here for so many other important things."

"And above all things have fervent charity among yourselves: for charity shall cover the multitude of sins."

"That's Psalms, isn't it?"

"Good try. First Peter. That word *charity* means love. The answer to just about every problem in the world is love. Do you get that? I'm telling you, baby, The Beatles were on to something."

Good one, Grandma.

"Just let her know you love her," Grandma Annie said. "And when it comes to everything you feel like she's done wrong to you, remember that you love her. Love can cover it all."

"Thanks."

When they arrived, Missy helped Grandma out of the van, up the steps, and into the house. After a quick visit with Daddy and Mama, Missy headed home to Ray and the kids.

The porch light was on when Missy got there, and as she walked across the yard, music came from inside. She dragged herself up the steps and inside the house where she found Ray rebuilding a carburetor on the kitchen table. At least he'd used one of her new, fluffy white bath towels to put down first. Piper sat beside him, painting her nails. A purple glop dotted the towel near where she worked.

The music came from the living room, where Little Bit danced around with an almost empty bag of tinsel. Shiny silver threads littered the room and even hung from Mr. Peanut's ears and tail. The dog scattered the tinsel around with his wagging tail as he greeted her, oblivious to his disgraced state.

"Hey, Mama," John Thomas yelled. "I'm having a dance party with the dog."

Missy sighed and pressed a hand against her cheek. "That's nice, baby."

She headed back to the foyer, plunked her bag onto the entryway table, and sifted through a stack of mail. The other two children were probably in their rooms. She'd go check on them in a minute. Missy dropped the mail and pressed her fingertips into her aching forehead. For sure there was no time for TV and ice cream. She'd have to get the vacuum out instead, and later try to bleach the stains out of the towel.

Love might cover all sins, Grandma, but it ain't gonna touch this mess.

Chapter Twenty-six

September 1966

$\mathcal{T}$HE METAL cradle clanged as Annie returned the payphone handset. "Barb says Thomas is fine, and that he's been a good boy. She's going to put him to bed soon."

"Wonderful." David placed a hand on her arm and the other on the small of her back. "Did you tell Barb that you are being a good girl, and also that you are blindfolded and have no clue where you are?"

"David, you know I didn't." Annie giggled. "You were standing right there the whole time." She felt for and grasped his forearm. "Wait—you *were* right there, weren't you?"

"Of course, I was. I wouldn't dream of leaving your side tonight."

He pulled her close and she felt the warmth and softness of his lips against her forehead. She imagined his wry smile and the twinkle in his eye. Annie felt for his chest then ran her palm up the lapel of his suit jacket, then his neck, until she found the smoothness of his cheek.

"It's a good thing I trust you, you know."

"I know. We're almost there, so you'll be able to take off the blindfold soon. You've been a good sport letting me surprise you like this."

David helped her back inside the car. Wherever they were headed, it was to be a complete surprise. She'd worn the eye covering since they'd left the restaurant, and her efforts to map the route in her mind and guess at each turn had failed. The filling station where they stopped to use the payphone could have been any one in Winston-Salem. The sounds of cars passing by, and the general smells of late summer air and motor traffic, offered no hints.

When the car came to a stop again minutes later, David helped her from the passenger seat. Then, after only a couple steps, he instructed her to step up.

"Be careful now. Just three more. Easy does it."

They passed through a doorway and into an echoey room, and soon through another doorway. In the new room, her voice got lost. This room was big.

"David, I'm getting nervous. Where are we? Is there anybody else here?"

"Don't be nervous, Annie. I promise, you're going to be fine with this surprise. Hopefully, much more than fine."

After turning right and then making a left, they walked straight for what seemed like a long distance. What kind of room had that much space? Maybe they were in a church. But the floor didn't feel like the old carpet of her church—their church, since he'd started going with her—and this place was much bigger.

He slowed and turned her with his arms.

"There's a few steps here? Are you ready?"

Annie nodded, and he helped her climb. Nervous excitement crescendoed from her toes. She reached the top of the stairs, and the floor beneath her feet seemed alive with an inexplainable magic. Familiar and yet foreign.

David stopped her and turned her ninety degrees.

"Now, you stand here. And don't take off the blindfold until I say, okay?"

She blew out hard, her lips trembling. "Okay."

Annie went up on the tiptoes of her pumps and came back down again. Even her heels clicking against the floor created an echo.

Where had David gone? Was he close enough to see if she raised the blindfold? The urge to peek overwhelmed her. She reached toward her face. *No.* She'd promised.

Just as the excitement began to manifest as an upset stomach, David spoke from somewhere in front of her.

"Okay, Annie. You can take off the blindfold now and see where you are."

Her shaky thumb slid beneath the soft fabric above her cheekbone, and she lifted it a centimeter per second.

Annie's hand went to cover her gaping mouth.

"Oh, my goodness. What are we doing here? What am I doing up here?"

"So, you know where we are?" David's smile covered the width of his face as he sat in the front row, separated from her by the orchestra pit.

She knew the place well. Rows and rows of seats in three sections on the lower level, five sections of chairs in the balcony, and four sections in the mezzanine with its concave front wall.

"Of course. We're in Reynolds Auditorium. But what am I doing standing on stage?"

He kept her in suspense still as she looked around. Behind her was a huge, whimsical, painted backdrop that featured a floating staircase so realistic she might have tried to climb it had she not been glued to the stage. Shock paralyzed her.

"What is this?" she called to David over her shoulder. "It's like something out of a dream."

"Well, in a way, it is," David said as she faced him again. "That's a backdrop the school is using for *The Nutcracker*. I plan to bring you when it opens in December."

"They're performing *The Nutcracker* here? Oh, how wonderful." Heartache crept in and threatened joy. For years, she'd imagined herself being Clara on stage. But those days had passed.

"The production is the last big event in honor of the town's two hundredth anniversary, I hear."

What a way to cap off the celebration. There had already been several events over the past year, in honor of the bicentennial. She'd even heard that Reverend Billy Graham would be speaking at the Memorial Coliseum in November for the Festival of Thanksgiving. Now *The Nutcracker*, too? But her question remained. "David, what are we doing here? It isn't to watch a show. And how did you even get us in this place?"

"Easy enough." He shrugged. "I called around, made some arrangements. Tonight, I want you to enjoy the stage, Annie. It's all yours." He spread his arms wide, then rested them on the seatbacks beside him. "You deserve to be the star of the show, and that's why we're here. You've become the star of my life, and I want to celebrate you tonight. You've lost or been forced to give up so much, and I want you to remember what the spotlight feels like. I want to watch you dance."

"You want me to dance? Up here? Now?"

"I have some friends helping me. There's someone backstage for the sound and someone back there for the lights." He pointed over his shoulder with his thumb. "But pretend they're not here. You can even pretend I'm not here if you want. This is all about you."

He was serious. The dream was real.

Annie looked down. Maybe her black pumps would work? No, not on this magnificent stage. It would be all wrong.

"But I can't." She pointed at her feet.

"Why not? Just go behind the backdrop, stage left."

She tiptoed across the stage and found a pink box where David had told her to look.

The black polyester of her baby doll dress tented over her knees as she squatted down and lifted the cardboard lid. She gasped. Brand new ballet shoes the same color as the box. She stroked one of the shoes as though she were petting a rabbit. How did he know? She'd never had a satin-covered pair. Only canvas.

"David," she said, bringing her attention back to where he sat straight, his forearms now draped across the armrests. "These are expensive shoes. And they're my size."

"Of course. You can't dance in wrong size shoes."

Her hands shook as she slipped them on and tied the ribbons around her ankles. Even if this was the only time she ever wore them, these shoes would be special forever.

"How do they feel?"

"Amazing."

"Ready?"

Her mouth gaped. "I—"

"C'mon, Annie. You know you want to dance."

She took a deep breath and gave a decided nod.

David held up his arm, and a bright light appeared. In the glare of the spotlight, David disappeared in the shadows. Annie walked to the middle of the stage where the beam of light rested.

Two hand claps sounded in front of her, and the music soon followed, first as the soft plucking of strings and then the unmistakable plinking of a celesta.

Tchaikovsky. *The Dance of the Sugar Plum Fairy.* "My girls used to do this for recital."

The familiar music awakened part of her soul and sent a charge to her feet, and she began to move. Annie pulled each step out of the recesses of her mind, just before it was time for the next one. Had anyone asked her yesterday, she would have told them that dancing again would only cause pain. That if she couldn't live it, she wanted to forget it. But the use of her body in such a way, the way she'd always thought it was meant to be used, was healing.

She'd lost her form, and her pointe was weak, but it didn't matter. Perfection was secondary to passion, and she had much of that.

The song came to an end, and Annie stood center stage, head down, hugging herself.

The house lights came up. David sat in the front row. Tears streamed down his face.

"You're magnificent, Annie. The most beautiful thing I've ever seen."

"Can we let the record play?"

He smiled and lifted an arm again. The lighting changed once more and at the sound of his clap, the music started. Could his friends see her dancing, too? Whoever they were, she wanted to thank them later. For now, she just wanted to dance.

Twisting, turning, bending, leaping—she did it all with abandon, only briefly wondering what she looked like on stage in her sleeveless, knee-length dress and those gorgeous shoes. She even danced to the songs written for male dancers and made up the steps as she went.

Perspiration gathered at the base of her neck. How glad she was that she had worn her hair up. Song after song she breathed in the music and exhaled with graceful movement. It would probably be the last time she danced on any stage, and she made it count.

The only thing that could make the evening more perfect was if they had her favorite Elvis record, too, but she hadn't told David about her "Peace in the Valley" routine.

When Annie had danced herself into exhaustion, she held the final pose until the last note, then she stood and shaded her eyes facing the audience. The houselights came on again and that magical beam of light that had chased her around the stage went away. And there was David. He stood and began to clap, starting slowly and then building to enthusiastic solo applause. The distance between them felt like miles. He had done this for her. He'd given her this incredible gift, and she needed to wrap her arms around him.

David held up a finger, then sprinted to right of the auditorium, the tails of his suit coat flapping behind him. Soon, he was there, in the wing. She met him halfway in an embrace.

"Thank you for this. Thank you so much. Tonight has been simply amazing."

His lips touched her ear. "You are incredible, and I'm so blessed to have you in my life. It was a joy to watch you dance, Annie. I love you."

"I love you, too, David."

She could stay there forever, in his embrace, except the other part of her heart was at home sleeping.

"What time is it?"

He held his wrist toward her.

"Oh, we've been here for almost an hour."

"I know you're anxious to get home to Thomas, but there's one more thing I want to do."

"More? This has been so incredible already. What more could you—"

"I wrote a poem for you. And I thought this stage would be a good place for you to hear it." He took her by the hand and led her back to the center of the stage. "It's definitely not Shake-speare, but it's from my heart."

David stood facing her, his dazzling blue eyes shining under the stage lights. He cleared his throat.

"A gem without price, the rarest of treasure," he recited. "A jewel with a worth that no man can measure.

"Flawless, magnificent, one-of-a-kind.

"A fortune that some search the whole world to find.

"In exchange for your love, I'll give you my life." He paused, then added, "My only desire is to make you my wife."

David took a step back and put one knee on the stage. Annie's already weak legs threatened to fail her as David produced a ring from inside his jacket. "Annie, I'll do my best to make you feel like the star of the show every day. Will you marry me? Will you and Thomas be my family forever?"

"Oh, David." She bent slightly at the waist, hardly breathing, taking in the sight of him holding the diamond. The small, marquise-cut stone in a white gold band gleamed. Bright like their future, she was sure.

Her heart screamed yes first, then her brain. Finally, the answer reached her lips. She *did* want to be Mrs. David Hall. Thomas would have the father he deserved. Aunt Brenda was right. Things didn't have to turn out the way she thought they should. Sometimes, they turned out better.

Chapter Twenty-seven

Saturday, December 16, Present Day

THE SQUEAL of air brakes made Missy jump. At least twenty people dressed in church clothes filed out of the bus and passed by them, heading toward the auditorium. Others came from the direction of the parking lot.

She shivered. The choir robe provided an extra layer over her dress slacks and sweater, but the wind still cut through to her skin.

"Ray, snap the picture already," Missy said between gritted teeth.

The man could take a car engine apart and put it back together, but he still looked cross-eyed at a smartphone screen half the time.

"Just give me a sec," Ray said. His finger tapped the screen then he held the phone up again.

Daddy and Mama stood on either side of Missy, next to one of six massive columns reminiscent of ancient Rome. She pursed her lips together and made the corners of her mouth turn upward. On that last one, she may have shown her teeth.

Light flashed from the back of the phone, and Missy slunk back into a natural pose as the kids traded places with Daddy and Mama.

"Ray, check those. I'm not sure you've been needing the flash. It's not quite dark out here yet."

"They're fine, Missy. It's on automatic." He held the phone out in front of him again. "Say cheese, everybody."

The kids pushed closer from all sides and yelled, "Cheeseburger!"

Emma huffed. "Y'all, that's getting old."

She had been the one to start the silly tradition, and now she'd outgrown it. Time marches on.

"Okay, now, let's have one with just my two girls." Daddy motioned for Erica to get in the shot.

"Hey, Mama, I need to ask you something." Joshua tugged on the sleeve of her choir robe.

"Not right now, baby. We're still taking pictures."

Erica stepped by him. "Hey, big guy. We'll be done in just a minute."

Joshua's eyes shined up at her. "Okay, Aunt Erica."

He hopped down the stairs and stood on the sidewalk with the other kids, between Ray and Grandma Annie.

Missy leaned toward Erica and spoke out of the corner of her mouth. "By the time we get done with pictures, it'll be time for the concert to start."

"And this cold air isn't great for your voice."

"I'm more worried about the muscles in my face from smiling."

"Okay, y'all. Get ready," Ray said.

Erica put her arm across Missy's lower back. Missy put her arm over Erica's shoulder. No, that wasn't right. They switched positions. That didn't feel right, either. They let their arms drop to their sides and faced Ray shoulder-to-shoulder.

Dad had his phone out, too, and he looked to already be snapping. Just one more to add to the collection of the oddball pair—the skinny sister and the chubby one, the traveler and the homebody, Miss Confidence and Mrs. Self-conscious. At least in this picture, both would be remembered as talented. Maybe she'd frame it.

"I'm really glad you came, baby sister." And she meant it. With everything in her, she meant it.

"Wouldn't have missed it." Erica gave her a quick hug and a pat on the back.

As the whole family headed toward the entrance of the grand theater, Joshua caught up to her and walked alongside.

"Mama, I have a question."

"I know, honey. Let's find your seats first and then you can ask me." She planted a kiss on the top of his head as they passed through the doorway.

Missy's heels clicked against the marble checkerboard floor of the lobby. Oh, why hadn't she worn flats? No doubt she would sing much better if she still had feeling in her toes.

Inside the auditorium, Ray led them down the aisle, holding John Thomas's hand. Forty-five minutes before the start of the concert and already so many people. Would it really be full at showtime? The nerves hit in a heatwave of nausea.

Missy turned around and waited for Daddy, Mama, and Grandma Annie to catch up.

"I'll help her, Daddy."

Missy took Grandma's arm, and Daddy and Mama went ahead.

"Hey, Grandma"—Missy leaned close and whispered—"remember how you prayed for me the day of Daddy's birthday party?"

Grandma Annie stopped in the middle of the aisle and smiled.

"Well, I figure it can't hurt tonight either," Missy said.

Grandma patted her cheek. "You got it, honeybee."

They started again, each painstaking step taking longer than the last.

"I never told you, I don't think," Grandma said.

Missy's stomach tightened. *No more secrets. Not tonight.*

". . . this is where your Grandpa David asked me to marry him."

"That's awesome, Grandma. No, you never told me. I bet it's a great story."

Tears shimmered in her eyes. "It's the best story. I promise to share it soon." Grandma Annie paused again, her eyes fixed on that big stage filled with risers. "Oh, I miss him so. There was no one else like him in the world." She sighed—a sound full of deep love and great loss—and started moving again.

When they reached the rest of the family, already filling a row of the brown fabric-covered folding seats, Missy helped Grandma Annie ease into a chair, then she said goodbye. She wouldn't see her family again until after the performance, so Missy drank in their words of encouragement. She slipped into the empty row behind them and side-stepped toward the other end until she reached Joshua's seat.

"Hey, real quick, baby." Missy sat. "What was it you needed to ask me?"

He rotated to face her and held onto the back of the chair. "Mama, Christmas is Jesus' birthday, right?"

Oh, goodness. Now?

"Um, yeah, that's why we have Christmas. Why?"

"Because Grandpa says that Jesus *is* God. But I've been wondering, if God created everything and lives in heaven, why was he born here as a baby?"

Aunt Erica on his right, and Piper on his left, seemed interested in the answer too.

"Well, honey, that's a really good question, but I have to get ready for the concert right now. We'll sit down and talk about it soon. Okay?"

Her son's face fell.

"Hey, I got this one, sis." Erica looked over her shoulder and smiled. "You go on and get ready." Erica put her arm across Joshua's shoulders.

Missy paused. She needed to get backstage for warm-ups, but what on earth would Erica tell him? The two of them hadn't talked about matters of faith, or the lack thereof, in . . . probably ever.

"Grandpa is right about Jesus being God," Erica said.

Missy scooted three seats down to the end of the row and waited.

"So, about your question; the simple answer is *love*," Erica said. "Jesus could have stayed in heaven where everything was perfect. But he chose to come down here as a baby because we needed a Savior, and He was the only one that could save us from our sins."

Is that what Mary Sue Montgomery had taught her in Sunday school? Is it what Daddy and Mama had told her all her life? It sounded *right,* yet too simple. And did Erica really believe everything she was telling Joshua? Missy wanted so badly for it to be true.

Erica continued, but Missy slipped out of the seat and scurried toward backstage. Time to get ready to sing.

*   *   *

"There's my star soloist." Henry greeted her in the warm-up room with his arms open. His voice was extra high-pitched. "How ya feeling about getting on that stage in a little while?"

"I'm not sure how I'm feeling, Henry. Mostly, ready to get it over with, I think."

Her head was so cloudy with confusion. Would she even remember the words?

"Oh, c'mon. Everything is gonna be all right. Better than all right. Fabulous. Here's the lineup." He handed her a program. "We're the third choir to go on in the first set. Then after intermission, we sing first. That's when we do *O Holy Night*."

"I know, Henry. You gave us the schedule before rehearsal last night."

"Just making sure. Now, we're just going to do a quick warm-up, then we'll wait back here until performance time."

Henry rushed to the music stand at the front of the room and tapped his wooden baton on the metal lip. Choir members stopped their chattering and faced the front of the room.

"All right, everybody. Let's get those pipes ready for our best praise, shall we?"

Everyone found a chair in their section. Carolyn and Wanda moved from the alto row down to the sopranos. When all the moving stopped, the pianist played a chord, and the normal warm-ups began.

Missy held back on the high notes. It would do no good to strain her voice before the solo. During the performance, she'd have to go clear up to the rafters and hold the note for two full measures. She nearly cracked every time.

After warm-ups, they sat, and the paper in Missy's hands rattled. She put it in her lap and gripped at the sides of her chair.

Carolyn, who wore Christmas-red lipstick and a kind smile, turned to her. "Hey, there. You doing okay? Nervous?"

"A little." Missy pushed at her glasses.

"Me and Wanda were just fixing to pray. I know I could use a boost of confidence. Wanna join?"

"Oh—um, okay. Sure."

Wanda smiled at her from the seat on Carolyn's left. She sat with her knees pointed toward Carolyn, and Missy copied. She closed her eyes.

The room continued to buzz around them, while Carolyn spoke just above a whisper, in the same tone she'd used with Missy. Like talking to a friend. It was so simple. A request for calm nerves and clear voices. Then Carolyn's voice raised.

"Let everyone in the auditorium feel Your presence. Let them know Your peace. Let them understand that You see them and that You love them. May our songs remind us all why You came."

Missy thought of Joshua's questions, and of her own. Erica *and* Carolyn had sounded so certain.

"Thank you," Missy said when Carolyn was finished with the prayer.

"You're going to sing beautifully out there." Carolyn reached and tapped her on the knee. "You've helped our choir so much with your talent."

Missy smiled. Maybe, but being part of the choir had helped her more.

*   *   *

"Okay, guys. Intermission is almost over. The first set was wonderful. Get ready to go out there and lift your voices up loud," Henry said.

A faint buzz came from Missy's pants pocket. She gathered the bottom of the robe and reached under to pull out the phone. A text from Ray.

Concert is great. Kids loved seeing you on stage. Little Bit getting restless but we're good.

She put the phone back in her pocket as someone grabbed her elbow.

Henry stepped around in front of her. His powder blue eyes were filled with anticipation. "You ready?"

"I think so."

"Thank you for doing this, Missy. It means a lot to me. Your voice is so lovely, I can't wait to hear you."

His words filled her spirit like air in a balloon. She stood up straighter, adjusted her glasses, smoothed the robe, and pushed the loose curls behind her ears. She smiled. "Okay, I'm ready."

"Hold on, sweetie. It looks like you got a tiny smudge of lipstick on your teeth there." Henry waved a pointer finger in a circle toward her face.

She ducked forward and rubbed at her teeth. "Better?"

"Yeah, you got it. Now go do your thing." Henry winked.

The emcee's smooth, rich voice came over the sound system, announcing the start of the second half of the concert. He welcomed the Bethabara Presbyterian Choir back to the stage.

Here we go.

The auditorium erupted with applause. Missy squinted into the spotlight as she made her way to the microphone at centerstage, trusting that the rest of the choir was filing in behind her. In that dark auditorium, with the blinding light in front of her, the only people she could see were Henry at the director's podium and the pianist at the grand piano at stage right. Everyone else was just a shape in a sea of faceless forms.

The melodic notes of the classic song's introduction made Missy's stomach tighten. Such a balance of beauty and pain in that moment. Art met panic there. The desire to create music faced down fear. The meaning of the song and the beauty of its lyrics collided with her doubt. In that moment before she opened her mouth, something stirred deep inside her.

I see you, Melissa Jo. I see you.

There was no time to answer the voice. The introduction had ended. Henry lifted his arm and cued her.

"*O Holy night,*" she sang, "*the stars are brightly shining.*

"*It is the night of our dear Savior's birth.*"

Perfect. Every note on pitch and beautiful phrasing.

"*Long lay the world in sin and error pining,*

"*'Til He appeared and the soul felt its worth.*"

Even as she sang the lyrics, different words began to work in her mind. It was as if she were two people in the same body. One vocalizing, the other having a silent conversation with herself.

Pining. That's what she had felt in her soul for so long, but she'd only just begun to realize it.

"*Fall on your knees; O hear the Angel voices!*

"*O night divine, O night when Christ was born.*"

The meaning of the words, the power in them, which she had rejected before, screamed to her. Her knees went weak. The weight of what she'd carried—secrets, shame, hurt, jealousy, self-doubt—pressed on her. Then the voice spoke again: *Lay it down.*

The choir came in, backing her up, proclaiming the divinity of that long-ago night with a majestic swell of sound. The chorus behind her fanned the spark of faith that had ignited on the first word of the song.

Was it really as simple as just believing?

The third verse came, and the emotion in her heart pressed its way into her voice. Whether it was good or bad for the performance she couldn't tell, but it didn't matter anymore.

"*In all our trials born to be our friend.*

"He knows our need, to our weakness is no stranger."

She'd always known it. People were weak. They made mistakes. And Sunday school teachers were no exception. All of them—every single one of them—needed a Savior.

The choir joined on the last few lines and their collective voices rang through the huge room with an energy Missy had never heard from them before.

"Christ is the Lord; O praise His name forever!"

She could say it over and over.

"His power and glory evermore proclaim."

She *would* say it over and over.

On the repeat, she held the long high note without wavering and finished strong on the last two words.

Movement came from the sea of forms in front of her as thunderous applause met her ears. They were standing. All over the auditorium, they were standing. And the clapping continued as tears slid down her cheeks.

She looked to Henry who stood with one hand on his chest, his head moving side to side. He gave her a double thumbs up, and with slow, exaggerated movements, mouthed one word: *amazing.*

Yes. Amazing. Grandma Annie had been right. Love could fix everything. Love *had* fixed everything. When Joshua had asked the question of why Christ came, Erica had told him the truth. And now Missy believed it.

Chapter Twenty-eight

September 1968

ADROP OF milk catapulted off a corn flake as Annie poured, and it landed on the counter next to the cereal bowl. She reached for the already-wet dish cloth draped over the sink divider and wiped the milk away as she gave thanks for the hundredth time. Their modern kitchen was so different from the one in her childhood home. Not only was it twice the size, but the yellow counters were so cheerful, and everything had a feeling of *new*. It made cooking and cleaning hardly feel like work at all.

"Honey, come get your breakfast." She set the bowl on the table.

Thomas, in his matching blue pinstripe pajama top and bottoms, ran into the kitchen.

"Mama, can I eat in there? Pretty please? Bugs Bunny and Road Runner just came on."

He stuck out his bottom lip. The new Saturday cartoon had become his favorite, and she couldn't resist that lip or his sweet little voice.

"Okay, I'll bring it. Just be very careful not to spill."

She delivered the cereal to the coffee table in the living room and stepped back into the kitchen as the phone rang. She wiped her hands on her apron and answered.

"Hey, Annie," the voice on the line said.

"Ruth Claire, it's so good to hear your voice. How are you, sweetie?"

"Can I come visit you? And David and Thomas Theodore?"

Annie's chest tightened. "Well, of course. Of course, you can. But is everything okay? Are Brenda and Cleet okay?"

"Yes."

R.C.'s matter-of-fact way didn't make conversation easy.

"Will either of them be coming with you?"

"No."

"Why not?"

"Cleet has to help Aunt Brenda on the farm. But he said he would buy me a bus ticket and drive me to the station. I'll be there next Tuesday. Here, Aunt Brenda wants to talk to you. Love you, Annie. Bye."

Annie managed to get out a farewell just before Brenda's voice came on the line.

"Hello, dear," Aunt Brenda said. "Sorry to spring this on you, but Ruth Claire is insistent. Is the timing okay? It don't have to be next week."

"Next week is fine, and I really want to see her. But she hardly ever wants to leave the horses, and she hates the noises on the bus."

"I think she just misses all of you. It's been a few months now. And she's been talking about Thomas a lot lately. Cleet and I wish we could come, too."

Ruth Claire had always been full of surprises, and this was a happy one. In just three days, Annie'd get to see her.

They worked out the times, then Annie hung up the phone and her mind went straight to planning as she wiped down counters. What kind of fun could she and Thomas and Ruth Claire get into next week? Definitely a picnic at Hanging Rock one day, and an afternoon at Tanglewood Park on another. And she could take R.C. shopping and out to eat. Annie hadn't worked outside the home since the wedding a year and a half ago, so she and Thomas would be free to spend Ruth Claire's entire four-day visit with her. One of the many joys of married life, Annie had been able to see Ruth Claire much more. She and Thomas had spent a week on the farm in the spring and loved it, except for missing David.

Maybe one day she'd start back to work. Maybe even find another job at the school, when Thomas, and any other children she and David might have, were older.

Other children.

She couldn't think of that now. Today was a happy day, not one for tears. She simply had to face facts. If it hadn't happened in more than a year of trying, it might never happen. Thomas was her miracle child in more ways than one, and David loved him as his own.

The door from the carport opened and David came in, his white tee tinted green and sprinkled with pieces of grass. Perspiration covered his well-defined brow.

"Hot out there already, huh?" Annie said as she put ice in a glass.

"Oh, yeah," he said.

She went to the faucet and filled the glass, then handed it to her husband.

"Ruth Claire called."

She'd caught herself before simply announcing that she had news. He might have thought it was baby news. They'd gotten their hopes up so many times.

"She's coming to visit," Annie said. "Next week. Can you believe it? By herself."

"That's great. We haven't seen her in a while. It will be nice to have her."

David set the glass on the table.

"Oh, I can't wait," Annie said. "Though . . . it does seem a little strange."

"What do you mean?"

"She's only visited by herself once before. And she just sounded a little, I dunno, different on the phone."

"Well, honey . . ."

"I know. But trust me. It was different for R.C. What if something is wrong and she's not telling me?"

"I'm sure everything is fine, honey."

David was forever the optimist. He kissed her on the forehead, keeping plenty of space between them, then headed for the shower.

She leaned against the door frame between the kitchen and living room. Her husband was probably right. Thomas sat on his knees beside the coffee table. He put a heaping spoonful of cereal into his mouth just as Wile E. Coyote ran off a cliff, and milk dribbled out and down his chin as he laughed.

R.C.'s eyes shined up at Annie through Thomas's. She heard R.C.'s laughter in his. So much of the little girl whom she had mothered throughout her teen years, though she was only four years older, could be seen in this little boy whom she loved with all her heart. Her miracle son.

*　　　*　　　*

Twenty-one-year-old Ruth Claire was such a different person than the sixteen-year-old girl that had given birth to Thomas. Five years, or marriage, or life in Georgia, or all of it, had changed her. Still beautiful. Still amazingly brilliant and unique. But with a measure of self-confidence Annie used to pray R.C. would have one day. Maybe that was it. Answered prayers.

"I can't believe you're getting' paid so well to break horses, Ruth Claire." Annie dipped a big helping of cherry yum-yum onto R.C.'s plate and slid it across the teak tabletop toward her.

"I don't like that word," R.C. said. "I never use that word. I know what it means, but it sounds bad. We don't break them. We help them. We're good to all the horses."

David smiled at R.C. across the table. "Of course you are. Otherwise, so many people wouldn't bring them to you to take care of. It's certainly impressive, R.C."

She smiled back, but with her face pointed toward her plate.

"I want to go back and ride the horses with Aunt R.C. They're fun," Thomas said. "And I like the goats and chickens, too. Mama, when can we go back to the farm?"

"Maybe in the spring."

"Yay."

Thomas had no idea that spring was months away, or even how long a month was. But he was satisfied, and Ruth Claire seemed to be, too. She shared an excited grin with Thomas.

"We're just so proud of you, R.C.," Annie said. "You and Cleet helping Aunt Brenda on the farm and starting your own business. I know Mama and Daddy would be real proud, too."

After dessert, Annie washed and put the dishes away while Ruth Claire read Thomas his bedtime story, but not before pointing out that the book used to belong to her. She was right, of course, because R.C. never forgot anything. Annie had read the Little Golden Book, *Scuffy the Tugboat*, to R.C many times.

Annie peeked in on them in the living room. They sat side-by-side on the couch, and R.C. held the book with both hands with her arms extended in front of her, elbows locked. Thomas craned his head to see the pictures.

"Thank you for the story," Thomas said as she closed the book. "You read good. But you don't get excited like Mama does when Scuffy goes out into the big ocean."

"Did I do it wrong?" R.C. said.

"No. Not wrong," Thomas said. "Sometimes Mama's loud."

R.C. smiled, and Annie stifled a laugh as she ducked back into the kitchen.

How could a child so young be so perceptive? He hadn't wanted to hurt R.C.'s feelings. Thomas truly was a remarkable boy.

David came out of the bedroom where he'd been grading papers. It was time to tuck Thomas into bed so Annie and R.C. could catch up more. After goodnight hugs and kisses, David took Thomas to his bedroom across the hallway from theirs, and Annie sat with R.C. on the couch in the living room.

"Did you get the letter I sent a couple weeks ago, R.C.? The one with the picture Thomas colored for you, and the photograph?"

"Yes. That's why I came."

Annie set her coffee cup on the end table and sat up straight. "What do you mean, Ruth Claire?"

R.C.'s brow furrowed. She was digging up the words. "The picture you sent. He's getting so big, I wanted to see him."

"Oh. Of course. You're welcome to see him any time."

"Annie . . ." R.C. pulled one knee onto the couch, under the folds of her long, blush-pink skirt, and turned to face her. "Cleet and I talked again about having children. I think he'd love to have a boy like Thomas Theodore."

A knot formed in Annie's throat.

"And what do you think?" Annie kept her tone even. She measured her breathing.

"I think taking care of a baby is hard. But Aunt Brenda and Cleet would help."

"That's true, they would."

"But it hurt a lot, Annie. I remember. I told Cleet I didn't want to do that again."

"And does he understand?"

"I think so."

They sat in silence for a while.

Ruth Claire picked up the storybook again and flipped through it.

Five years. In all this time, no talk of giving birth, or of being Thomas's mother at all. What if she was starting to regret her decision to let Annie be his mother? What if Cleet had decided he wanted to help R.C. raise Thomas? The room began to spin, and Annie felt faint.

Ruth Claire looked up from the book. "Do you want to watch television? Red Skelton should be on now."

"That's it? Wasn't there anything more you wanted to talk about?"

R.C. gathered her long, wavy hair to one side and twisted it into a rope. "Um . . ."

"It's okay, R.C. I just thought you were trying to tell me something else . . ."

No. She'd been *afraid* her sister was trying to tell her something else.

"Oh, yeah. There is something else," Ruth Claire said. "Thomas Theodore will be five years old in four weeks and two days and"—She checked the skinny black watch on her wrist—"one hour and six minutes. If it's okay, Annie, I want to plan his birthday party."

"How sweet, Ruth Claire. But you don't have to do that. We'll have him a little party here with the kids from church and a few from the neighborhood. You're welcome to come back for it."

"But I want to, Annie. I want to do it for him. You get to take care of Thomas Theodore, but I want to do something for him, too. And birthday parties are fun."

Annie drew a slow, deep breath. Her hand inched toward R.C.'s face. Annie stroked her cheek with the back of her fingers, and R.C. didn't flinch.

"I could never deny you something that means so much to you. And you're right—birthday parties *are* fun."

"You can help me with it, and he doesn't even have to know that it's my idea. But I'm going to pay for it, since I make my own money now." Ruth Claire's eyes brightened. "And if I do a good job, maybe you'll let me do it again. Every five years? When he's five, ten, fifteen, twenty, twenty-five, thirty—"

"I understand, Ruth Claire. And I'm sure you'll do a good job. Do you have anything in mind? We don't have much time to plan."

"I want him to have a big party. With a big cake. And I was thinking of a petting zoo, with pony rides. There's room in the backyard. Right, Annie?"

David might not like animals tearing up his grass, but there *was* room. Annie smiled and nodded.

"And balloons. No, I don't like balloons. They're loud when they pop. *Games.* What kind of games would he like?"

Annie chuckled. "Hold on, baby sister. Let me get a pencil and paper. And I guess we'll need the phonebook to search for ponies." She stood, then paused, captivated by the joyful expression on her sister's face.

"You are always full of such fun surprises, Ruth Claire. Just nobody quite like you in this whole wide world."

Chapter Twenty-nine

Sunday, December 17, Present Day

$\mathcal{T}$wo more Sunday morning services at Henry's church. Then what?

Missy supposed it would be time to turn Jeannie Wallace's choir robe over to someone else. One thing she knew: she wanted to be in church somewhere. And she prayed it would be somewhere she could use her voice to praise the One who gave it to her.

She leaned close to the bathroom mirror, and her breath fogged it as she stroked her tiny eyelashes with the bristles on the end of a mascara wand to paint them black. Then she put her glasses back on and inspected the job. *Not bad.* Maybe a little more powder under her eyes and . . . *perfect.*

She closed the compact and dropped it into the pink bag on the bathroom counter as a list of possibilities ran through her mind.

It *might* be Henry's church, or maybe Daddy and Mama's. Maybe somewhere brand-new. The six of them could search together, somewhere that felt right to all of them. She prayed it would be the whole family. But Ray might need time to come around, and she couldn't blame him. She'd take the kids by herself if she had to, but . . .

Ray came back into the bedroom with a stack of folded clothes just as she stepped in from the bathroom.

"Little Bit's on his fourth pancake," he said. "You better go get one before they're gone."

She put a hand on her hip and smiled. "They always eat more pancakes when you make 'em. I can't figure out why yours are so much better."

Ray looked over his shoulder at her as he placed his shirts into a dresser drawer. "I guess it's on account of my secret recipe."

"And why don't *I* know about this secret recipe?"

"'Cause it's a secret."

She laughed.

Missy watched him in the mirror as she put on earrings. He finished putting the clothes away and started to leave the room until she called his name. He looked at her reflection.

"Thank you for making breakfast," she said, then she turned to face him. "You're a good father, Ray, and I don't tell you often enough."

He raised his eyebrows and his eyes got big, then his face relaxed into a look of contentment. "Thank you, honey."

Missy sat down on the edge of the made-up bed and patted at the spot next to her. "Ray, I need to talk to you." *And maybe the kids won't interrupt.*

Noise from the television in the other room meant they were entertained. For now.

Ray hesitated. "Okay."

When he sat, Missy ran her fingertips over the softness of his flannel sleep pants as she rubbed his knee. "You know, this really is a nice bed," she said. She looked back at it over one shoulder then the other. "I think I'll buy some decorative pillows for it."

"Is that what you want to talk about? Pillows?"

"Well, no, but I've been thinking that I—well, I never thanked you for buying it for us."

Ray scooted over and kissed the back of her neck. "Well, you could tell me now . . ."

She giggled. "No, I'm serious."

His playful smile and raised eyebrows said: *So am I.*

She stroked his cheek.

"I need to leave soon, but there are a couple things I need to talk to you about. It's not the ideal time, but . . ."

Now his brow furrowed. "What's up?"

"First of all, last night at the concert, I felt something that I hadn't felt in a long time. It was . . . well, it was God speaking, Ray. That's the only way I can explain it. And I know it might sound strange, but I don't think I ever really *stopped* believing in Him. I think I was just mad and the anger blinded me."

"Was blind but now I see, huh?"

She studied his posture and his expression. Analyzed the tone. There was no sarcasm.

"Yeah, basically."

His breath came out hard then he pulled his lips inward.

What would he say? What would she have said a month ago if the tables were turned?

"I knew you seemed different this morning," he finally said. "And I guess if believing makes you happy, then I *want* you to believe. I don't know exactly how that changes things around here, with us, with our family. But, to tell ya the truth, that music got to me a little last night, too. The words, they get you to thinking sometimes, you know?"

She smiled and nodded. "I know."

Baby steps.

She gave him another few seconds to process, basking in the quiet. He hadn't told her she was crazy, that it was all in her head. He hadn't tried to talk her out of it or remind her how many times she'd scoffed at other peoples' belief. He'd actually hinted that he'd felt God's presence at the concert, too. He may have called it *the music,* but Missy knew it was the Spirit who spoke through those melodies and lyrics, and through so many of the voices that carried them forth. Even through the fingers of the pianist.

She took another big breath. Would the next revelation go as well as the first?

"There's something else that's happened, Ray, and I know it will be surprising. It was a few weeks ago, and well . . . I've been keeping it a secret."

A look of horror spread across his face.

"Oh, it's not really about *me,* honey." She waved her hands back and forth in front of her. Even if had assumed the worse, at least he cared enough to be concerned.

"It's something that I learned about Grandma. But she and I talked and—and we both decided that it's not the kind of secret a wife should keep from her husband. You need to know what I'm going through right now. Same with me. I need to know the things that you go through. So we can help each other. And Grandma trusts you with her secret, too."

"You're scaring me, Missy. Annie means the world to me. What kind of secret could she have that's so serious?"

Missy looked toward the door, then turned back and whispered. "My daddy was adopted, and he doesn't know it. I found some papers that proved that Grandma didn't give birth to him, and then she admitted it to me."

Her own words clamped at the corners of her heart and squeezed.

Ray couldn't have looked more stunned. She knew the feeling.

"Was that the folder that—"

She nodded.

"Ruth Claire is Daddy's biological mother and"—She blew out a breath—"my grandmother. Grandma Annie raised Daddy as her own. And even though she didn't give birth to him, she's the reason I'm alive, that our kids are alive."

Missy told him the whole story—at double speed to get it all out before she had to leave—including the part Grandma Annie had shared only days ago, about how upset Great-Grandma Leeta had been at first over the pregnancy, and how she questioned if the baby should even be born.

Oh, the thought.

But it had been Grandma Annie who had reminded Great-Grandma Leeta of the value of life; and knowing that had given Missy a brand-new perspective on, well, pretty much everything. Maybe that's what had made her receptive to the new life she'd been given last night.

"And if Daddy had been put up for adoption, he wouldn't have grown up here and met Mama. But God had a plan, and He worked all of it out. I see that now. Or I'm starting to."

For a moment it seemed Ray had stopped breathing. He stared at his hands, then looked back to Missy. "This is nuts."

"I know it is. I cried for days when I first found out. It still hurts, but not as bad. I just don't want to carry it alone." She touched his knee again, rubbed the softness of the material between her fingers. "But I don't know if I should tell Daddy. I don't want to hurt Grandma, but I feel like he has a right to know."

Ray sat straight and rubbed at the back of his neck. "Well, if you think about it, you would never have found out if you hadn't been snooping in her things, so . . ."

He wasn't wrong. But how could she just pretend she didn't know?

"And, I guess, you could ask yourself, would *you* wanna find out something like that at his age?"

Somehow, she hadn't asked herself that before.

Ray was so much more helpful than she'd given him credit for. That had been much of the problem in their marriage. Not giving him enough credit. Her nosy, bow-tied little friend had been right.

John Thomas burst into the room like a tiny ninja and jumped onto the bed between them.

"More pancakes, Daddy."

Missy bound up and took a step back. No doubt John Thomas had syrup on his hands, and she wouldn't have time to clean it if he touched her clothes.

"I think you've had enough pancakes, Little Bit," Ray said. "And the kitchen's closed until lunch. Maybe go get a banana."

He scurried out as fast as he'd come in.

Missy stood in front of Ray and kissed him on the top of the head. "It's time for me to go. I know I dropped a lot of big news on you this morning. You okay?"

He wrapped his arms around her waist and pressed the side of his face against her stomach. "Yeah, baby. I'm good." He looked up. "I'm glad you told me all of it."

She eased away from him and slipped her feet into the shoes at the end of the bed. If she didn't leave soon, she'd be late.

"You know, I don't remember ever seeing a picture of your grandma's sister," Ray said.

"We set one out at Daddy's party."

"I must have missed it." He sighed. "It's a real shame we didn't get to meet her. Though I can't imagine what it would be like for you now if she were here. I think the truth would be a whole lot harder if you literally had to come face-to-face with it."

Chapter Thirty

May 1984

A WARM BREEZE made the long-stemmed white roses in Annie's hand dance, and tiny raindrops blended with the tears on her cheeks. The other mourners had long-since left the graveside, but she and Thomas remained, if for no other reason than that her brain wouldn't tell her feet to move. She couldn't leave R.C. alone out there yet.

Thomas's arm rested across her shoulders. Such a fine man he had become.

"Thirty-seven is too young. I'm so sorry, Mama." He handed Annie a handkerchief from his pocket, just like his father did whenever she cried. David had taught him well.

"She'll always be young to me. She was so childlike and innocent. So full of life." Annie turned and pressed her face near the breast pocket of his dark suit jacket. The smoothness of the fabric on one cheek and the handkerchief pressed against the other steadied her. "R.C. thought she could tame any animal. Oh, it was amazing to watch. And she almost could. Almost."

Annie dabbed the corners of her eyes again and looked up at him. "Did I ever tell you about the time I stopped her from petting a timbler rattler?"

He smiled and nodded.

"I never imagined that years later . . ." A metaphysical ache rolled from Annie's stomach upward to her chest, and the muscles along the same path tensed in a sequence like dominoes falling. "She was a horse whisperer, for sure. But that one. That wild one . . ."

"Uncle Cleet said the owner had the horse put down."

Annie sniffled. "I know. And R.C. would have *hated* that. She loved all of God's creatures so much. I wish I could have stopped them. But Cleet was grieving, too."

The spring shower stopped, and the sun broke through the clouds in front of them. Annie reached and grasped the pendant of her sister's necklace that now rested around her neck, as a rainbow popped into the sky in front them in a perfect horizontal bar of colors.

Annie sighed and patted Thomas on the back. "I've never been one to look for signs, son. But I'll certainly take them when God hands them out." She pointed to the sky. "I knew that Ruth Claire was okay and with Him. Now I feel it, too."

She handed one of the roses to Thomas, and they each laid their flower down on the red, just-tilled earth, an offering to her memory.

"Let's go inside," Annie said.

Mother and son linked arms and headed toward the little fellowship hall of the church, where the rest of the family was probably already eating.

"I'll always remember how much she liked to have fun," Thomas said as they walked. "I loved watching her at my birthday parties. So excited. At least the last couple that I remember well. Especially last year. I didn't expect a shindig like that just for turning twenty."

"She loved your birthdays, Thomas. And she loved you so much." Annie stopped and faced him. "Thomas, R.C. wasn't just an aunt to you. She was—she was a very *special* aunt, and she would have done anything in the world for you. I know she didn't show it the way some do, but it was there. From the moment you were born."

"I always liked your sister, Mama." He shrugged and looked off in the distance. "I know she was a little . . ." He locked eyes with Annie again. "Uh—she was unique. Like a really *rad* kind of different, though. Like how she always called me by my first and middle names."

She smiled, trying to reassure him that she believed him. Thomas was genuine, not insincere, and Ruth Claire had been different. She made being what most people considered *normal* seem utterly boring. And the world would be a better place if there were more people like Ruth Claire in it.

The heels of Annie's black shoes began to sink in the moist dirt, and she started walking again, blowing a kiss to Mama and Daddy's graves as they passed. Cleet and Aunt Brenda had been so kind to let R.C. be buried there near them, instead of back in Georgia.

Annie and Thomas entered the white vinyl-sided fellowship hall that sat behind the church and to the left of the graveyard, where family and friends sat at long rows of tables partaking in the customary funeral meal. The spread was true to form for the ladies of their church. Casseroles, fried chicken, sides, cakes, pies. The women who bustled about the kitchen wouldn't stand for anybody to leave grieving *and* hungry.

With their plates filled, Annie and Thomas sat in the metal folding chairs David had saved for them on either side of him at the end of a long rectangular table. The pastor and his wife sat across from David, next to Aunt Brenda and Cleet. Annie took the seat at the very end and Thomas took the one next to his father.

David looked up from his banana pudding and asked her with his eyes if she was okay. She gave him a half smile as she nodded and patted his arm.

Annie thanked the preacher again for a beautiful service then stared at the plate in front of her. It all looked so good, but she couldn't muster the energy to lift the fork.

David nudged her forearm, and she turned toward him. He gestured to the other side of her, and when Annie looked in the direction of his glance, it took a moment for recollection to catch up with her eyes. A man in his late thirties stood near her. He wore a dark suit and a nice smile with maybe just a hint of mischief to it. And his eyes were so familiar. She'd known him once-upon-a-time, she was sure, but the grief had left her in a fog. No. No, it wasn't the grief. It was all those long years. And the eyes were the same as her son's.

"Annie," he said, "I hope you don't mind me coming. I heard about R.C. from one of our former classmates. They'd seen the obituary in the paper and remembered that she and I used to be friends."

"Tommy Jacobs."

He nodded.

Annie extended a shaky hand and he accepted it, holding it in his through a long, awkward silence.

She cleared her throat. "Tommy, this is my husband, David Hall." Annie's breath caught as she pulled her hand away and lifted it toward David and then to Thomas. "And this is our son." Their son and their precious gift. Hers and David's. The only child they shared, though they'd never figured out why other children hadn't been possible. Not that it mattered. The three of them together were as complete as any family could possibly be.

Tommy stepped behind her chair, and she rotated in the seat as he extended a hand to her husband. David stood as he accepted the handshake with one hand and gripped Tommy's forearm sincerely with the other hand. David knew the name of Thomas's biological father, but had he caught the name?

David returned to his seat, his eyes never leaving hers, as Thomas took his gentlemanly turn in standing as David had taught him, his matching eyes smiling.

"Nice to meet you, young man," Tommy said.

"Thomas," her son said. "Thomas Hall." Tommy's hand gripped Thomas's, then relaxed. His Adam's-apple bobbed as he swallowed hard. Annie fought to keep herself in the seat and she tamped down the illogical urge to yell, "He's mine!" and whisk her adult son out of the room. Her stomach tightened and the world around her stood still as her son's hand slid from his biological father's. "It's nice to meet you, too, Mr. Jacobs," Thomas said.

Then it was over. The same polite ritual Thomas had done so many times that day.

But to Tommy Jacobs, it was much more. Tommy knew it and so did Annie.

Tommy came back to the end of the table where he faced her again. She looked to Brenda and Cleet. Thank goodness they were talking with the pastor and his wife and wouldn't expect an introduction to one of Ruth Claire's old friends. Annie pleaded within her heart for Tommy not to say anything that would—

He opened his mouth and she braced herself. "You have a real nice family, Annie." Tommy's words were slow and deliberate. "And your boy is a very handsome young man. I know you're proud."

"Thank you, Tommy." Annie pressed her lips together as tears threatened to spill. "If she could know it, Ruth Claire would be very happy that you came. She was very fond of you."

His eyes narrowed as he smiled. Those eyes. David had always had similar enough features to pass for Thomas's father, but seeing Tommy—would anyone else notice the eyes?

He reached for her hand again and held it while he stared past her to Thomas with a wistful look.

"You have my condolences, Annie." Tommy's voice cracked as he added, "I'm so very sorry."

Chapter Thirty-one

*T*HE LIVING room armchair looked ready to erupt as Missy stood in front of the pile of towels, underwear, and clothes the kids referred to as Mount Saint Laundry. Smaller than Everest, but more volatile.

Piper plopped onto the opposite end of the couch from Emma with a huff. "It's not fair that Emma gets to go shopping with Aunt Erica, just the two of them. I want to go shopping, too."

No sooner had Missy put an end to the boys' latest squabble than the girls had started. Now she had to fold laundry *and* play referee.

"Honey, they've had this planned for a long time. Since Erica wasn't here for Emma's birthday, she wants to take her out as a special treat. Plus, your sister might be buying you a Christmas present. Did you think about that?" Missy shook her head as she held up the white bath towel in the light. Evidence of grease spots and fingernail polish remained. Might as well let Mr. Peanut have this one.

Piper rolled her eyes and flipped her dark hair over her shoulder. "I doubt she's shopping for *my* present. But it's not fair anyway, Mama. Emma gets to do fun things all the time just because she's the oldest. And because she's *your* favorite."

Emma dropped her tablet onto the couch beside her and jumped to her feet. "No way you think I'm the favorite, Piper. That's just plain dumb. You get all kinds of attention. Tons more than me. With all the cute things you say and all your cute little outfits. Everyone *oohs* and *aahs* over you all the time. *Piper Grace this* and *Piper Grace that.*" Emma was incredulous.

Missy dropped the towel she'd been folding on top of the pile and sat on the couch between the girls. "Girls, stop." She held a hand up toward each of them, then with just a pointer finger, directed Emma to sit back down. "Piper. Emma. You have got to understand that there are *no* favorite children in this house. I dislike both of you equally." Missy threw her head back and laughed, then put an arm around each of their shoulders and pulled them close. "I'm kidding. I couldn't resist."

Piper giggled, and the slightest hint of a smile showed on Emma's face.

"Now really. Listen to me. I love all my children as much as is humanly possible. And there's not even a tiny possibility that I love one of you more than the other. Or that I even *like* one of you more. I mean it. I don't have a favorite. And neither does your daddy."

"You promise?" Piper scooted to the edge of the couch and put a hand on her hip.

Missy held a crooked little finger toward Piper. "I pinkie swear."

Piper's hand froze mid-air. "You mean you pinkie swanny, Mama."

Missy paused. "What?"

"You remember, Mama. You told me that Southern women never swear. So we have to pinkie swanny instead."

"So I did, baby girl."

Heavens to Betsy. How many times had her own mother said, "I swanny" to avoid taking an oath? She'd never realized how much it had rubbed off.

"I could have stuck with 'I promise,' but all right." Missy sighed. "I pinkie swanny." She hooked her little finger with Piper's and held the free hand toward Emma. "You in? I can't play favorites with pinkie swannies either."

Emma tossed her head to one side and paused. "All right." She locked little fingers with Missy, completing the chain.

"You are both so talented and special, in your own unique way. Don't compare yourselves to one another. God knew exactly what he was doing when he made you. He wanted the world to have a Piper, and he wanted the world to have an Emma. No mistakes."

"I still wish I could go shopping," Piper said.

"I know you do, but I'm sure you'll get your turn. You could try being happy for your sister."

"Hey, and I might bring you a treat from the store." Emma leaned forward and smiled across Missy at Piper.

"Really? A new lip gloss or a pack of candy?"

"Why not?" Emma shrugged.

"Good girls." Missy squeezed their shoulders again.

"Can I go get ready now, Mom?" Emma said.

"Just one sec. There's something else I wanna say." Missy leaned back against the couch. Maybe it was too much for a thirteen and a ten-year-old. But she needed to say it for herself, too. "I know I don't always act like it, but raising my girls to be the women you're meant to be, and helping your brothers grow into the men they're supposed to be, is the most important job I can think of. Even when I forget it, I know it here." Missy put her hand over her heart. "And I wouldn't trade my job for any other job in the world."

Her girls snuggled close, just like when they were tiny. She kissed them each on top of the head, wishing she could capture every detail of the moment in her memory. They wouldn't always be here. One day, she'd miss the sound of their squabbling. She'd miss those rare teaching moments. She'd miss always having them close enough to hold. This season was proving shorter than she could have imagined on that day her first child was born, especially since she and Emma had done so much of their growing up together. She didn't want to take any moments like these for granted.

Thank you, God, for my children.

*   *   *

"Emma, can you grab that bowl of party mix and put it on the table?"

The heat from the oven smacked Missy in the face as she drew out the second pan of sausage balls. She placed the pan on the stovetop, and the savory smells of baked meat, bread, and cheese made her mouth water and her stomach growl at the same time. "Aunt Erica will be here any minute."

"But we're going shopping, Mama. Not staying here for a party." Emma's brow furrowed.

"I know, but I thought she might want to visit for a few minutes before you go. And I felt like making Christmas food anyway."

That was only half the truth. Whether Erica knew it or not, a reckoning was needed, and hard tasks were always easier with good food at hand.

The grating voice of a kid sitcom character assaulted her ears from the other room. Missy sighed. "Hey, Joshua," she called out, "turn the television down, please."

"Sorry, Mom. I hit the wrong button on the remote," Joshua called as the television quieted.

That had been a close call. So far, she'd kept up the *no yelling* streak for an entire day. She deserved a pat on the back. Sure, they'd only been home from school for an hour, but . . .

The doorbell rang.

She's here.

The defender of the house let out an eardrum-splitting *woof* that continued as an incessant *bark* until Missy opened the front door. "Good boy, Mr. Peanut," Missy said, bending down near his head.

She pushed open the glass storm door and welcomed Erica inside. They managed an honest-to-goodness, two-arm hug before the kids swarmed, yelling greetings. They tried to hug her all at once and nearly knocked her backward.

Erica's white teeth gleamed behind a wide smile as the assault continued. Finally, the mob released her.

"Come on in," Missy said. "Want a snack? I just made sausage balls."

"I can tell. They smell wonderful."

"You smell good, too, Aunt Erica," John Thomas said.

Erica tussled his hair. "Thank you, Little Bit."

Erica followed Missy to the kitchen, and the kids came along in lockstep.

It had been months since her sister had been in her home. And of course, John Thomas had dumped a bucket of building bricks in the kitchen floor just before she got there.

Missy had never even seen Erica's apartment in Nashville. Only pictures. But she imagined that right now it looked as put together and perfect as Erica did. With her pristine makeup and a messy bun that looked anything but messy, plus an ensemble of skinny jeans, a stylish sweater, and knee-high boots, Erica could step onto a magazine cover and fit right in. Missy usually shopped in sneakers and a hoodie.

"Watch your step," Missy said. She pointed to the minefield of colorful plastic bricks.

"Ooh, these look great," Erica said, picking up a sausage ball from the table. "I guess I shouldn't eat too much since me and Emma are going out to dinner before we go shopping, but . . ."

Erica filled the small paper plate with snacks. How she managed to stay so small with her appetite had always been a mystery.

"Want some sweet tea?" Emma asked.

"I'll get a cup," Piper said.

"Thanks, girls." Erica smiled at her nieces.

They all ate while Erica told stories of Nashville and the celebrities she'd run into at shows and around the city. Ten minutes or so passed before Emma asked if they could leave.

"Baby," Missy said, "I know you're anxious to get going, but—I need to talk to Aunt Erica a minute." She raised her brow. "Just us."

The kids must have thought it was about a Christmas surprise, because they darted out of the kitchen without complaining.

Missy sat sideways at the table with her knees pointed toward Erica's chair. The heat on her cheeks was like a beam of sun through a magnifying glass.

"So, what's up?" Erica took a bite of sausage ball.

"Erica, I owe you an apology."

"Missy, I've already forgiven you for what you said on the phone. Forget about it. I was pretty upset at first, but I decided to let it go. I'm not going to let one conversation ruin our Christmas together."

"That's good, but it's—it's not what I'm talking about." She shifted in her seat. There was no other way to do it, than just to do it. "I've been carrying a lot of resentment and for a long, long time. You've been out there living your dream, and as happy as I am for you, I have to admit that, well, I've also been jealous. Like, why couldn't it have been me? Even knowing full well that I would never leave my babies to trade places with you."

Erica blinked. She opened her mouth and closed it again then took a napkin from the table and brushed a stray crumb from her painted lips. "I don't know what to say." Erica leaned forward, her pretty eyes searching Missy's.

"That's okay. I just hope you'll forgive me for being bitter. You must have felt it sometimes. But I've realized, it's not all about being jealous. It's also—and maybe mostly because—I miss you. I miss us. You were such a help to me when Emma was born, even at fourteen. And especially when Piper was born. But then you went to college and so soon after to Nashville."

"I miss y'all, too. All the time. Being away isn't easy, Missy," Erica said. "I'm sorry if I've made it seem like it is."

John Thomas ran into the kitchen and stood next to them, his eyes wide. "Y'all done yet? Emma told me to ask."

"Almost." Missy smiled and gave him a nudge, sending him back to the living room.

"I know you've gotta go," Missy said to her sister, "but there's one more thing." She took a deep breath. "I heard what you said to Joshua at the concert. About Christmas. And I've just been wondering . . . do you really believe all of what you told him? Do you believe the Christmas story?"

"Um, yeah. Of course. I've believed since we were kids." Erica's tone made it sound like a no-brainer, as commonsensical as remembering her address or phone number.

"I guess I assumed you left all that behind when you moved to Nashville."

"You can't leave something that's part of you, Missy. No matter where you go. I mean, I'm not perfect by any means, but I've been reading the Bible more lately, and praying. I haven't made it to a church in a while, but Tamara's dad is a pastor, and we watch the live stream of his service when we're on the road." She leaned even closer. "Don't *you* believe?"

Missy could never have imagined welcoming the question like she did. "Well, I had a lot of doubts for a while, but not anymore," she said. She clasped her hands in her lap and let out a contented sigh.

A sweet, genuine smile spread across Erica's face.

"Since we're on deep subjects, big sister, I guess I owe you an apology, too. And a thank you." Her sweet smile changed to a coy grin as she leaned back and pushed the sleeves of her sweater to her elbows. "Remember when we were kids, how you saved me from getting in trouble when I messed up your painting? And countless other times. I was always pestering you when we were little."

Gracious, the watercolor of the dogwood tree. "I haven't thought of that in years. And yes, you were, but that's all behind us now. Hey, maybe while you're here, we can spend some time together, just the two of us. I'll leave the kids with Ray, and we'll have our own girls' night."

"Sisters' night." Erica popped a handful of party mix into her mouth.

"Sounds good."

"And we can sing in the car at the top of our lungs like we used to," she said as she crunched. "You know, that reminds me. Katy's getting married soon and she's talked about quitting the band. I could put in a good word for you if Justin needs somebody. You've got the talent."

Pride welled in Missy's chest. "It's nice to know I'd have a shot, but I think I'll leave the professional singing to my amazingly talented little sister. My job is here." She tapped the tabletop with one finger. "At home."

Emma tiptoed into the kitchen. "Okay to be in here?"

"Yes, baby. We're done because it's time for y'all to go have fun now." The chair screeched across the linoleum as Missy stood. She began to clean the crumbs and stray pretzels off the table. As she raked a pile into one hand with the other, Erica stood and wrapped her arms around her. The crumbs fell to the floor, and Missy returned her sister's embrace as Mr. Peanut sucked up the food around their feet.

"You're a good big sister, Missy." Erica sniffed from over Missy's shoulder.

Oh, how she didn't want Erica to go. Missy squeezed tighter. She could have gone on talking all night now that the walls had been torn down. Now that she'd unburdened herself of one secret—the hidden resentment and jealousy that God had healed. Soon. They would make time to talk more soon.

Chapter Thirty-two

July 1993

"**M**AMA, THIS is so hard. I wish something would happen already."

Annie's son sat beside her in the hospital waiting room. He pressed the heels of his hands into his face and cupped his fingers over his eyes. When he removed his hands, fast-fading blotches of red marked the area. How she longed to take his pain.

"I know, darling. But when you meet that little girl, all the waiting won't matter one bit. You'll hardly remember it at all. And when you hold her in your arms for the first time, it will be a moment you remember for the rest of your life."

"JoAnn is having such a hard time."

"Your wife and daughter are going to be fine. Your Daddy and I have been praying for all of you."

Annie had been there for hours, and the update Thomas brought her wasn't what any of them wanted. *No progress.*

Without looking at her, Thomas said, "What was it like when you had me, Mama? Was it really rough?" He took a long drink from his bottle of water.

Annie looked to David on the other side of her. He squeezed her hand and gave her a reassuring smile.

"Oh, your birth was a hard delivery, for sure, but worth every bit of the pain, a hundred times over."

"Thanks, Mama." Thomas leaned over and kissed her cheek. "I better get back in there. I'll update you again soon."

David stood and grabbed Thomas in a hug. "We'll keep praying, son."

As Thomas walked away, Annie felt herself spiraling. This happy day was bound to bring out complex emotions. She'd tried to prepare herself.

"Stay calm. I know what you're thinking." David caressed her forearm.

"I didn't lie, did I?"

"No, Annie. We've been over this a thousand times." He spoke close to her ear. "You are his mother, and I am his father. You've never actually told him that you gave birth to him. You didn't lie. And it would do more harm than good now if he knew."

The family on the other side of the room surely knew she had a secret, despite how she and David whispered, and the fact that the family appeared otherwise focused on the game show on television.

"I know you're right." She laid her tired head on David's shoulder. "I never want to hurt our boy. But I don't want to be guilty of breaking the ninth commandment either."

"You're only guilty of loving your son and taking wonderful care of him for his whole life and teaching him how to be the amazing parent we know he's going to be. You and I are about to be grandparents, Annie. Just focus on that."

The thought brightened Annie's spirit. She sat up straight and pulled her shoulders backward, tensing all her muscles on the inhale and relaxing them as she breathed out. They were going to be grandparents soon.

"I'm going to go find coffee, sweetheart. Do you want to go with me?" David asked.

"I think I'll stay, just in case. Bring me a cup?"

He patted her hand and smiled. "Be back in a flash."

As soon as David had left the waiting room, Tom Brokaw's distinctive voice pulled her attention upward. Time for *Nightly News* already? She'd been in that same room since the noon report but had mostly ignored the television mounted high in the corner, preferring to flip through old copies of *Southern Living* and *Better Homes and Gardens*.

"Political news this evening out of North Carolina," Brokaw said. "State Senator Julian Lane, often touted as the likely winner of the next United States senate race in the state, is under investigation due to allegations of tax fraud. This news comes on the heels of the senator's damaging admission of an extramarital affair. With more on this story, let's head to our Southeast correspondent..."

As the image on the screen switched to a shot of Julian, shielding his face from cameras as he got into a car, thirty years vanished. In her mind, she saw him just as he was outside the dance studio when he'd told her there was someone else.

Annie had seen him in person only twice since that day, though a few times on television. The last time—about eight years back—she'd been at work, just like the time before at Thalhimers. As administrative assistant at the School of the Arts, she'd helped coordinate use of facilities there for a campaign stop, and she would never forget the look of regret in his eyes when he saw her.

David entered the room holding a Styrofoam cup in each hand. He must have read her face because he froze and looked to the television.

"Wow." David took the seat that Thomas had sat in before. "That fella's got himself in some trouble, huh?"

There were so many things he could have said. *Aren't you glad you didn't marry that guy? It's a good thing you have me instead of that slimeball. Look at how your old boyfriend turned out—mister bigtime politician involved in another scandal.* But David's words were true to his heart—an honest statement without guile or malice, and even with a hint of empathy. That's why she loved him.

She patted his knee and rubbed at the soft cotton of his slacks. There was no comparing her forever love to her first love. How true that all things work out for good, and unanswered prayers are sometimes a gift from a merciful, all-knowing Father.

The news switched to a story on the winner of the Tour de France—a third-time champion from Spain. David reached for her hand as the piece ended, his head leaned back, and his eyes closed. She bowed her head. He didn't have to ask her to pray with him. She just knew.

After a while, her earnest praying became peaceful snoozing, though it wasn't long. When she opened her eyes, the clock on the wall read only a few minutes later than the last time she'd checked. Just then, Thomas appeared in the doorway of the waiting area and called to them, his mouth turned up beneath his dark mustache.

"She's here. The baby is here, and they're both doing great."

Annie and David met Thomas in the middle of the room in an embrace.

Joy bubbled up in Annie's chest and spilled out as happy tears. "We're so thankful."

"I'll come back and get you when we're ready for company, okay?"

Annie nodded at Thomas, then he was gone.

If only Ruth Claire could have been here on this happy day. Another thought sprang up in Annie's mind. "David, do you have the phone card in your wallet?" Annie said.

He reached into the back pocket of his slacks in response.

"I'm going to go call Cleet," Annie said. "He'll want to hear the good news."

*   *   *

"She's perfect, Mama. She's just perfect."

Her grown-up Thomas stood, holding his little girl with such tender care. He was a natural, cradling her body and supporting her head, and Annie's heart grew full to overflowing at the sight them.

"Do you want to hold her?"

"Oh, you know I do. But first . . ."

Annie walked to the side of JoAnn's bed. Her daughter-in-law's eyelids sunk halfway down over her green eyes, and her wispy brown bangs clung to her forehead.

"Thank you for bringing this little one into the world for all of us to love on. You did good, sweetheart."

JoAnn smiled up at her, and Annie kissed her on the top of the head then went to Thomas. David stood beside him admiring the baby.

"What's her name?" Annie said. "You've had us guessing this whole time."

"Mama, this is Melissa Jo." He placed the wrapped-up baby in her arms. The weight of the child, the newness of the skin, the fineness of her hair, the overwhelming miracle of new life, it all took her back thirty years to an old farmhouse in Georgia where she had held Thomas for the first time. Instant love filled her heart just as it had that day.

David put his arm around her and kissed her cheek. He stroked the top of Melissa's head. "She's beautiful, isn't she?" David whispered.

"Beyond words."

Annie lifted her granddaughter close to her face. "God has great things in store for you, little one. I believe it with all my heart."

Chapter Thirty-three

Sunday, December 24, Present Day

"*A*ND THE *angel said unto them, Fear not: for, behold, I bring you good tidings of great joy, which shall be to all people.*" Daddy's voice rang through Missy and Ray's living room, and it carried a joyful tone that no doubt matched the angels on that long-ago night.

"Hey, that's what they said in the Christmas pageant at church this morning," Joshua said. His eyes sparkled.

"That's right, buddy." Ray gave Joshua a thumbs up.

All the kids had especially liked the nativity play at Henry's church.

"*For unto you is born this day in the city of David a Savior, which is Christ the Lord,*" Daddy continued. He sat beside the Christmas tree, perched on a stool that had been brought in from the kitchen, and the kids sat on the carpet in front of him in a row, with their knees pulled up to their chests and their heads tilted toward him. The light of the tree and the excitement of the season made their faces glow.

The girls sat shoulder-to-shoulder, looking so much like Missy and Erica had when they, as children, had listened to Daddy read the Christmas story.

"I love our Christmas Eve tradition," Missy whispered in Ray's ear. "And it means more this year than it ever has before."

He snuggled in closer on the couch and put his arm around her. "Merry Christmas Eve, baby."

When the reading was over, the kids scattered, and Missy turned to Mama on the couch. "How's the shoulder today?"

Mama smiled and lifted her arm away from her body, stopping just short of a right angle.

"It's pretty good, baby." She patted Missy's knee. "I'm getting there. Slowly. I've even been playing a little piano. As a matter of fact, I think it's time for a sing-along right now."

Missy waved toward Erica who stood behind Grandma Annie's chair. "Hey, baby sister, you up for a duet?"

"How about 'Silent Night'?" Erica said.

Missy smiled and nodded as she stood.

For sure, the piano would be out of tune. Christmas was almost the only time it was used. But even those bad keys were part of the tradition, and this year, Erica wouldn't sing alone.

Missy and Erica stood beside the upright piano as Mama sat down on the wobbly bench. Mama started low and played a run up the keyboard for an intro. On the first verse, Missy lead and Erica sang low harmony. On the second, Erica took the lead and Missy surprised herself by finding the high harmony. The whole family joined for a final verse, all gathered there, and when the song was over, the skin on Missy's arms was covered in goosebumps.

As soon as the clapping ended, Joshua said, "Hey. Me and John Thomas have a song, too."

"Yeah," John Thomas said. "Wanna hear it?"

Before anyone could answer, the boys broke out with a spirited version of "Grandma Got Run Over by a Reindeer" and the room filled with laughter.

"Just which one of your grandmas are you singing about?" Grandma Annie said.

The boys covered their faces and giggled, and their mischievous expressions made Missy think. She hadn't posted a single thing on social media all day. Not one. She'd been too busy enjoying her family. There needed to be more days like this, making fun memories, and less time spent manufacturing memories to get a reaction from people she barely knew.

Missy checked her phone but only to see the time. It was getting late. Most of the family headed to the kitchen for one more cookie or sausage ball before calling it a night as she went to Grandma sitting in Ray's recliner and whispered. "Grandma, do you feel like coming out to the garage with me for a minute?"

Grandma drew her head back and raised her shoulders, giving Missy a wary look.

"No, it's not that." Missy laughed. "I promise, I've given up smoking for good. Just come with me."

Missy helped Grandma up, then they went through the kitchen and threw out the excuse of "Christmas secrets" as they went to the garage.

"I want to give you a Christmas present," Missy said as she closed the door behind her. She stepped close to Grandma and looped their arms together.

"I thought we were exchanging gifts tomorrow at your daddy and mama's."

"We are, but this is something special I want to give you tonight. And it's a secret."

Missy pulled the unwrapped gift from her pocket and placed it in Grandma's hand.

"It's a key." Grandma cupped her fingers over the piece of metal and her eyes filled with questions.

"Yes, but not just a key. It's a key for a safe deposit box I rented for you. And I have a key, too. You and me and no one else."

Missy grasped Grandma's hand that held the key as understanding flashed in Grandma's eyes.

"And you'll keep my papers for me there?"

Missy nodded. "And whatever else you need to keep."

"Does this mean—"

"Yes, Grandma," Missy whispered, pressing their foreheads together. "You were right. It would do more harm than good to tell Daddy now. So, Ray and I will keep your secret safe, at least until—well, I don't like to think about it. But at least until after you and Daddy have both gone to be with Jesus. Until you're with Grandpa David and Ruth Claire." She straightened. "I don't know how things like that work in heaven. Maybe she'll get to tell him herself. But what I *do* know is that he won't be hurt or upset about it up there."

Grandma's lips parted and the corners turned up. She looked like a prisoner set free. Like she'd stepped into the sunshine for the first time in ages, and she radiated joy. Grandma pressed her forehead now onto the top of Missy's shoulder, and Missy laid her cheek on Grandma's soft hair.

When they faced each other again, they had tears in their eyes.

"I have something for you, too, Melissa." Emotion doubled the shakiness in her voice. Grandma moved her glasses and wiped the tears. "I was planning on giving it to you tomorrow, but it's in my purse, and I think now is the right time. Let's go in. This garage is chilly, anyway." She smiled.

Missy helped Grandma into the house and followed her back to Missy and Ray's bedroom where everyone had laid their coats and purses on the bed. Grandma sat on the bed, reached inside her purse, and pulled out a small, black velvet bag. It had a drawstring closure, and Grandma worked to separate the fabric at the top. She retrieved the gift from inside and held it out toward Missy.

"Oh, Grandma, it's your locket. The one you wear all the time."

Missy sat down beside her.

"Yes, dear. This is very special to me." She ran her finger over the chain in Missy's hand. "I gave it to Ruth Claire when I left her in Georgia, right after your father was born. I've worn it ever since she died, to have her close to me."

Emotion clamped down on Missy's throat.

"Are you sure you want me to have it now, Grandma?"

The gift was too special, too valuable. There was too much meaning behind it. She wasn't worthy of such a gift.

"There's no one else that I'd rather have it. Now that you know what Ruth Claire is to you, maybe this necklace will make you think of both of us. And there's a special verse written inside, on a little piece of paper. I hope it will be special to you, too. One day soon, I'll tell you the story about why I did that."

"Oh, I'd love to hear it." Missy worked to secure the clasp behind her neck. "I've been enjoying your stories so much. Until a few weeks ago, I thought I knew everything there was to know about you. I guess I thought your life didn't start until I was born."

Grandma chuckled. "Well, it did improve a whole lot after that. But you know what's funny? Most people don't even know all there is to know about their own selves. But God does. He knows what we're gonna do before we do it—right and wrong. Makes it all the more amazing that He loves us so much, doesn't it?"

Missy nodded. It sure did.

"Thank you for the necklace, Grandma. I love it. And I'll take real good care of it. I promise. One day, I'll give it to one of my girls, and I'll tell them how brave you were for our family. How you sacrificed for us. And how strong and brave Ruth Claire was, too."

Grandma squeezed her hand, and its familiar warmth made Missy smile.

"Knowing that someday your children will hear Ruth Claire's story, too, well, that's a gift I never knew I needed. My sister was an amazing person, and she deserves to be remembered."

Missy turned as Erica peeked around the doorframe. "Speaking of amazing sisters . . ."

Erica smiled. "Grandma, you about ready to go? Daddy asked me to check."

"Oh," Grandma Annie said with a slap of her hands against her knees, "I guess I need to go tuck him in before Santa Claus comes."

What a precious thought. Though she was only joking, at sixty, Daddy was still her baby.

He always would be.

Missy gave her grandmother a kiss on the cheek. "I love you, Grandma."

"I love you, too, sweetheart."

Behind them, Erica gathered up coats and pocketbooks as the whines and cries of children who didn't want the night to end came down the hallway. Missy understood how they felt.

Grandma used Missy's offered hand to push herself into a standing position, then she turned back with a wry grin.

"I couldn't have done that on that old waterbed, you know." She winked.

286

Missy chuckled. "You're right about that, Grandma."

She helped Grandma into her fluffy black coat with the pretty Christmas wreath pinned to it. Soon it would be time to put her own children to bed.

"Hey, whatcha got there?" Erica stepped toward Missy and pointed at the locket around her neck. "Is that Grandma's necklace?"

"Um, yeah. It's a Christmas present."

"That's so sweet. And it looks great on you."

Erica's gorgeous brown eyes sparkled. Not a hint of jealousy or insincerity. Just sisterly love that Missy treasured now more than she ever had.

She gave Erica a side hug as Grandma watched with the most contented smile.

Maybe someday Missy would tell Erica about the locket, explain how much it meant. Maybe she'd share Grandma's secret when she and Erica were both old and gray.

No.

Even then she'd protect her, like a good big sister. She'd bear the truth for them both.

Missy lifted the locket and looked down, rubbing the etched cross in the center with her thumb. *Someone* needed to know about Grandma and R.C., and about Great-Grandma Leeta and her sister, Brenda, who had taken R.C. in to live with her.

She'd write it down for her girls. That's what she'd do.

And she'd keep the written record in the safe deposit box with the adoption papers—the story of how an unplanned baby was given a chance, thanks to a group of brave women who saw more value in God's creation, and in family sticking together, than they saw trouble in their circumstances.

For now, she'd honor them by living out the lessons they had taught. By continuing their legacies of love.

Epilogue

A CHRISTMAS MIRACLE—THAT'S what the children called it. Missy had to agree. Only once before had she seen snow on Christmas day. And this wasn't just any snow. The falling flakes looked like floating chicken feathers, and all of them had accumulated into a solid foot of white, wintery goodness. While the kids played outside, she and Ray exchanged gifts, sitting side-by-side in the floor of their living room with their backs propped against the couch.

"You did good picking out my new boots, honey," Ray said.

"I'm glad you like them. And I love the new scarf." She stroked the fluffy, multi-colored fabric. "I can't believe you went to the mall for it."

"Well, there's a couple more gifts to open. Why don't I go check on the children, then I'll get your other presents." Ray winked as he stood.

Missy's jaw dropped and she smiled up at him with her eyes. He'd already given her so much, the best of which was his promise to start going to church as a family. If there were no gifts at all, wrapped with paper and ribbon, she would have been just as happy.

Ray came back carrying a printed shirt box with a red bow. "Kids are fine. Happy as pigs in slop out there." He handed her the box.

Missy slid her index fingernail under the edge of the box lid and split the tape. The tape on the other side acted as a hinge as she opened the lid and pulled back the white tissue paper. She ran her fingers over the black sequined top inside. Rows and rows of shiny adornments that sparkled in the light of the Christmas tree. A quick peek at the tag confirmed he'd even bought the right size.

"Ray, it's beautiful."

"I thought you could wear it to regional conference, for when they call your name for that level-up ceremony."

"Yes, it's perfect. Thank you. I can't wait to wear it." She leaned and gave him a peck on the lips.

"I bet it won't be quite as exciting now, though, since you're already use to being on a big stage."

Missy laughed. Such a sweet and thoughtful gift, she could hardly believe it. And it really was an exquisite blouse.

"Okay, let's get this paper cleaned up, then go play outside." She placed her fist on the floor and leaned onto it as she swept her feet behind her and pushed herself up on her knees.

"Not so fast. There's one more." Ray stood and slid a large box from behind the couch.

"What? How long has *that* been there?" Missy's bottom came down and squished the heels of her fuzzy slippers.

He grinned and laid the box on the carpet in front of her.

Missy's heart raced as she reached under a flap of paper on the end of the box and ripped. A peek at the outside of the box left her gasping. "Ray! This is unbelievable. A *guitar*? But how?" The picture on the box, of a smiling musician and the gorgeous instrument, filled her with joy. "Did Henry tell you I wanted a guitar?"

"Henry? No, you did, silly."

"What are you talking about? I've never mentioned wanting a guitar."

"Sure, you did. Back when you were pregnant with Emma." He sat on the edge of the couch and leaned forward. "The first Christmas we were married. I couldn't afford it then, but I remember you said that, even if you *could have* the guitar you'd always wanted, your pregnant belly would get in the way anyhow."

Missy shook her head, and her hand rested on the box as if it would disappear if she didn't keep hold of it. "You remember a conversation from thirteen years ago?"

"Maybe not all of them, but I remember that one for some reason. Something about the way your eyes lit up when you talked about learning to play."

Now her eyes welled with tears, and her hands shook until she clasped them together.

"Well, open the box. Let's see it," he said.

Ray helped her remove the thick cardboard lid. Missy gasped again, then pressed one hand against her chest. The acoustic guitar inside had a honey-colored finish and the inlay around the sound hole was a gorgeous, iridescent abalone. She lifted the instrument from its foam packing, closed her eyes, and brushed her fingernails across the metal strings.

She laid the guitar back in the box as the sobs reached her throat.

"Hey, what's the matter? I thought you'd be happy." He sat on the floor near her.

"Oh, Ray. I *am*. I'm so happy. It's just . . ." Missy fought to catch her breath. "Y'all have never gotten in the way. I hope you know that." She sniffed and rubbed at her eyes. "That stretched-out belly *would* have made it hard to hold a guitar, but my family has never gotten in the way of me doing anything important. Y'all *are* what's important. And I wouldn't change a single part of my life if I could. None of it. I hope you know that."

"I know it, honey," Ray said, bringing his forehead to hers. "I know you wouldn't. I wouldn't either."

She reached up and touched his cheek and he did the same. In that moment, more love filled Missy's heart than her seventeen-year-old-self could have ever imagined.

The sliding door to the patio slammed closed, and they looked toward the doorway of the living room. All four kids gathered there, talking at the same time while stomping their wet shoes. Clumps of snow fell around them, but Missy was too happy to yell.

"Oh, cool guitar," Emma said. "Is it yours, Mom?"

"Yep. She's all mine." Missy patted the edge of the box. "Wasn't it sweet of your daddy?"

Ray smiled.

The kids gathered round, each begging to try the guitar as Missy moved to sit on the sofa, then rested the instrument across her knees. She promised each they'd get a turn later, after she'd had a chance to play, and Ray offered to make hot chocolate for them to have while they waited.

"So, what song do you think you're gonna learn first?" Ray said as he stood and stretched.

"I know exactly what song to learn." Missy strummed her nails over the strings again as she smiled up at her husband. "My new favorite song—'Amazing Grace.'"

THE END

Author's Note

WHEN I WAS A LITTLE GIRL, traveling an hour away to Winston-Salem was an event to be anticipated and remembered. Winston-Salem had a mall with toy stores and fancy clothing shops. The city had Krispy Kreme doughnuts and an arcade. It felt big and important and being there made me feel the same way. Winston-Salem was where people went if they were very sick, often transported from our much smaller hospital to the one referenced in this book. And it's where we took school field trips to Old Salem, to learn more about our state's history and to see how Moravians lived in 1753. I traveled to Winston-Salem just to have a "fancy" dinner before my high school proms, as did many in my small town.

Winston-Salem is where lots of people from my neck of the woods migrated because there's not much work to be found in a small town unless you're a teacher, police officer, nurse, or mechanic. Such was the case for me years ago when I moved to the outskirts of the city. For many years, my home has been the town of Lewisville, near the highway that leads me a short drive into the heart of downtown, or the other direction, back home to the foot of the mountain. I remember when the highway to Winston-Salem was a two-lane road, and that hour drive seemed to take at least two. Now I drive an easy forty minutes at least once a week, often more, on a four-lane road, back home to the church I grew up in.

While I'm proud to be a Wilkes County native (from just across the Surry County line), I love that my children are Forsyth Countians by birth. There's a rich history here, just like the rest of the state, and much to be proud of, like having the first Arts Council in the country—a fact that is referenced in the story. For those of you who also call this city or the surrounding area home, and to those who have been fortunate enough to visit, I hope you enjoyed the references to actual businesses and landmarks, and I trust you'll find them accurate.

Winston-Salem has been known by many names. Where I come from, people just say they're headed to "Winston." Some people call it "The Twin Cities," since it was formed from a merger of Winston and Salem in 1913. Camel City is a popular moniker—a reference to a brand of cigarettes made here by R.J. Reynolds Tobacco, whose founder was at one time the wealthiest man in our state. A few people, so I've heard, call it "The Dash," which is the name of our minor league baseball team and a reference to the punctuation between Winston and Salem. But in 2014, Winston-Salem adopted an official slogan, taking on the name, "The City of Art and Innovation." The University of North Carolina School of the Arts, and the arts in general, play important roles in the region's history and in this story.

In writing this book, I greatly enjoyed learning more about R.J. Reynolds Memorial Auditorium, built by Mrs. Katharine Smith Reynolds in memory of her husband. This architectural masterpiece, completed in 1924, is a treasure to the city, and it has a fascinating, but also tragic history that I encourage you to research.

This book is my second to have started as only a title. The words came to me in the shower one day, seemingly out of nowhere. I had no idea what the story would be about, though I did picture in my mind an older model convertible and a happy couple, as if they were out for a Sunday drive. I didn't know that image would turn into the first scene with Annie and Julian, in Chapter Two.

Songs for a Sunday is my fifth novel, but it is my first story with a dual timeline. What a fun and special challenge it was. And when I say challenge—much of this novel was written in 2020, which brought challenges to most of the world. But 2020 was also the year I became a mother of four when our youngest child was officially adopted. The Lord saw us through every challenge and added blessing on top of blessing during this unique period in our lives.

As a singer, my prayers and my praises to God, in good times and bad, are often communicated through songs. Especially the old hymns of the faith. Songs like "Amazing Grace," which Missy sang, have been a source of inspiration to me for as long as I can remember. One of the hardest parts of writing this book was imagining how Missy could sing "Amazing Grace" without being moved by its meaning at first. It was difficult to relay a scene in which a person sings about grace yet doesn't accept it. But of course, that was the point. May it be unfathomable to you as well. Whether we sing it loudly or simply whisper it within our spirits, may we most of all live each day in wonder of it.

How precious did that grace appear, the hour I first believed . . .

Acknowledgments

To you the reader, *thank you*. I am sincerely grateful that you have invested your time and interest in my work. It is my great hope that this book brought you enjoyment, and, though it is fiction, that it caused you to reflect on the goodness and mercy of God.

To every person who read any of my earlier novels and encouraged me to keep going, then stuck around to see this book through to publication, you mean so much to me. The worth of a faithful cheerleader is impossible to measure. I'd give you each a hug if I could!

My sincerest thanks to my amazing editor. Being able to work with Eva Marie Everson on this project was a dream come true! I can't say it enough—an absolute dream! Eva Marie, you once told me at a conference that my writing sample had too many exclamation marks. You were right, of course, and I've not forgotten the lesson, but I hope you'll forgive them here. Thank you! Thank you! Thank you! I am immensely grateful that you said "yes" to this story and then put your special polish on it. Thank you for handling my words with such care. I look forward to learning more from you.

Thank you to my publisher for the opportunity to tell this story. I am thrilled to be part of the Iron Stream Media family.

Many, many writing groups, courses, and conferences have shaped my writing journey so far. One of those is Word Weavers International. I am thankful for my friends in this group, and I especially want to acknowledge the president of the North Carolina Piedmont Triad chapter. Renee Leonard Kennedy, you are without a doubt, one of the most generous people I know. Thank you for believing in me.

One of the first people to read this story, other than my editor, is a very special beta reader for whom I am thankful. Charlene Yarger, though we've never met in person, I am so happy to know you. Thank you, friend, for your help.

Thank you, always, to my parents, Bobby and Barbara Norman. After six published books, they are still the best word-of-mouth marketers I could hope for. Who else carries copies of my books to hand out to people they meet? I am so blessed.

To my sisters, Jennifer and Brittany, to whom this book is dedicated—thank you for so many wonderful memories that fed into much of the emotion of this story.

To my four children—Elizabeth, Sarah, Daniel, and Benjamin—though you didn't realize you were doing it, thank you for inspiring many of the characteristics of Emma, Piper, Joshua, and John Thomas. (For the readers, if you haven't heard which two funny scenes were inspired by something two of my kids *actually* did, feel free to ask.) And to my husband, Alex, for your dedication through all the crazy. We make a great team. I love you all.

Special thanks to Hanging Rock State Park Ranger Jason Anthony for answering my questions about the history of the park, and to local historian Molly Rawls for her incredible website, www.winstonsalemtimetraveler.com, as well as to the North Carolina Room of the Forsyth County Public

Library, for the invaluable collections of photographs and articles that assisted in my research about Winston-Salem in the 1960s.

And as always, I am grateful to my Lord for His lovingkindness. Thank you, God, for giving me a voice, and for continuing to patiently teach me to use it.

Heather Norman Smith

Book Club
Discussion Questions

1. Does the hint of self-pity from Missy in the beginning of the story help you relate to her character, or does it make her unlikeable at first?

2. How does Annie's hiding the truth from her son make you feel about her character? Do you sympathize with her actions?

3. Did you relate more to Missy or to Annie? In what ways?

4. What did the story teach/remind you about forgiveness of others and forgiveness of oneself?

5. Do you think Ruth Claire had a clinical problem, or was she simply *different*? Did you automatically diagnose her with a certain condition, and did her character follow the characteristics of that condition that you would expect?

6. Do you feel the title of the book relates well to the story? What would you title it?

7. Is there anything you would change about the story-line? If so, what?

8. Do you think you would have reached the same decision about sharing Grandma's secret if you were Missy? Why or why not?

9. Have you had a Mary Sue Montgomery or Miss Melinda in your life? How did their actions or attitudes affect you?

10. What was your overall impression of Henry?

If you enjoyed this book, will you consider sharing the message with others?

Let us know your thoughts. You can let the author know by visiting or sharing a photo of the cover on our social media pages or leaving a review at a retailer's site. All of it helps us get the message out!

Email: info@ironstreammedia.com

 @ironstreammedia

---

Iron Stream, Iron Stream Fiction, Iron Stream Kids, Brookstone Publishing Group, and Life Bible Study are imprints of Iron Stream Media, which derives its name from Proverbs 27:17, "As iron sharpens iron, so one person sharpens another." This sharpening describes the process of discipleship, one to another. With this in mind, Iron Stream Media provides a variety of solutions for churches, ministry leaders, and nonprofits ranging from in-depth Bible study curriculum and Christian book publishing to custom publishing and consultative services.

For more information on ISM and its imprints, please visit
IronStreamMedia.com